John Francome has been Champion Jockey seven times and is regarded as the greatest National Hunt jockey ever known. James MacGregor is the pseudonym of a practising barrister, who also has an avid interest in racing.

John Francome and James MacGregor have been a successful writing partnership for three previous bestsellers (*Eavesdropper*, 1986, *Riding High*, 1987 and *Declared Dead*, 1988), which have been greeted with increasingly enthusiastic critical acclaim:

'Rattling good storytellers' *Horse and Hound*

'The racing feel is authentic and it's a pacy, entertaining read' *The Times*

'Splendid racing scenes and a tight storyline. Gripping stuff . . . a must for all racing fans and a fun read for others' John Welcome

'A thoroughbred stayer . . . cracking thriller' *Independent*

D0680762

Also by John Francome and James MacGregor

Eavesdropper
Riding High
Declared Dead

And by John Francome

Safe Bet
High Flyer
False Start
Dead Ringer
Break Neck
Outsider
Rough Ride
Stud Poker
Stone Cold

Blood Stock

John Francome and James MacGregor

HEADLINE

Copyright © 1989 John Francome and James MacGregor

First published in 1989
by HEADLINE BOOK PUBLISHING

First published in paperback in 1990
by HEADLINE BOOK PUBLISHING

10

All rights reserved. No part of this publication may be
reproduced, stored in a retrieval system, or transmitted,
in any form or by any means without the prior written
permission of the publisher, nor be otherwise circulated
in any form of binding or cover other than that in which
it is published and without a similar condition being
imposed on the subsequent purchaser.

All characters in this publication are fictitious
and any resemblance to real persons, living or dead,
is purely coincidental.

ISBN 0 7472 3416 7

Typeset in 10/12½ pt English Times
by Colset Private Limited, Singapore

Printed and bound in Great Britain by
Mackays of Chatham PLC, Chatham, Kent

HEADLINE BOOK PUBLISHING
A division of Hodder Headline PLC
338 Euston Road
London NW1 3BH

Blood Stock

Chapter One

He took the spade and started digging. The asparagus bed had been his father's pride and joy, yet since his disappearance Fergus had not had the energy or the enthusiasm to do anything with it. In fact, he had only entered the walled garden a handful of times in the past eighteen months and, as a result, the vegetables and fruit which his father had so lovingly planted and tended had been sadly neglected. Save for frequent assaults by the birds, the produce had just withered away untouched and unappreciated.

Fergus had spent a year and a half waiting for his father to return, like a dog waits for its master. Every time he heard a car pulling into the drive he would rush to meet it, longing to see his father's face behind the wheel. Each time the telephone rang he would snatch it up, yearning for the sound of his father's voice – there would be some simple explanation as to why he just left without saying a word. But it was never him.

'No secrets, no lies.' That's what his father had always told him and that's how it had always been, which made the whole thing even more difficult to understand. They had been more like brothers than father and son. Then he had just vanished and left Fergus feeling like someone whose best friend had unexpectedly committed suicide without leaving a note: eighteen months of living in a void. He had cried on more occasions than he cared to admit through just missing him. The Gardai had long given up their inquiries, and it was now up to him to run the stud as his own.

For no reason that he could put his finger on, he had woken that morning with a fresh resolve. He couldn't go on moping about for ever, and, as a symbolic gesture of his new-found independence, had decided that the asparagus bed had to go. He had never liked the stuff anyway.

As he began digging, he pondered on his main problem of how and where he was going to find the money to survive and continue breeding racehorses. His mother would certainly want no part of it. As far as he could gather from their occasional conversations, her sole concern was how long the courts would take before declaring her husband dead so that she knew where she stood – financially. Fergus had always known that one day he would inherit Drumgarrick – his father had told him that since he was barely out of nappies – but he had never expected it to be so soon. There was now no chance of carrying out the long-held plan of going around the world visiting studs, gaining experience and broadening his knowledge of the racing world. He was now the master of Drumgarrick, and as such he was going to try his damndest to make a success of it.

He decided to put money worries out of his mind for the time being and attack the earth beneath him; after all, hadn't the morning started in fine style? He had risen early and taken Tongue in Cheek, the horse his father had given him as a foal on his eighteenth birthday, for a gallop out across the fields. He had always known that Tongue in Cheek was a good horse, but he was prone to breaking blood vessels. In fact, because of that he had only been able to run half a dozen times in the two seasons that he had been racing. On the one occasion that he hadn't broken, which had been at Punchestown, he had given the season's leading novice a real run for his money. He stood well over 16.2, and was completely black except for a small white sock on his near hind. Fergus had been convinced that most of his problems with breaking blood vessels had been due to his weakness, and for that reason had turned him out in March to benefit from the early spring grass.

After four months turned out in the field the change in him had been staggering. He no longer looked like two boards stuck together and now had a body to match his frame. Fergus had then set about getting him fit: months of trotting on the roads, and long, steady canters. And then this morning had come his first serious piece of work. He had only galloped for a little over a mile, but at the end of it Fergus got the feeling he could have gone on for ever. As he let Tongue in Cheek ease back to a steady canter, Fergus had a smile on his face from ear to ear; a mixture of pride and pleasure.

When he arrived back at the yard, Joe was waiting with a bucket of warm water and an anxious look on his face.

'How did he go?'

'I should think he must have improved about two stone since last year.'

Joe's face lit up. 'Didn't I tell you he was a racehorse? We'll stick to the plan then, and give him a couple of runs down the field to make sure he's fit and to get his weight down the handicap. Then we'll put our heads down and go for our lives in the Ladbroke on New Year's Day.'

Fergus was almost as close to Joe as he had been to his father. Joe had worked for Patrick Kildare, Fergus's father, for the past thirty years. A former jump jockey, it was Joe who had taught Fergus how to sit properly on a horse and had encouraged him in his ambition to be a really good amateur rider. Together they had spent their evenings, after Joe had fed the horses, talking about the stud groom's experiences as an apprentice in stables in England, and planning the day when they would pull off the coup of a lifetime which would clean out the bookies. Tongue in Cheek had it in him, Fergus had felt it that morning, but he was still apprehensive.

'Isn't the Ladbroke aiming a bit high for a horse that hasn't even won a race yet?' he said. 'Why don't we just go for a touch in an ordinary novice hurdle?'

'Two reasons. First, if we go for the Ladbroke we'll get a very good price. And secondly, that's how good I think he is. And so do you, you as much as said so.'

'What if he breaks a blood vessel again?'

'If he breaks, it won't matter what race he's in, he'll get beaten and we'll both be looking for jobs.' Joe looked at Fergus and grinned.

Fergus grinned back, buoyed by Joe's confidence. 'This stud certainly needs a large injection of cash. Maybe this horse will fill the syringe for us.'

Fergus was dreaming now of the big race at Leopardstown as he laboured away with his spade. He pulled off his shirt in anticipation of the sweaty task ahead. He was almost five foot ten but could ride at ten stone seven pounds given a few days' notice. There was no doubt that he was his father's son, with the same tight, blond, curly hair that was cut short and those enormous blue Kildare eyes.

As he set about his task, the late October sun warmed his lean body and hopefully helped heal some of the scratches on his back that Emma had given him as a token of her appreciation of his lovemaking.

Emma Ballantine was a typical fiery red-head, who needed sex the way junkies need a fix. He had met her in his second year as an undergraduate at Trinity College, Dublin, when she had been hanging around the Philosophy Department in search of what she called 'imaginative thinking', and to escape the rages of her father, who was a judge in Kerry. Her mother was more agreeable, although her life was consumed by three-day eventing and the ten days of obligatory gossiping which followed every competition.

Emma wasn't a student at the university – she hadn't passed an exam in her life – but she was already by then a graduate with honours in love-making and the art of sensuality. Within a couple of months Fergus realised that he had fallen madly in love with her. She was tall and athletic-looking with the loveliest, curliest red hair he had ever seen. Her face was one that you would expect to see advertising fruit or some other healthy type of food, and was dappled with freckles that covered the tiny nose between her large green eyes.

That had been three years ago. She was still as dangerous and flirtatious as ever, but Fergus had come to realise that she had long tired of their respectability, if living in sin can ever be called that, and had been allowing her eye to roam. In fact, he was certain that her body had gone on ahead and that her interest in Hugo Fitzwilliams who trained on the Curragh was more than just platonic. Fergus had always known that one day he would have to let Emma go, only until now he had been afraid to be on his own. Perhaps that time had also now arrived.

He began singing an old Beatles number called, rather inaptly, 'She Loves You', and dug the spade into the ground with renewed vigour. He was down about eighteen inches, shaking the roots free from the soil as he went, when his spade hit something hard, jarring his wrist. There was over twelve feet of the most fertile soil in the world where Drumgarrick was situated, which was the reason it had become a stud in the first place, and Fergus hadn't seen a stone of any size there ever. He dug his spade in again, only this time behind the last mark so as to get under whatever it was. As he pulled back on the handle, a long white bone sprang through the dark loam. He thought he must be unearthing one of the dog's hiding places. Then he saw the tip of something else showing through beside it. This time, as he levered the spade in underneath and jerked the object to the surface, he froze momentarily while his brain lost the battle with his eyes as to what he was seeing. As he stood over the hole, gaping, he felt like someone was pumping chalky water into his body through his stomach. He spun round and vomited.

He stood there, his legs astride and his head hanging down, until he recovered from the shock. Then he went back to have another look, like a criminal who goes back to the scene of his crime.

As he stared down, the tears began to well in his eyes. There, lying on the surface, was the skeletal hand of a human being, the index finger missing, the thumb no more than a stump. He had just disinterred his own father.

Chapter Two

Jack Hendred leapt out of bed and with his left hand held firmly across his mouth ran down the corridor of his flat to the bathroom. He just made it to the loo in time before his stomach disgorged the excesses of the night before. Why, he asked himself, did he keep going on these binges? And what had happened to the pretty girl he had begun the evening with? From somewhere deep in the back of his mind flashed a picture of a restaurant with a waiter trying to throw him out with the help of a tall Swedish-looking girl. Then it all came back to him. Why did these foreigners never have a sense of humour? He had only suggested that if she paid the bill he'd take her home and make love to her as a joke, and she had suddenly had hysterics. The pounding inside his head made him try and recall whether or not she had hit him, but as far as he could remember she hadn't so he must have gone somewhere else afterwards and consoled himself with yet more whisky.

He staggered over to the washbasin to wash himself and to do the usual bit of stock-taking in the mirror. The Swede had been right when she had said during dinner that he looked a bit like Harrison Ford. That was when they had still been on speaking terms. Maybe his eyes weren't so close together and his face a little flatter, but there was more than just a passing resemblance. Jack was five foot nine and tried to remember whether the actor was taller or shorter. Whichever it was, H. Ford couldn't boast a half-inch scar running laterally across his left cheek just below his eye. Jack used to tell people he had won it in a brawl with a Greek ship's captain whom he had been investigating for scuttling his own ship. In fact, he had been hit by his elder sister with a poker in a fit of jealousy when he was just four years old.

The shrill call of the alarm in his bedroom shook him out of his self-absorption. Today was to be particularly important. In just under an hour, at half past eleven, he was due to have a meeting with the lawyers to discuss his progress in the Moondancer case.

He didn't expect too much of a reception. There was a tendency among the professional classes to regard private investigators as a necessary but otherwise disagreeable evil and to consider their work something which only a social misfit or disturbed personality would willingly undertake. In Jack's case neither description would have been accurate or fair and perhaps that explained his great success. While at university he had taken a vacation job working for an insurance company, which had involved helping the claims manager investigate a case of suspected arson. The discovery that the policyholder was also the arsonist had opened his eyes to the world of fraud and thereafter he had devoted himself, in return for large fees, to investigating suspicious claims all over the world. He disliked failure and it was for that reason he was more than a little apprehensive about the day ahead.

Moondancer was a famous racehorse who had been insured in London by his owners for five million pounds, and one day he had been found dead at Drumgarrick Stud, his brains decorating the walls of his box. Every dram of instinct that Jack had distilled over ten years of inquiring and probing into his fellow man's machinations told him that there was villainy at work and he was now going to have to persuade the lawyers and his clients, the underwriters, to give him just a couple more months to come up with the truth. If he could only find that bloody Irishman, Patrick Kildare, who owned the stud, he was convinced he would crack this whole business. Nobody except white rabbits and magicians' assistants disappeared into thin air without a good reason and Patrick Kildare's was the one face he would like to see in the witness box.

A sudden searing surge of pain behind the eyes made Jack congratulate himself for having typed up his report the previous afternoon and not done his usual trick of rising early and knocking it off at the last moment. He felt dreadful and not in the least bit confident that he would be able to withstand rigorous questioning without having to make a bolt for the door. Solicitors and barristers didn't tend to find that kind of thing very funny.

Ten minutes later he was dressed and rummaging through his desk in the spare room which doubled as his office. Papers were scattered everywhere and he vowed that this weekend he really would clear the place up. He probably needed a secretary to look after him but over the years he had come to enjoy working alone and not sharing his secrets. He heard his own confessions and that way no one else was ever at risk or, for that matter, in a position to betray him. When you were dealing in claims worth millions of pounds the usual niceties didn't apply; the scar on his cheek could easily have been earned in the way he pretended.

He played back the answerphone from the evening before; except for a call from his mother it was blank. He knew she wanted him to go and stay with her for the weekend and was becoming anxious lest he should cancel for the third time running. He made a note to call her later and confirm that this time he really would be coming. Then he left a message and the telephone number of the solicitors in case anybody wanted him urgently. That done he gulped down a

BLOOD STOCK

cup of black coffee and a brace of aspirin, grabbed his report and headed for the Temple and the all-important meeting in counsel's chambers.

Some chap falling under a train on the District line held him up and he was twenty minutes late when he was ushered into the room of Rupert Croke. The overweight, grey-haired Queen's Counsel barely acknowledged his arrival as he continued recounting a story to the couple already seated opposite him. From what Jack gathered it was of the 'what I told the judge' variety and ended with Croke roaring with laughter at the punch line. Quintin Arthur, the senior partner of the solicitors' firm which bore his name, joined in the guffaws. Even lawyers must have been children once, Jack thought to himself. He was relieved to see that the pretty dark-haired girl on Arthur's right, sitting with her legs crossed and a note pad at the ready – presumably Arthur's new secretary – had either not seen Croke's joke or had preferred not to join in the fun. Jack looked round the room and took in the sombre collection of legal prints which covered the drab mustard-coloured walls. Perhaps it wasn't the done thing to have cheerful surroundings.

Croke, who had quite happily let Jack stand like a lost soul in the middle of the room as he talked, now motioned him to an upright leather chair beside Quintin Arthur. The solicitor acknowledged his late arrival with a knowing shake of the head and the resigned air of a man who, having known Jack for years, had long ago given up hope of instilling any manners in him.

'I'm glad you're here at last, Jack,' he said. 'We've been amusing ourselves in your absence. I don't think you've ever met Mr Croke before. He's advising the underwriters in this matter.' Arthur stopped there. He didn't seem to think the girl warranted an introduction. Croke rose from his chair and shook Jack's outstretched hand with such resolution that in his present uneasy condition he felt he was going to fall apart.

'I've heard a lot about you, Mr Hendred. Mr Arthur here is always singing your praises as the best investigator in the business. I'm just sorry that our first case together is not looking too healthy.'

It was apparent that not all the talk had been social before Jack's arrival, and he was going to have to fight his corner from the outset.

'I wouldn't say that. You're the barrister, I know, but if you ask my view' (and you're going to get it anyway, he thought to himself) 'it's certainly not nearly as cut and dried as it seems.'

'Really?' Croke . was obviously unconvinced. 'From what Mr Arthur has just told me and from what I've gathered from these papers and my instructions,' he said, waving his hand in the direction of a huge bundle of documents stacked on the desk in front of him, 'we are faced with a trial in about four months, an insurance policy which obliges my clients to pay out in the case of accidental death or misadventure and no evidence whatsoever to establish that it was the work of any of the policyholders. A pretty expensive treble, I'd say!' he added, grinning at his use of the gambling term.

Jack ploughed on. 'I appreciate all that and it's of course why I'm here today. You seem to overlook the fact that this very expensive animal had about as much future as a stallion as a donkey on Brighton beach.'

'I'm sorry, I don't follow you.'

'No sensible owner would send any mare of any value to be serviced by him.'

It was clear from the barrister's vacant expression that horse breeding wasn't high among his leisure interests. Jack continued: 'Let me explain. A stallion is judged by his ability to put mares in foal and to produce through them good-looking and fast-running offspring. That, put brutally, is his sole function in life. In his first season, Moondancer was all the rage as a sire and had a respectable striking rate. Unfortunately his progeny tended to have poor conformation and to walk as if their legs were tied together. Worse still, when they reached the racecourse, an experience denied to the majority in fact, they ran even more poorly than they looked. Ugliness and slowness are an unbeatable disincentive when it comes to attracting the owners of brood mares. By his third year at stud Moondancer had become positively unfashionable. In these circumstances the only way his owners could hope to recover all the money they had paid for him was by killing him and claiming on the insurance. Money is money and no one likes losing large dollops of it in a bad investment.'

Croke didn't appear to warm to Jack's robust approach. 'Mr Arthur says you've prepared a report. I had hoped to have it last night so I could have digested it before this conference.'

'Yes, I'm sorry. The old copying machine packed up yesterday afternoon.' A little fib now and again didn't harm anybody, thought Jack to himself. 'But I've brought it with me.' He reached into the inside pocket of his jacket and produced a scruffy wad of paper.

Croke was unimpressed. 'Is that it? And only one copy?'

Jack nodded, and immediately regretted the sudden movement of his head as he felt the stabbing pain behind his eyes again.

'It's hardly fair to Mr Arthur and Miss Frost if I see your report and they can't,' Croke said tetchily. 'As we haven't got all day, why don't you read it out? It's not too long, is it?'

Perhaps the silent Miss Frost was more than a secretary, thought Jack as he opened up the folded sheets. Reading out loud was the last thing he wanted to do. His eyes ached, his throat was dry and parched from the alcohol of the night before and he really didn't believe he could manage a twenty-minute monologue. He looked appealingly at Arthur who nodded paternally and sat back in his chair waiting for the performance to start like some benign schoolmaster. Jack clearly had no option.

'All right,' he said, 'if you insist. What I've done is set out a brief account of Moondancer's history, followed by a description of the interested parties, the evidence to date, and suggested future lines of inquiry. Most of it of course won't be new to you . . . Perhaps I should save time and go straight to the last part?' he ventured hopefully.

'No, I think it would be best if we heard it all,' answered Croke. 'As the man in the field, your views are of particular . . .' he hesitated for a moment, and Jack mentally dared him to say importance '. . . interest.'

Jack began to read. To his surprise the words came out reasonably clearly: 'I have been asked by Messrs Arthurs, solicitors, to investigate the circumstances surrounding the death of a stallion called Moondancer at Drumgarrick Stud. Messrs Arthurs are acting on behalf of the insurers who wrote a policy in respect of the horse and are now facing a claim of five million pounds sterling as a result of his death. Moondancer began his stud life at the age of four, having retired as a racehorse five months previously as a three-year-old. He was therefore nine at the date of his death, all horses having their birthdays on January the first. As a two-year-old he was unbeaten in four starts and as a three-year-old he won both the English Two Thousand Guineas and the Irish Derby. A training accident prevented him from running in the English Derby for which he had been the ante post favourite.

'When in training on the Curragh in Ireland, he was owned by a Texas oil millionaire who subsequently syndicated him at the end of his racing career for five million Irish punts. There are only ever forty shares in a racehorse syndication, and with the collapse of the oil price the Texan chose not to retain a single one of the shares himself.

'Moondancer was sent to stand at Drumgarrick Stud, which for the last fifty years has been in the ownership of the Kildare family and has been run by Patrick Kildare for the last twenty-five. This was regarded in racing circles at the time as a somewhat unusual choice of stud, as Kildare, though much liked in the bloodstock world, was primarily a breeder who kept half a dozen mares, and whose only previous stallion had been a National Hunt sire called, rather aptly having regard to his owner's precarious financial circumstances, Cheque in Post. Drumgarrick Stud itself was in a state of disrepair and a large sum of money had to be spent erecting suitable quarters and facilities for Moondancer.' Jack looked up from his report. 'Shall I read on?'

'If you're coming to the bit about his failure as a stallion, I think we've got all that sorted out now,' Croke said amiably, looking to Arthur and Miss Frost for confirmation. 'Perhaps you could go on and deal with the circumstances leading up to the death?'

Jack cleared his throat, discarded some of the sheets of paper and continued: 'Yes, well, come January of last year, the prospects for Moondancer were extremely bleak. Only half a dozen mares were booked in to him and there was no real chance of any serious increase in that number during the covering season, which ends in June at the very latest. At the same time, Patrick Kildare began receiving telephone calls at the house from a woman claiming to be calling on behalf of the IRA. She demanded the payment of a large sum of money in default of which Moondancer would be killed; in short, protection money. Patrick Kildare reported the calls to the Gardai, the Irish police, who agreed that if they continued, they would provide some additional security at the stud. According-ing to a statement he subsequently made to the Gardai, Patrick Kildare did not take the threats seri-ously. In any event, both he and the other owners of the horse had nothing to lose and a lot of insurance money to gain if the horse was killed, and that's exactly what happened. One Sunday morning, the fif-teenth of January, Moondancer was discovered dead in his stable, his head blown off by a shotgun blast. It appeared that he had been slipped a quantity of aspirin during the night and once he had fallen fast asleep he had been executed. On the face of it, therefore, a very fortuitous escape for the owners, and a *bona fide* claim against the insurers. Once the suspicious circumstances leading up to the death had become known, however, it was decided that further inquiries were necessary before any pay-out could or would be authorised.'

'So presumably that was when Mr Arthur called you in?' Croke clearly resented anyone else talking too much.

'That's right.' Jack went back to reading. 'Mr Arthur asked me to carry out the necessary investigations and two weeks after notification of the claim I went to County Limerick. My brief was to discover all I could about the true ownership of the horse and investigate thoroughly the Kildares and the whole set-up at Drumgarrick to see if there was anything dishonest or untoward going on.' Jack heard a rustling movement. He looked up to find Croke with his feet on the desk staring blankly out of the window into the courtyard beyond. 'Am I going too quickly for you?' he asked.

If Croke heard the sarcasm, he ignored it. 'No, it's fine at this pace. When are you coming to the owners of the horse?'

'Now.' Jack returned to the report. 'The insurance policy had been taken out on behalf of the owning syndicate by Kieran Steele, a wealthy Irish entrepreneur who has had several horses in training over the years. Steele purchased ten shares at a cost of one and a quarter million pounds. The sale was arranged by Eamon Fitzwilliams, one of Ireland's leading blood-stock agents, and he himself retained ten shares. Another ten were purchased by an Englishman called Guy Pritchard.' Jack paused. 'If I was making a book,' he said, eyeing Croke's elevated feet, 'I'd have this guy in at even money favourite. He's an East End boy with not much past but lots of money, most of which, I'd say, he's obtained by terrorising people.'

Jack now had Croke's full attention. 'You mean he runs a protection racket?' he asked.

'No. From what I can gather, and judging by the way people suddenly forget things when you mention his name, he physically intimidates people himself. He's almost fifty but still works out every day in a gym, and I would guess he'd be up to taking a shotgun to his own mother if she were insured for enough.' He went back to reading from his report. 'The other ten shares in Moondancer were divided between Eamon's son Hugo, who had trained the horse at his stables on the Curragh, and who also, by the way, trains for Steele and Pritchard; and Patrick Kildare, the owner of Drumgarrick Stud.'

'Do people normally take such large shareholdings in a stallion? Isn't it all a touch risky?' Croke was again staring out of the window as he talked, only this time he was also cleaning out his right ear with what appeared to be a gold Parker pen. At least the lovely Miss Frost was giving Jack her full attention. He began to wonder how he could manoeuvre lunch with her without old Quintin being present . . .

'You're right, although it can vary greatly, depending on the wealth or greed of those involved. In this particular case the moving spirit was Eamon Fitzwilliams who took the view that Moondancer was seriously undervalued on his breeding and racecourse performance and was convinced the horse would be a great success at stud. His reasoning was simple: the fewer owners, the bigger the share-out. After all, nobody who discovers what he thinks is a goldmine wants to start handing out shovels to every Tom, Dick and Harry.

'Having received instructions from Mr Arthur and established the background of the owners,' Jack read on, 'I immediately began investigating their movements on the night before or morning of Moondancer's death. It so happened that on the weekend the horse was killed they were all staying at the stud. But there was still nothing to link any one of them directly or even indirectly to the shooting. When challenged, somewhat languidly, by the Gardai, each claimed to a man that he had been fast asleep throughout the night and heard nothing.'

'Are you saying the Gardai didn't take the investigation very seriously?' interrupted Croke, turning to face him.

'Let's put it like this. The IRA theory was a distinct possibility and since the horse was insured and no protection money had ever been paid, there was a limit on the amount of manpower which could be justified in pursuing any detailed investigation.'

'I see,' said Croke doubtfully. 'Please continue.'

'I decided to concentrate my early inquiries on the staff at Drumgarrick, beginning with Joe Slattery, the head lad. Slattery had once been a professional jump jockey in England, having come over from Ireland as an apprentice. He returned home when he was thirty, being quite a good rider, I'm told, and was nicknamed "the crack" for his ability to keep his head when the money was down on the horse he was riding. He's worked for the Kildare family ever since and is now aged about sixty. He's well-liked locally, although prone to the occasional prolonged drinking bout which can lead to fairly heated but never violent arguments with his wife Moira. Despite this matrimonial discord they have eight children, all now grown up and living away from home.

'Dressed in my roughest clothes I managed to strike up a conversation with Slattery in his local in Drumgarrick High Street. After a few drinks the subject turned to racing and breeding and once he had his head, Slattery started talking freely about Moondancer and what a terrible blow his death had been to the stud and his governor, as he called Patrick Kildare. What principally emerged was that the horse

23

had been absolutely fine in himself right up to his death, whereas the same could not have been said of Kildare. According to Slattery, Kildare had been in a state of nerves in the week leading up to the death, and very depressed afterwards, drinking more than usual and being aggressive to the other staff. Since then they've all gone, bar one lad who lives in the village. I arranged to meet Slattery again the following night but events were to determine otherwise. As I was walking back to the house where I was taking bed and breakfast, I was followed by two extremely menacing individuals who proceeded to frog-march me down a dimly lit alley. Shoving me up against a wall with a strategically placed knee nestling in my groin, they asked me what my business was in town and why I was nosing around asking questions. The term "Prot" featured a little too often for comfort in their questions. I couldn't very well tell them the truth so I said I was on holiday from doing a postgraduate course on Irish history at London University and had decided to come and see some of the great Irish castles and meet the people for myself. They didn't find that very convincing and when one of them mentioned the words "Army spy", I thought my time was up. I was saved by the local police who luckily drove down the road at that very moment and the two men ran off. I decided the time had come for me to leave. I packed my bags that night and drove off at the crack of dawn to the anonymity of Shannon.'

'But you didn't leave it there surely?' asked Croke.

'No,' Jack replied, without bothering to look up from his report. 'About six weeks later I telephoned Mr Kildare, posing as the owner of a brood mare who was wishing to board her out. He was absolutely charming and invited me round to the stud on the following Monday.

'When I arrived at the house nobody was at home. I walked round the yard and caught sight of Slattery in one of the surrounding paddocks with a brood mare who appeared to be heavily in foal. I didn't want him to spot me so I returned to the house, found the back door unlocked and trusting to the hospitality of the Irish, went and made myself at home in the kitchen. About half an hour later Mrs Kildare arrived and was clearly very surprised to find me there. I explained that I had come to see her husband. She said that she knew nothing about it and that he had gone away that weekend to look at some horses in the south, and hadn't yet returned. She didn't seem too worried by his absence and I gained the distinct impression that this was normal behaviour on his part. In fact, as we now know, Kildare never returned from that trip. He just vanished into thin air and for the last eighteen months there hasn't been sight nor sound of him.'

'All very interesting, Mr Hendred,' said Croke, 'and I'm sure very upsetting for his relations. But the problem is, unless you have made some other progress which you have yet to tell us about, we are no nearer establishing that Moondancer's death was the work of the policyholders than we were at the beginning of this conference.' The Queen's Counsel stared at Jack. 'I appreciate you have a suspicious mind, but lawyers can only deal in facts, and my clients have their reputation to protect. With the trial due to be heard in February, the time has come to face up to reality.'

'But if only we can discover the whereabouts of Patrick Kildare. I can't believe his sudden disappearance is a coincidence. Every one of the owners of Moondancer, including Kildare himself, had a reason for wanting him dead. But it's only Kildare who can give evidence about those phone calls from the IRA. If you accept the calls were made up or merely a subterfuge, then—'

'But my dear man,' Croke interrupted, rising to his feet and walking up and down in front of the window, 'if we are going to plead fraud and that it was the policyholders who killed Moondancer, then we have to do it soon and on the basis of hard evidence. I've no doubt that in the past your hunches have been right on many occasions. Mr Arthur wouldn't recommend you so highly otherwise. But High Court judges are lovers of fact not theory, however plausible. I'm sorry, but I do think I'll advise the clients to pay up.'

Jack was fighting hard to hold back his temper. He calculated that with one leap he could be on the desk and from there he could land a well-placed right hook on Croke's perfectly formed nose. He resisted the urge and decided to be conciliatory.

'I can see the force of that but I just want one more month to go back to Ireland to try out an idea of mine. If that fails, then I'll throw in the towel.'

Croke looked towards Quintin Arthur. The solicitor always chose his words carefully and there was the usual pause before he started speaking: 'I agree with Mr Croke. It all sounds very plausible, Jack, but when it boils down to the nitty gritty you have nothing concrete to go on. My duty is first and foremost to the underwriters on this syndicate. We have already run up costs of thirty thousand pounds in defending and investigating this particular claim. I think the time has come to put an—'

The phone rang. Croke picked up the receiver impatiently: 'You know I'm in conference. What? For Mr Hendred? It's for you,' he said, handing the receiver over to Jack.

The investigator blinked in surprise. 'Yes, Jack Hendred. Oh, it's you, Seamus. What's happened?' Jack nodded his head as he listened. 'When? This morning. Where? At the stud itself? And do they know what the cause was?' He shook his head and couldn't resist a smile. 'Thanks, I'll catch the first plane over and phone you from Shannon. You're a good man.' He put the phone down and took in the expectant faces of Croke, Arthur and the suddenly even more attractive Miss Frost. 'I'm sorry about that.' He was going to make them wait a second before he broke the news. 'That was a friend of mine who has a contact in the Gardai who slips him the odd bit of information. A body's been discovered at Drumgarrick Stud this morning. A man. His skull's been smashed in. They're treating it as murder.'

'But whose body?' asked Croke, trying hard to appear relaxed.

'Didn't I say? I'm sorry. Patrick Kildare's. Now, can I continue with my inquiries?'

28

Chapter Three

By one o'clock Drumgarrick was no longer a sleepy stud in a remote part of southern Ireland. For the past three hours police cars had been tearing up the bumpy half-mile drive which led to the house and parking area in the huge cobbled courtyard at the rear. On either side of the courtyard there were twenty stables, all of which had been refitted and repainted four years previously to house the mares who came to be serviced by Moondancer. Nearly all the stables were empty but every now and again one or other of the four remaining brood mares owned by Fergus's father would look nonchalantly over the top of her stable to see what all this sudden commotion was about. The atmosphere, pregnant only with gloom, was in stark contrast to the frenetic excitement which had preceded the stallion's arrival to take up his duties.

The pathologist was expected at any moment and the Gardai had already erected a makeshift tent about four yards square out of sheets over the spot where the body had been discovered. One of the sheets was pink and added an incongruous touch of prettiness to the scene. Over at the far end of the courtyard, by the entrance to the walled garden, stood a defiant and fresh-faced young Gard from the village who had been placed there with strict instructions not to let anyone pass. Not that anyone wanted to.

Fergus had been waiting with his mother in the drawing room for the past hour for the super-intendent, who was due to arrive with the pathologist. He was still in a state of bewilderment and shock. On discovering the body, he had run into the yard calling for Joe who had come out of one of the stables and hurried over to the walled garden. Together they had stared down at the skeleton, its cavernous eyes looking beseechingly up at them.

'Are you so sure now it's the guv'nor?' asked Joe in a whisper, taking off his flat cap and running his left hand through his mop of curly dark hair. Fergus fought back the tears.

'Look at the left hand, the thumb and missing finger. It's him all right. I wish to God that it was someone else. Why on earth would anyone want to do this to him?'

Joe said nothing, merely made the sign of the cross against his chest.

Fergus regained his composure and began to get his thoughts together. 'How the hell am I going to break this to my mother? I'm sorry, Joe, but would you mind staying here while I go and make a few calls? I have to phone the Gardai.'

'I'll do whatever you want, guv'nor.'

It was the first time that Joe had ever called him by that title. Even during his father's absence when Fergus had run the stud, it had always been Master Fergus.

Fergus walked to the door of the walled garden and, as he opened it, turned round to see Joe sinking to his knees and bowing his head as if in prayer. Then, tears running down his cheeks, Fergus hurried across the courtyard towards the kitchen and the telephone. Fortunately, his mother and Emma were both away and he was thankful that he at least had some time to grieve by himself. He would be able to contact his mother at Tipperary where she was staying with friends. As for Emma, she would just have to wait. He wondered if she was in bed at that moment with Hugo Fitzwilliams, and then chided himself for having such a venal thought at such a time.

He managed to contact his mother and tell her to come over. From the tone in his voice she must have guessed that something was very wrong, but she didn't press him for an explanation on the phone. When she arrived at the house, he led her into the study, his father's favourite haunt, and broke the news.

Her only reaction was to ask him to take her to what

she termed the grave. Joe was still on guard and on seeing her he put on his cap and then immediately took it off again as a mark of respect. She asked both Fergus and Joe to leave her alone. Ten minutes later she emerged from the garden and strode purposefully without saying a word back to the house. Fergus noticed as she brushed past him that there was soil on her skirt and that her hands were muddy too. He said nothing and having asked Joe to return to his vigil he followed her indoors.

Now, three hours later, they were waiting together in silence in the drawing room, his father's least favourite room. They had only used it on rare occasions during his childhood and never at all during the last eighteen months since his father's disappearance. His father hated formality and what he called starched rooms and had opened it up only when it was absolutely necessary. Occasionally he had served drinks there to the owners of brood mares who were thinking of sending their valuable pieces of bloodstock to be serviced by Moondancer, and who had come to inspect the stallion. Even then such visits had tailed off as Moondancer's progeny failed to shine on the racecourse. Like the stables out in the courtyard, the drawing room, with its ornate oval ceiling, had enjoyed a fresh coat of paint before the stallion's arrival, but Patrick Kildare had drawn the line there – if he hadn't, his bank manager would have done – and the relative smartness of the walls only made the

32

faded Edwardian velvet curtains and the elbow-beaten armchairs look even more weary. All the decent furniture had long gone to pay for Fergus's school fees and for nominations for the brood mares; all that remained was a large ornate French commode standing incongruously in the corner. That, too, would soon find its way to an auction house. Fergus had always been proud of his father for putting those he loved before material possessions.

Sitting on a dark green chaise longue in the bay of the drawing room's large french windows, Fergus was unable to believe that this was really happening to him. His mother, who on her return to the house had changed into a simple black woollen dress, was seated on the chintz sofa on the other side of the room beside the blazing log fire. Fergus had quickly made it up before her arrival. She was flicking through an old photograph album, clasping a white silk handkerchief in her left hand and taking the occasional sip from a large glass of brandy. Every few minutes she would dab a tear from her eye, a gesture which for some inexplicable reason annoyed her son intensely. Even confronted with death he felt that she was mistress of her emotions and, if anything, more beautiful than ever, with her long, raven hair pinned up with tortoiseshell combs, setting off the pale, smooth skin of her face. She was now approaching fifty but looked much less, and moved with the supple grace of a much younger woman. He wondered what she would do with her life now.

Superintendent Brogan was shown into the room by Mrs Magee, the Kildares' belligerent daily from the village. The police officer stretched out his hand in turn to Fergus and his mother and offered his condolences. He was a huge man, well over six foot and broad as a tree trunk, and Fergus instinctively suspected that his avuncular air was a trap for the unwary. He invited the officer to sit down in the armchair opposite his mother and went and stood beside the fire.

'This is a terrible terrible thing, Mrs Kildare, Mr Kildare. At some stage I'm afraid I'll have to be asking you some questions, but you may rather I left it till later.'

Fergus didn't give his mother an opportunity to reply. 'As you'll appreciate, Superintendent, my mother's in a state of shock and naturally I'm anxious she should be spared any hurtful or upsetting questions for as long as possible.'

'Of course, I appreciate that. The pathologist is with the body now and it might be best if we defer any discussion until the cause of death has been established.'

Mrs Kildare stared up at the superintendent. 'My son's being over-protective, officer. I'm quite happy for you to start asking questions now if they're necessary for your inquiries.'

'Are you sure?' asked Fergus.

'Fergus, do stop treating me like a child. Fire away,

34

Mr Brogan. I'll tell you if they become too painful.'

'Thank you, madam. We'd better start with your husband's disappearance last year. Now that was,' he took a notebook from his pocket and began reading from it, 'in March. I believe it was a couple of weeks before you reported him missing.'

'That's right. My husband was extremely depressed after Moondancer was found dead in his stable in mid-January and he had begun drinking rather heavily. One weekend in early March, the eighth I believe it was, he told me that he had heard of a horse for sale in Sligo which might make a good hunter and he was going to go and have a look. I was away myself for most of the weekend and he never returned. We now know why.'

'Did he take his car with him?'

'It wasn't in the garage and as I expect you know it was subsequently found at the station near the coast.'

'Did he ever say who he was going to visit in Sligo?'

'No, but that wasn't unusual, I've never really shared my husband's love of horses and we didn't discuss business together. I never asked and he never volunteered.'

Fergus nodded in agreement. When it came to bloodstock his parents were chalk and cheese. Given Patrick Kildare's love of horses it had always struck his son as strange that he had married a woman who had no interest in them. Fergus suspected that his mother had married his father for Drumgarrick, not realising that behind that grand façade stood a mountain of debt.

The superintendent continued in his soft, almost melodic voice: 'I'm sorry to ask this, but was your husband in financial difficulties?'

Fergus butted in before his mother could reply. He was beginning to resent the detached way she was dealing with the superintendent's inquiries. 'As you can imagine, this is an expensive place to keep up and my father had gambled on Moondancer being a success as a stallion. There was no reason after his racecourse performances and on breeding why he wouldn't be right. My father's share of the horse cost him more than half a million punts and you can add on to that the money spent on bringing the place up to scratch. He had to borrow heavily from the bank to pay for it all.'

'Was the horse insured?'

'For five million. My father's share of that is an eighth, which would just about cover his debts.'

'So in a way your father was a beneficiary of Moondancer's death?'

'If you're suggesting that my father might have had something to do with Moondancer's death, I bitterly resent it. He loved animals and nothing, and I mean nothing, would induce him to harm a hair on any animal's head, even if it meant his own financial ruin.'

'And have the insurers paid up?' the superintendent pressed on.

'Not yet. Unfortunately shortly before my father

disappeared they intimated that they were not satisfied with the circumstances surrounding Moondancer's death and we've had to go to court over the policy. Our lawyers are expecting settlement any day now.'

'One last thing and I'm afraid I have to ask both you and your mother this. Do you know anybody who had a grudge against Mr Kildare, anybody who could have wanted him dead?'

'Nobody,' Fergus's mother said emphatically.

Fergus shook his head. 'My father had no enemies. He was a good man, perhaps too naive or romantic about his business affairs, but that's what made him the man he was. I can't believe that anyone other than a maniac could have a reason for taking his life.'

'I understand how you feel, you and your father were obviously very close, but we have to face up to the fact that someone wanted him dead. Hopefully we'll get some help from pathology or when we've checked the area. I apologise for intruding at this time and once again may I say how sorry I am that this terrible thing should have happened.'

Brogan rose and made for the door. As he reached it he turned and spoke again.

'I trust that neither of you were thinking of going away at the moment?'

They both assured him they weren't. Typical, thought Fergus. Why is it the Gardai always suspect the immediate family?

*   *   *

'Would you like a brandy or something?'

Amy Frost shook her head. 'I've drunk too much as it is and I've got a lot of work to do this afternoon.'

'Drafting wills and settlements and all that kind of stuff, I suppose?'

Jack called the waitress over and ordered a Remy for himself. His initial instinct had been right. This was a very stylish and unassuming girl. Although she had readily accepted his invitation for lunch she had allowed him to do the talking, throwing out the odd barbed or mocking comment. He immediately warmed to anybody who did not take him in the least bit seriously.

'Sure you won't change your mind?'

'Positive,' Amy replied. 'One slip of the pen could lead to heartbreak for an expectant beneficiary. Is this a typical boozy lunch or are you just celebrating the discovery of a body and the relaunching of your investigation?'

'Don't be unkind. I won't deny that phone call was welcome. I've never bought that IRA rubbish. They gave up horse kidnapping and all that protection money business after the Shergar fiasco. The trouble is that horses are in the same category as women. You can't trust their nearest and dearest to come up with the money.'

'So you're a cynic as well, are you?'

'No, just a hardened realist. I wish man's nature was all sweetness and light but over the last ten years

38

or so all the milk of human kindness I've seen would fit comfortably onto a teaspoon. It's self-interest which motivates man and insurance companies are regarded as legitimate fodder in its pursuit.'

'Isn't that inevitable? Just look at Lloyd's. Lots of rich people putting up money to make more money. It's just a merry-go-round where only the wealthy can have a ride.'

'Were it all so easy. Not every syndicate makes a profit and the worst thing you or anyone sane would want is a state-owned insurance body where there was only one rate on offer and then it was take it or leave it. There would be no quick pay-outs then, you know.'

'I'll take your word for it. So now you're off to Ireland?'

'This afternoon, provided I can get a flight. I'll meet my contact in Shannon and hopefully find out what the pathologist has had to say and then go and stay within striking distance of Drumgarrick. I can't see the family wanting to see me, but you never know. Given time, this chap Fergus might be so upset about his father's death that he would welcome any help in tracking down his killer.'

'How can you be so sure the body is Patrick Kildare's? There can't be much of it left that's immediately recognisable after all this time.'

Jack sipped his brandy. Amy was right, Seamus had said that the skeleton hadn't in fact been

positively identified yet, but Jack saw no reason to
let her know that. He'd bet odds on it was Patrick
Kildare. 'My contact's source is usually reliable,' he
told her, hoping she wouldn't press him for details.

She didn't. 'You intend to get really involved in
this?'

'I'll get involved in anything which shows this is a
crooked claim. I'm not suggesting all the owners are
in it but at the moment all five, including old man
Kildare, had a reason for wanting that horse dead and
each one remains a suspect.'

'What if the events are unconnected?'

'You mean the horse's death and the old man's?
Every instinct in this rugged frame tells me they are.
It's going to be a long haul and I just hope the insurers
don't do something stupid like settling. Arthur's not
going to give in, is he?'

'You don't expect me to disclose legal secrets do
you?'

'Yes, to be honest.'

'They say there's no such thing as a free lunch. I
should have refused when you asked me but you
looked so miserable during that conference.'

And I felt it, thought Jack. 'All right then, don't
tell me,' he said. 'It's just that barrister fellow worried
me with all his settlement talk.'

'He's no different from the rest of them. They are
professionally cautious, they have to be, now that
they can be sued along with the rest of us for negligent

advice. As to your question, I think you ought to know that Mr Arthur is going into hospital for a minor operation and won't be directly in charge for the next couple of months. He's deputed responsibility to a junior partner who will of course report to him on any progress, or lack of it.'

'And who's to judge if I'm making progress? This worries me. A new Pharaoh came into Egypt who did not know Joseph and all that. Is there some spotty-nosed chap to whom I have to report my every movement?'

'Not spotty-nosed, but extremely hard and demanding. I wouldn't count on you two getting on too well.'

Jack's spirits sank and he downed his brandy in misery. 'When will I have the honour of being introduced to my new master?'

'You already have.' Amy smiled and looked at her watch. 'We don't want you to miss that plane, do we?'

Chapter Four

Jack paid for lunch and promised to telephone Amy from Ireland as soon as he had any news. Before taking a taxi back to his flat in Notting Hill Gate he telephoned his local travel agent to find out if they had managed to book him on a plane to Shannon or, failing that, Dublin. He was in luck. The Aer Lingus flight to Shannon had been delayed owing to a technical problem and there were two cancellations in business class on the flight which was now due to leave at five thirty. The girl said they had grabbed one of them and he had to check in at Heathrow by five o'clock. That left him an hour and a half to return home, tie up one or two loose ends in other matters he was dealing with, shove a few things into a travelling case and then get to the airport in half an hour. Tight, but manageable.

The traffic had been appalling and with time running against him, he ran up the stairs to his flat

on the fifth floor and flung open the door. The blow
which caught him on the chin sent him reeling into
the lobby. Before he could find his balance a hand
tugged him inside, closed the door and threw him
down onto the floor.

Jack was fit but he wasn't a fighter and initially
the terror of being attacked took over his whole
body. His assailant, who was over six foot and
well built, was now on top of him with a length of
sash cord taut between his enormous hands. The
incapacitating weakness of fright disappeared as
Jack suddenly realised he was fighting for his life.
An image of being strangled rushed through his
mind as simultaneously his brain was asking why
someone should want to kill him. He bucked and
wriggled like a Brahmin bull in a rodeo, trying to
prevent this life-threatening hulk from getting the
noose round his neck. Jack managed to get his
fingers between the rope and his windpipe in an
effort to keep the air flowing to his lungs but
whoever was tightening the cord was much too
strong for him. As he lost the battle the rope bit
quickly into his skin. Jack struggled to breathe but
couldn't and made one last, futile attempt to free
himself. Somewhere, through the fog and the pain,
he heard the telephone ringing, and his last thought
was to wonder who was trying to contact him while
he was being murdered.

*   *   *

'Are you all right, Jack?' He looked up to see the anxious face of Dorinda, his Spanish daily, kneeling over him with a wet sponge in her hand. He forced himself up off the floor and onto one knee, his throat burning with pain. 'Here, I'll get you a glass of water.'

She returned from the kitchen with the glass. As he swallowed, the pain was excruciating.

'What are you doing here?' he asked, realising that she had somehow saved his life.

She pointed to a pile of laundry by the door. 'Tomorrow I go to the doctor first, so I thought I bring your laundry back today. I no bear you wearing those dirty clothes. When I open door I see this man lying on top of you. When he hears me he gets up, pushes me away and run down the stairs.'

'Did you get a look at him?'

'No. He had a stocking over his head, you know, like on the television.'

Jack stood up and gave Dorinda a hug. She had undoubtedly saved his life.

'Shall we call the police now?' she asked.

'Yes.' He changed his mind. ' No. I'll do it later. I've got a plane to catch.' His voice croaked like a sick frog's.

Dorinda headed for the kitchen. 'I make coffee.'

'Good idea,' said Jack, but first he wanted something stronger. He walked into the sitting room

45

and helped himself to a double brandy. Apart from the fact that he was big and strong he had not the slightest clue as to his attacker's identity. He ran a mental check of all the cases he was involved in where his continued presence was unwelcome. The most likely was those fires in Soho, which he was convinced were arson and where the insurers were refusing to meet the claims on his advice. The claimants, from what little he could discover about them, were hardly more than gangsters and wouldn't think twice about putting a premature end to his investigations.

'You must go to the doctor,' said Dorinda who had come into the sitting room bearing a large mug of coffee. 'Your face is a terrible mess.'

He went to the bathroom and stared at the mirror. The Harrison Ford look-alike had given way to a Mike Tyson victim. His chin was badly marked and his lip swollen and cut; there was nasty and extensive bruising on his neck too. He ran his hand round it in gratitude that he was still alive to feel it, vowing to give Dorinda a big pay increase. It just had to be his lucky day and Ireland beckoned.

Remembering the ring of the telephone as he was being strangled he checked the answerphone. It was Seamus in Ireland saying that the dental records had positively identified the body as Patrick Kildare's, the pathologist had confirmed that it was murder and that Kildare's skull had been crushed by a blunt instrument wielded from behind. Jack fetched his coffee from the sitting room and drank it. The warm liquid helped. He then contacted the insurance brokers in the arson case and told them under no circumstances were they to pay out on that claim, and finished off by cancelling his appointments for the rest of the week. That done, he dictated a message onto his answerphone, giving no idea as to where he had gone or when he would return, merely asking the caller to leave his name and telephone number with a promise to get back as soon as he could. He thought about ringing his mother to cancel his weekend visit, but decided he didn't have time. He would send her a postcard from Ireland if he wasn't back by the weekend.

It took him only five minutes to pack. He led Dorinda down the stairs and found a taxi. He insisted on dropping her at her flat in Bayswater and gave her a couple of hundred pounds, telling her not to come in for a month. For all he knew, the attacker might pay a return visit or think that she might be able to recognise him.

He sat back in the cab as it hurtled down the M4 to Heathrow. So far it had been a day he would never forget. He sensed it was high time he increased his own life cover.

The plane was already pretty packed as he took his seat by the window in business class. He gave his fellow passengers only a cursory glance. He was feeling shattered and all he wanted to do was catch up on some sleep before reaching Shannon. He fastened his seat belt and was asleep soon after take-off. He woke up to find the stewardess shaking him and asking him to push his seat upright as the plane was about to pass through some turbulence. That familiar ping sound was followed by the flashing 'fasten seat belt' sign. Although his job meant he spent a great deal of time flying, he still dreaded the idea of crashing and the prospect of making that journey across the Styx with a whole lot of people whom he had never met before. Normally before take-off he would look around to see whom he would eat if the plane had to put down in the desert or some other remote spot.

He gave up on the idea of any more sleep and instead read the *Sporting Life* which he had shoved into his jacket pocket before leaving the flat. He wondered where the racing was in Ireland the following day and whether it would be worthwhile fitting in a visit to the track to hear if any rumours were going round about Kildare's death. Horse-racing and breeding, he had come to realise, were very incestuous occupations and you never knew what you might hear in the owners' and trainers' bars.

He glanced at the front and then the back pages. The yearling sales were in progress at Newmarket and the *Life* recorded the transactions of the

previous day. One headline caught his eye:
'Fitzwilliams pays top price for Sadlers Wells
colt'.

Hugo Fitzwilliams, of course, had been the trainer
of Moondancer, and his father Eamon had been the
bloodstock agent who had arranged the stallion's
syndication and its taking up duties at Drumgarrick.
Both had retained substantial interest in the horse
and were among the plaintiffs in the insurance claim.
Clearly they still had clients with money to splash
about. Jack read the article quickly: 'Eamon Fitzwilliams was again in action yesterday when he gave
the top price of five hundred thousand guineas for a
beautifully bred Sadlers Wells colt out of Ascot
winner Indecency. The Irish bloodstock agent was in
unusually reticent mood when asked to disclose the
identity of his client. All he would say was that the
yearling will be going into training with his son Hugo
on the Curragh.'

Jack whistled to himself. He knew there had been
numerous yearlings sold over the years for well into
the millions, but five hundred thousand guineas still
seemed a heck of a lot of money. Incredible to think
that the price of one unproven piece of bloodstock
could be equivalent to well over what he would earn
in a lifetime.

He turned to the inside pages and found the
runners entries for the next day's racing in Ireland.
There was a National Hunt meeting at Tipperary

which he reckoned would fit in very nicely with a trip to Drumgarrick village in the morning. He would have to wait a while before he could chance snooping around the stud itself. He looked down the list of runners and riders. There in the second race, a handicap hurdle, he noticed that Tongue in Cheek was down to run. Owned by Mr Patrick Kildare and due to be ridden by the amateur Mr F. Kildare, claiming seven pounds. That, Jack concluded, was bound to be a non-runner under the circumstances. Only a heartless sod would go and run a horse the day after his own father and the horse's owner to boot had been found murdered.

'Could I have a glass of champagne, please?'

Jack recognised that voice. He whipped round in his seat to see Amy sitting immediately behind him.

'What on earth are you doing here?' he asked, making no attempt to hide his surprise.

'Travelling to Ireland. I hope your powers of detection are a little more subtle than that, Mr Hendred. And what happened to your face? You look terrible.'

Jack instinctively put his hand to his throat. 'A little accident with my front door. You haven't answered my question. Are you telling me that you had a seat booked on this flight all along?'

'No, I'm not that devious. When I returned to the office after our excellent lunch – thank you again, by the way – Mr Arthur told me that the clients wanted a report from the scene and as there was so much money involved in this claim, he wanted me to go personally. There were two seats cancelled on this flight and my secretary booked me on one of them.'

'And I got the other. You're not going to follow me around, are you? This could all turn very nasty. Murders have been known to come in pairs.'

'No, Mr Hendred, don't worry about me. I'll do my job and you do yours. Just make sure you remember about that spotty partner you have to report to.'

Jack signalled to the stewardess. 'This turbulence is getting to me. Could you make that a large brandy as well please?'

The pathologist left Drumgarrick with Superintendent Brogan just after three thirty, shortly followed by an ambulance carrying Patrick Kildare's remains. Fergus had insisted on being present when the skeleton was placed in a plastic bag and then onto a stretcher and had even asked if he could lay a blanket over the remains. He trembled at the thought that his father was being taken away to be picked over somewhere in a pathologist's laboratory with cold and analytical detachment, and decided that the only way to deal with such a macabre prospect was by banishing it from his mind. What was important was the memory of his father and what he stood for as a man. Now he, Fergus, had to do everything in his power to ensure that those responsible were brought to justice. It was not that he distrusted the Gardai. They would do their best under difficult circumstances, but his father was just one of many cases and had no special personality of his own.

His mother had retired to her room as soon as the questioning had finished, making it quite clear that she did not want to talk about the day's events for the time being. He and his mother had never been very close and save for the occasional pleasantry, they inquired little of each other's business. Fergus always felt that she would have been happier with a daughter or perhaps even no children at all. The last thing she had wanted was a son who was in many respects a replica of her husband. Since his father's disappearance they had adopted a ménage of convenience – he sharing a bedroom with Emma and his mother living virtually her own life at the other end of the house. Occasionally, more by luck than any planning, they would have dinner together.

Fergus decided to go for a walk round the estate which surrounded Drumgarrick, just as he had done so many times before with his father. The leaves on the trees were turning to that yellowy-brown colour which heralded the arrival of autumn and which made Limerick such a beautiful and romantic spot at this time of year.

He walked to the front of the house and set off across the lawn and then to the fields beyond. There was a small flock of sheep grazing there which he would send off to market in November and raise some much-needed ready cash. Now that his father was officially dead and not just missing, their financial problems had to be tackled forthwith. Provided the insurance money came through on Moondancer, he was in the clear. If not, he would be in deep trouble.

He ran through the available assets. His aim had to be to save the house and try and continue the stud as a going concern. That would be difficult. Two of the four brood mares owned by his father were barren and the other two, although still fertile and capable of throwing good-looking foals, were into their early teens and had become what his accountant called wasting assets. There was only a hundred acres of land left, yielding an income of about five thousand pounds a year; he could probably raise twenty or thirty thousand by selling the bottom two twenty-acre fields to old Geraghty over the hill – exchanging capital for income, as the bank manager had loved to remind his father. The trouble was that once sold, never recovered, and it went against the grain to think of that grasping oaf Geraghty getting his hands on

53

Kildare land. It would have broken his father's heart.

Fergus crossed the stream which meandered right through the estate. If he raised fifty thousand, that still left a considerable sum owing to the bank and nothing for his mother. He was fairly confident that his father had had life insurance. He would phone the solicitor tomorrow and find out for sure. Even then the situation was bound to be gloomy, bordering on the desperate. It now seemed more important than ever that they pulled off a coup with Tongue in Cheek. Joe was confident that they could but his father hadn't trained a winner for the last four years and if you don't have other horses to gallop against in your yard, how do you really know how good your fellow is? Fergus had to admit Tongue in Cheek felt top class but he himself had only ridden two winners under Rules, although countless more at point to points. His second race had been over hurdles at Punchestown on Tongue in Cheek last year and he had come in second. Tongue in Cheek had given Fergus a marvellous feel that day, half a ton of sheer power beneath him. Someone had once told him that the difference between the English and the Irish was that an Englishman yearns to own a Rolls-Royce and an Irishman a top-class racehorse. He was right. One comes from Mammon, the other from God.

Joe had had it all worked out to the last detail how

they were going to pull off the coup. The plan had been to give Tongue in Cheek his first of two runs the next day at Tipperary. That would be enough to get him in at near bottom weight in the big Ladbroke hurdle at Leopardstown on the fifteenth of January. It would mean his dieting and wasting for the next three months but when they had concocted the plan it all seemed worth it – fifty thousand pounds first prize and a hefty amount of the sponsor's money in bets. If, as Joe claimed he could, they managed to get ten thousand-odd pounds on at fifty to one, their problems were over. If. But now all that had gone to pot. There was no way he could ride Tongue in Cheek tomorrow, and they couldn't allow another jockey to have the ride. Jockeys have loose tongues and Tongue in Cheek's potential and ability had to remain a secret.

Fergus sat down under an oak tree and allowed his mind to roam over his life with his father. At the moment, just thinking about him brought tears to his eyes but he hoped that with the passage of time this immediate sorrow would give way to the warm glow of the love they had shared. Fergus tried to recall the particular weekend that his father had disappeared. He had been up at Trinity and had talked to his father on the Thursday before. He had mentioned a hunter he had heard about down in Sligo and said he was going to look at it. He knew he couldn't afford it at the moment but fancied a day out. Fergus had encouraged him. Since the disaster involving Moondancer, his father's health and state of mind had worried him and there had even been occasions when he half suspected that his father knew more about the horse's death than he was letting on. He had certainly become very depressed when he heard that the insurers were not prepared just to pay out and were sending out some kind of investigator.

His mother hadn't made it any easier. She was bored at Drumgarrick and now to crown it all her husband had blown all their money. She had liked the idea of standing a top-class stallion there but when it proved to be a failure her enthusiasm turned to scorn. She spent more and more time away with her friends and the only occasions she brightened up were when the Fitzwilliams clan turned up to visit. Eamon Fitzwilliams was a well-known ladies' man, glib-tongued and urbane, and he paid her gratifying attention. Like father like son. Fergus wondered what Emma was up to at that moment in Newmarket. He leant back against the tree and contemplated the lonely nights ahead.

By the time he pulled himself together it was gone seven o'clock. He decided to check Tongue in Cheek. He walked swiftly back across the fields to the rear of the house and down the pathway which led to the stallion box, with a covering area at the back, which had been built for Moondancer. This palatial establishment had now been given over to Tongue in Cheek, an appropriate successor in the circumstances.

The top door of the stable was open and inside Joe was talking away to the horse. Fergus poked his head over the bottom door.

'Hello, Joe. You should be home by now.'

Joe shrugged, his expression sombre. 'I'm in no hurry.'

Fergus entered the stable and walked over and put his arm across the groom's shoulders. 'I'm sorry, I know how fond you were of him.'

'It's a crazy world. How anyone could do that to the guv'nor. I just hope they'll be catching them pretty quickly.'

'So do I, Joe. So do I.'

'I blame it all on that damned stallion. I knew the day that horse walked into the yard, the cocky bastard, that he'd bring no good with him. I told the guv'nor that and he laughed. Said he would make our fortune and now see what's happened. They're both dead. It's a bloody tragedy, that's what it is.' He patted Tongue in Cheek and then turned to face Fergus. 'You look tired. You'd better be getting some rest if you're going to ride our boy tomorrow.'

'What do you mean?'

'I took the liberty of declaring him, seeing you had so much else on your mind.'

'But I can't ride him tomorrow, I mean I'm in no state and what will people think?'

'I don't do much caring for other people's thoughts. We can't give up our plan now, guv'nor. If anything, it's more important than ever if you want to keep Drumgarrick.'

Fergus had no need to tell Joe about the parlous state of the stud's finances. Joe hadn't been paid his proper wages for over a year.

'But there are other races we could run him in.'

'A plan's a plan. The going's right, it's a big field and you can lose him tomorrow in the ruck and no steward's going to blame you for riding a misjudged race in these circumstances. Your father would have wanted it this way.'

Fergus sighed. It struck him as wrong but more than anything he wanted to save Drumgarrick.

'All right. You drive the horsebox and we'll leave as soon as the race is over.'

'Agreed.'

'Thank you, Joe. And thank you for guarding him today. It meant a lot to me.'

'That was my honour. There's just one last thing, guv'nor.'

'Yes?'

'Well, as I was sort of kneeling by the spot, you know, where you found him, I noticed this.' He held out a silver brooch with two initials framed on it in rubies.

'Did you mention this to the police?'

'No, I didn't think it was my business to.'

Fergus took the brooch and clasped it tightly in his hand. He had recognised it immediately. The initials C.K. stood for Colette Kildare. It belonged to his mother.

Chapter Five

Jack couldn't make up his mind whether he was angry or pleased that Amy had come over to Ireland. He certainly had nothing against attractive intelligent girls, indeed a large part of his life had been dedicated to being in their company, but on the other hand he could only do his job properly if he was left to his own devices. The idea of having a partner or even having to furnish daily reports was anathema to him.

He had offered to carry Amy's bag as they disembarked from the plane and now as they walked towards the arrivals' hall at Shannon he wondered how he was going to get rid of her without causing offence or jeopardising any possible future relationship.

'Do you know where you're staying tonight?' he asked.

'Somewhere called the Shamrock Hotel. It's about five miles out from the airport on the Limerick Road.

I'm only there for a night while I liaise with the solicitors in Limerick who are going to act as our agents.
I'll then go on to Dublin to see the brokers who originally placed the Moondancer insurance. And you?'

'Oh, I'll probably hire a car and find myself a hotel
between Drumgarrick and Tipperary and start
sniffing around. You must give me a number where I
can get hold of you.'

'Yes, I suppose I must.' Jack was surprised that she
did not appear more enthusiastic and thought perhaps
he had misjudged her potential to be a nuisance.
Either that, or he had upset her by his offhand manner on the plane. The last thing he could afford to do
was alienate her; that could lead to the plug being
pulled on his investigations.

'Do you like horseracing, by any chance?' he asked
as they reached the hall and he put down her bag.

'A lot. I come from a family that's been certified
horse mad. I prefer the jumping game to the flat. Why
do you ask?'

'It's just that there's a National Hunt meeting at
Tipperary tomorrow and I thought it might be fun to
go along and see if we could pick up any gossip about
the murder. It's a long shot but you never know.
Young Kildare was meant to be riding a horse owned
by his father but I somehow feel that'll be a non-
runner. I've never met the chap, and only seen a
photograph of him in his riding kit. It would be nice
to have a look at him from close quarters. You can

often tell a lot from someone's face and mannerisms.'

'Lawyers call it their demeanour. Personally I think you can tell a lot from what people do with their hands.'

Jack felt his own go clammy. 'I've never heard that before.' He thought he detected a slight smirk pass across her face. 'The first race is at one o'clock, so shall we meet outside the front gate at, say, twelve thirty? We could have a sandwich and a drink and I can give you my first report.'

'Okay, that should give me time to brief our lawyers. Someone's waving at you over there.'

Jack turned round to see a short, plump, round-faced young man in a duffel coat rushing towards him. With his ginger hair, freckled face and round gold-rimmed spectacles, he had all the air of an over-grown schoolboy.

'Seamus, what the hell are you doing here?' asked Jack.

He shook Jack's hand like a long-lost friend and bowed respectfully to Amy.

'I phoned Mr Arthur's office. Did you get my message?'

'I did, thanks.'

'Quite a turn-up for the book, eh?' grinned Seamus.

'I'll tell you later.' Jack's tone was clipped; he did not want to say anything in front of Amy.

Seamus understood and turned towards Amy. 'I

don't think I've met your friend,' he said, holding out his hand.

'Amy Frost, this is Seamus Pink.'

'At your service,' said Seamus.

'Miss Frost is a solicitor acting for the insurers in the Moondancer case. She is co-ordinating the investigations and is over here on business for a couple of days. She's staying at the Shamrock Hotel on the road to Limerick.'

'That's a bit of luck. I've booked you in there tonight too, Jack, I didn't think you'd want to drive all the way over to Drumgarrick this evening. Anyway, the place is bound to be crawling with police and reporters. I'm told that even the odd member of the racing press has turned up to study the form. Perhaps you'd like a lift, Miss Frost? I can't guarantee you'll get a taxi.' Seamus bent over to pick up Amy's case.

'Thank you,' she replied. 'That's very kind of you, Mr Pink.'

'Please call me Seamus, everybody else does. Is this your first trip to Ireland?'

'Yes, it is.'

'It's a beautiful country. You'll find the people very friendly here.' As they marched off ahead of him, locked in animated conversation, Jack began to think that the fates had decided to intervene in his life and there was no point at the moment in putting up any resistance.

Half an hour later he and Seamus had accompanied

Amy to her room on the fourth floor of the hotel and agreed to meet downstairs for drinks at eight thirty before having dinner. Jack wasn't that pleased to have been given the room next door but he had no intention of making a scene at reception. The first thing he did on entering his room was to tap the dividing wall. It sounded pretty hollow.

'What's up, Jack?' asked Seamus. 'She's not the kind of girl to listen in to your conversation.'

'You can never be too careful. I just hate the idea of anyone listening to my conversations. It's like sleeping in someone else's sheets.' He put his head to the wall and listened again. 'It's all right, she's running a bath. What else have you got to tell me?'

'We've had one major piece of luck. Patsy Flynn is on the murder team investigating the death. He owes me one after the help I gave him on the Killowem kidnap and has agreed to keep me informed of developments. The only *quid pro quo* is that I don't breathe a word of it to anybody. He doesn't know about you and if he did he'd kill me.'

'Don't worry. His secrets are safe. Who's leading the investigation?'

'At the moment Superintendent Brogan. He's clever and efficient but a Grade A shit in the process.'

'Has he formed any views?'

'Give him a chance. They only found the body this morning. I talked to Flynn on the phone before meeting you and he said that Brogan knows that it could be tied up with the stallion's death.'

'In what sense?'

'Possibly that the IRA are behind it, that Moon-dancer was killed because Kildare refused to pay out protection money and that Kildare was subsequently liquidated to teach him and other breeders a lesson as to their future conduct.'

'All very cosy and bad news for the insurers, if true. Do you buy it?'

'Not really. It's all too easy to blame them and if they really wanted to use Kildare as a warning to others, why bury him in a spot where he was unlikely to be found?'

'And where was that?'

'In the walled garden, in the asparagus bed of all places.'

'Maybe they thought that the body would be found much quicker. How were they to know the rest of the family didn't eat asparagus?'

'I know, but it doesn't feel right. I'm convinced it's something to do with this insurance sting.'

'What more have you got on how he was killed? In your message you said he was hit by a blunt instrument.'

'That's about all I know. He was struck from behind, crushing his skull, poor bugger.'

'How long had he been there?'

'Flynn didn't really know but it's his guess that it was since the old man disappeared. The pathologist will have a better idea in a couple of days but even then you can't be precise with a skeleton.'

'So where's all this leave us?' Jack chose to answer his own question. 'Presumably with the same list of suspects as before. The five owners of the stallion, now reduced to four, and we'd better add on Kildare's wife and son for good measure. How have they taken it?'

'Flynn only knows what Brogan told him after he had the first interview at the house. She by all accounts is a pretty cool customer, although it might just be that the discovery has come as a relief after all the months of not knowing. The son is more excitable, very upset by the whole thing, particularly having discovered the body in his own garden. He wants immediate action to find the killer.'

'Don't they all. Was there any life insurance?'

'Don't know. I'd have thought that's something your clients would be able to find out.'

'Not necessarily, insurance companies don't operate a mutual benefit society. Make a note to ask your pal Flynn. He's bound to know. Like a cigarette?'

'No thanks, trying to give up. I thought you were going to.'

'Tried but failed. Still need them now and again to calm the nerves and make me think straight.'

'That girl's pretty nice, isn't she? Chat her up on the plane, did you?'

'She's all right. I would be grateful if you didn't

talk shop over dinner. She'd never believe you were a private investigator anyway. That duffel coat would fool anybody. You can keep her amused with some of your racing stories and a bit of Irish folklore.'

'I'd be delighted. I might even end the evening with a song or two if the mood takes me.'

Jack's face fell. 'Is that a threat or a promise?'

It was past midnight before an extremely merry Seamus was coaxed out of the lounge bar of the Shamrock Arms and into his car outside. Amy agreed to join Jack for a nightcap which in his case consisted of yet another Irish coffee and in hers a cup of decaffeinated tea. She had been extremely good fun throughout the evening and had laughed at Seamus's jokes without the slightest inhibition. There was no doubt she had real style. Jack wanted to tell her that behind the Irishman's boyish exterior was a very professional investigator who was an expert in karate, surveillance and wire-tapping. He doubted if she would have believed him.

'I'll be leaving early in the morning, so I doubt if I'll see you at breakfast. Are you still on for the racing?' he asked.

'Subject to any hitch in meeting these lawyers. I'll hire a car and drive on afterwards up to Dublin and spend the night there. Before you go to bed, there are one or two questions I'd like to ask. I brought the file over and was reading it up in the bath.'

68

Jack did his best to look helpful. 'I could have read it over your shoulder.'

Amy continued: 'I see that Patrick Kildare's car was originally found abandoned at the station in Sligo. Do you know whether the police checked it over at the time for bloodstains or anything?'

'The car was inspected at the time by the Gardai but at that stage they were not treating his disappearance as suspicious. They hadn't ruled out suicide but no one was dreaming of foul play. I don't know where the car is now but I'll make a note to find out in the morning. If the Kildares have kept it, the Gardai are bound to want to examine it again.'

'Good. What steps do you intend to take to investigate the whereabouts of the other owners on the weekend of Patrick Kildare's disappearance? If I've got it right, that's Eamon Fitzwilliams, his son Hugo, Kieran Steele and Guy Pritchard.'

'I'll make inquiries about their movements but since I don't have the power of search or questioning like the Gardai I have to use more indirect methods.'

'Do you have any contacts with the police? Sorry, the Gardai?'

'Officially no, unofficially yes. Obviously as soon as I have anything important I'll let you know.'

'Is that your link with nice Mr Pink?'

'Seamus? No, he's on the claims side of the insurance business. Far too nice a chap to be involved in the messy side of things.'

'So tomorrow you're going over to Drumgarrick?'

'Just to the village, to get the feel of the place and listen to the locals. The day after I'll start finding out about how successful the Fitzwilliams' bloodstock business is and whether Mr Steele or Mr Pritchard have any skeletons in their cupboards.'

'And finally, what about Mrs Kildare?'

'She's not out of it. She's young compared with her late husband and good-looking, and for all we know might have another man on the side. It might even pay to tail her for a while.'

'How long do you propose to spend over here?'

'As long as you and the insurers let me.'

'Five million punts is an awful lot of money. Just make sure you deliver.'

Chapter Six

After leaving Joe and Tongue in Cheek together in the horse's stable Fergus returned to the house and made straight for his father's study. There was no sound or movement coming from upstairs and he had no intention of going up to his mother's room to see if she was still awake. When he was young she had frequently retired to her room complaining of migraines and he had become accustomed to treating her chosen solitude as sacrosanct. He began rummaging through the contents of his father's desk. He didn't really expect to find anything of interest although he thought he had once seen some cream parchment with a ribbon round it which could have been a will. He didn't mind how his father had disposed of the estate – the house would be his in any event – but he was curious to know what provision, if any, he had made for his mother.

His search proved to no avail and not feeling at

all hungry he decided to go straight up to bed. He thought he might have heard from Emma but presumably she was having a good time at Newmarket and there was no reason to think that the news of his father's death had reached England yet. No doubt it would be reported in the morning's papers. In a way he was glad she hadn't called. He no longer felt close enough to her to want to share his grief and she was bound to ask all sorts of questions and offer to come home. She loved excitement and intrigue and the last thing he wanted was anyone to dramatise his father's death. He was alone now and that was the way he wanted it to be for the moment.

He emptied his pockets onto the chest of drawers beneath the window, including the ruby brooch which Joe had handed to him. He had temporarily forgotten about it. He looked at it and noticed that the letter K was damaged; the bottom of the upright had snapped off. His father had given it to his mother as a birthday present about ten years previously; Fergus remembered how pleased he had been at having found a brooch with her initials on it.

Fergus undressed, washed himself in the old basin in the corner and then slipped into bed. Lying on his back he tried to remember when he had last seen the brooch on his mother. She had definitely worn it at his twenty-first four years ago, and he thought she had worn it at the Limerick Hunt Ball the year before his father disappeared. He racked his brain to think of any more recent occasion. What about that big dinner they had held to celebrate Moondancer's arrival at the stud? All the owners had been there and a few top breeders who had promised to send their brood mares to be covered. His father had been in cracking form that night. It was the evening Emma had met Hugo Fitzwilliams and he could see the trainer now, chatting her up over dinner. After the meal they had all gone into the drawing room for a photograph.

He leapt out of bed and ran downstairs to the study where the albums were kept. He remembered that he and Emma had spent an evening sticking all those photographs in it. He quickly found the right album and turned the pages. The photographs of his father at Christmas time brought back happy memories. He carried on with his search and came across one of Moondancer arriving at the yard and being led out of the horsebox by a smiling Joe. He turned over the page and there was the photograph he wanted. His mother was standing beside Guy Pritchard, her head towards the camera, but she was looking over her shoulder and the front of her dress where the brooch would have been was not visible. Disappointed, Fergus returned the album to its drawer and went back to bed, thinking once again of the mud on his mother's skirt as she had left the walled garden that morning.

* * *

Colette Kildare's face was drawn and pale when she came down for breakfast but she was in a more talkative mood than the day before.

'Fergus, you'll have to take charge of the funeral arrangements. I think it should be immediate family only, and no flowers.'

'We ought to let Joe come, he was so fond of Father.'

'Must we? You know what I think about that man. You can do it all through Mulcready's in Limerick, they're very efficient.'

'I'll get on to them this morning, although I'm not sure yet when it can take place.'

'What do you mean?'

'The Gardai will have to give their okay. The pathologist has to examine the body and then there's the inquest. It's not like an ordinary death. Sometimes it can take weeks.'

'What's the pathologist going to find?'

'I don't know, Mother. They'll want to discover precisely how Father died and see if the body yields clues about the identity of his killer.'

'From a skeleton?'

Fergus thought he detected a hint of anxiety in his mother's voice. The business with the brooch and the photograph had unnerved him. No doubt if he asked her, everything could be explained. He decided to leave it to a more opportune moment.

'I agree it seems highly improbable and I expect

nothing will come of it, but the Gardai have to start somewhere. No doubt they'll be out combing the grounds looking for the murder weapon.' He found himself studying her face, watching for the slightest reaction.

'How can you be so clinical about it? He was your father.'

'Mother, I'm just being realistic. I don't believe anyone loved Father more than I did. If we weaken now we'll never be able to survive the months ahead. You know as well as I do that Drumgarrick is as good as bankrupt and I'll have to contact Gleasons this morning about the will and things.'

'Drumgarrick is yours, you know that.' His mother's voice betrayed no hint of resentment.

'And hopefully my son's after me. I think there's some life insurance and of course the money from the insurance on Moondancer.' Fergus chose not to add that as far as he knew the shares in Moondancer were pledged to the bank.

'What's happening on that? The litigation appears to be dragging on for ever.'

'The last thing I heard was that the other side are about to cave in.'

'That's what lawyers always say. I think I'll give Eamon Fitzwilliams a call and see what he has to advise. He's got rather more business sense than you or your father ever had.'

Fergus stopped himself rising to the bait. 'If you

insist. Don't go telling him anything other than the bare details of Father's death.'

'For heaven's sake why not? He was a close friend of your father's.'

'It's just that I don't want people gossiping or having pity on us.'

'I never could understand you,' she sighed and changed the subject. 'We've no food in the house. Could you pop into town this afternoon and get some? I can't face talking to the butcher and people.'

'I'm sorry, I'm going to the races.'

'To the races? I don't believe it! The day after your father's body has been found. What will people think of us?'

'I don't really care what people think,' Fergus replied, echoing Joe and suppressing his own misgivings about appearing at Tipperary. 'Tongue in Cheek was due to run and Joe and I felt that Father would have wanted it this way.'

'I don't see how a groom would know what your father would have wanted. You at least should know better.' She rose from the table and strode out of the room.

Angry and chastened, Fergus went outside into the courtyard. At the far end the Gardai and two men in plain clothes were talking outside the barn where his father's car had been stored. He presumed that they were about to examine it for fingerprints or other clues. He walked up towards them and then turned left towards the walled garden. The young Gard on the gate allowed him to go in. The makeshift tent was still in place and beside it several officers were chatting together over a cigarette and a cup of coffee. They stopped laughing when they spotted him. He retraced his steps and went to the stables of the four brood mares, peering in and talking to each in turn. Simon, the lad from the village, had already mucked out and was busying himself with the two foals who in a couple of months would be going up to Goffs for the December sales.

Still angry with his mother, Fergus strode down to Tongue in Cheek's stable. Joe was grooming the horse and preparing him for the trip to Tipperary. Fergus had never felt less like riding in a race. Tongue in Cheek was still on the burly side, as Joe was leaving quite a lot for him to work on before having him truly fit. Even so, Fergus knew he would need all his strength to hold him back and finish in the ruck. Thank God he had eleven stone six pounds to carry and hadn't needed to lose any weight.

'Don't forget it's the first race, guv'nor,' said Joe. 'If we leave in twenty minutes it'll give us plenty of time to settle him down and you could even walk the course if you fancied it.'

Fergus nodded. Joe always insisted that he walk the course before riding in a race; whether or not he fancied it didn't really come into it.

*   *   *

Jack's morning had been singularly unproductive. His visits to the butcher, general stores and baker in Drumgarrick had yielded a steak, half a dozen eggs and a loaf, but precious little information on Patrick Kildare. The feeling was one of shock and anger at the murder of such a decent man; the common view was to put it down to a homicidal maniac. An afternoon at the races was now just what Jack needed. He had taken Amy to the bar up in the grandstand which overlooked the winning post and told her about his morning activities.

'Occasionally this kind of field work pays dividends,' he concluded. 'Now is the one time when the locals are likely to gossip with a complete stranger – not that they had much to say on this occasion. Come on, drink up. Fergus is due to ride in the first and if we go now we can catch a glimpse of him in the parade ring – if he decides to turn up, that is.'

They went down the steps and across the enclosure, where on all four sides the bookmakers had their pitches. They arrived by the parade ring which was right next to the course as the horses were being led round. Tongue in Cheek was there, carrying number six. Jack pointed him out.

'Nice-looking horse, isn't he?' he said.

'Beautiful. He looks more like a chaser than a hurdler. His lad seems a bit crusty.'

'That's Joe, the stud groom. He's the one I chatted

up in the pub. Lean and wiry. You can believe he used to be a jockey.'

'Here come the jockeys now. Is Fergus among them?'

'Yes, he is,' said Jack, surprised to see him. 'Over there. He's the one wearing the yellow cap with purple spots.'

'He's good-looking too. I like the Roman nose.'

'Do you think he's the type who could kill his father?'

'He looks too nice – unhappy as well. This must be a terrible ordeal for him.'

'It can't be that bad,' answered Jack. 'He didn't have to run the horse or at least he could have put up another jockey; I suspect our Mr Kildare has a heart of stone.'

'Are we going to have a bet before the race?'

'I'll have a fiver on him just in case. The tote's over there. The minimum's a couple of quid or so.'

'Thanks, but I'll keep to the bookies. See you by the winning post.'

Amy went off to the bookies and Jack soon lost sight of her among the other racegoers. Tongue in Cheek was on offer at odds varying from four to one to two to one and Jack liked the fact that there seemed a far greater spread than on English courses. Sometimes you felt there that the chalk which marked up the prices was on auto pilot. Tongue in Cheek was drifting in the betting and no sooner had he wagered a tenner on at fours than he saw sixes marked up. It was a locally trained horse called Hoolahan's Folly which was attracting all the money and Jack watched as his odds tumbled from seven to one down to five to two. He was just building up the courage to have twenty pounds on when a roughly dressed man, a gypsy judging from the ring in his ear and his dark sallow skin, pushed past him and had a monkey on in dirty fivers. Jack couldn't believe he had five bob to call his own let alone five hundred pounds. Two to one was now the best on offer and cursing himself for having missed the best price Jack walked back to the members' enclosure and found Amy in the stands. He was about to ask her if she had bet when the starter called the runners in.

Down at the start Fergus put his father's death to the back of his mind and concentrated on the job in hand. It was the first time he had ever stopped any horse from winning and he was beginning to get nervous. He and Joe had two plans. The first was to let Tongue in Cheek whip round at the start, lose a few lengths and then let him get stuck behind a few no-hopers. Tipperary was quite a tight left-handed course, and so that should be easy, but in case it wasn't, they had Plan B which was far less subtle. It consisted of simply pulling Tongue in Cheek up quickly at any point during the latter half of the race if there looked to be even the slightest chance of his finishing in the first half-dozen. With his past record, the stewards wouldn't need much convincing that Fergus had thought the horse had broken yet another blood vessel.

Fergus made sure he was one of the first to have his girths checked so that he could get where he wanted to be at the start, and then when everyone was ready and the starter called all the runners to line up, he deliberately put Tongue in Cheek's nose right onto the white tape and waited. As the starter pulled the lever and the tape shot up, Tongue in Cheek sprang backwards in fright as the other runners raced past him towards the first hurdle. By the time Fergus got him going again he was some fifteen lengths adrift of the last horse and, for the first circuit, that was where he remained.

Fergus then made the mistake of getting a little closer. As they turned down the far side for the second and last time, Tongue in Cheek suddenly realised that he was meant to be racing and really caught hold of the bit. As he passed the first tail-ender, he began to get even stronger and it was obvious he had no intention of going along with Fergus's wishes. He barged his way between the next two horses in his effort to get to the front. As they turned for home with two hurdles left to jump he was only twenty lengths off the leaders when finally, and much to Fergus's relief, he ran out of breath and stopped pulling.

Jack switched his attention from Tongue in Cheek, who clearly had no chance of winning, to what was happening at the front of the field. Hoolahan's Folly had ranged up to share the lead approaching the final hurdle, and Amy was shouting in encouragement. His jockey was riding as if he had a double handful and hardly moved a muscle as he pinged the last flight and passed the grey who had led throughout. A roar of delight went up from the crowd and Jack began to feel that he was the only man in Tipperary who wasn't on this particular certainty. He, that is, and the jockey on board the grey. Standing up like a policeman and riding for all his worth, he drove his mount back into the lead with a couple of cracks on the backside. Suddenly, Hoolahan's Folly wasn't going as easily as his supporters had imagined, and his jockey quickly picked up the stick in his left hand and hit him down the shoulder. Hoolahan's Folly immediately veered away to his right, losing valuable ground. Not wishing a repeat, his jockey resorted to riding with hands and heels only, quickly getting the horse back on an even keel. Hoolahan's Folly stuck out his neck and strode out gamely for the line. For the last fifty yards of the run-in they were locked together and as they reached the post it was only on the nod that the winner was decided.

'Yahoo! He's won!' screamed Amy. 'How about that!' She gave Jack a huge grin and beat the air with pleasure.

'That was fantastic,' he replied, trying to appear to all the world as if he himself had backed the winner as well. As he looked on to the course, he spotted Tongue in Cheek finishing strongly through tired horses. To describe that as late progress, he thought to himself, would be an understatement.

'What made you back old Hoolahan then?' he asked Amy, trying to convey a sense of familiarity about the horse.

'A real piece of luck. I was about to have a couple of pounds on Tongue in Cheek when this wily looking Irishman in front of me asked for a hundred pounds on Hoolahan's Folly. I put on my most innocent face and asked him if he knew something and he winked at me and said it was a certainty. So I had a little flutter.'

'I suppose you only got the five to two?'

'Is that what it started at? I found this nice bookie who gave me eight to one. Judging by the way you cheered him home, I guess you backed him too? What fun!'

Jack couldn't bring himself to admit he hadn't. 'Just a little saver. I didn't want to desert Tongue in Cheek, although I somehow don't think that Mr Kildare joined me with his money down. The horse was hardly drawing breath when they finished. Come on, if we're quick we'll catch them dismounting and just see if the damned animal's even sweating.'

Fergus was delighted with Tongue in Cheek's performance, considering it was his first run of the season, and his only problem had been in restraining him. He wasn't cut out, mentally or physically, for pulling horses. His arms were aching from his effort. He exchanged a few brief words with one or two of the other jockeys and then jogged back from past the finishing post towards the area where the unplaced runners were being unsaddled. Joe was waiting for him with a sponge and rug, looking suitably serious.

'Everything all right?' he asked, grabbing hold of the bridle as Fergus hopped off and began undoing the saddle to go and weigh in. Joe patted Tongue in Cheek lovingly on the neck. 'That's a good boy.'

'Fine, he really enjoyed himself. This will have brought him on a treat.'

'You finished a bit well.'

'Couldn't hold him back any longer. The others were all going backwards and he was full of running. What's the matter?'

Fergus noticed that Joe was staring suspiciously towards the paddock rail about ten yards away. 'Don't look now, but see that man and woman over there? I think I recognise him.'

Fergus turned round with his saddle in his hand. 'I see them. So?'

'Just before your father disappeared, that chap was hanging around the bar in the village buying me drinks and trying to get me to talk about Moondancer's death and asking questions about your family.'

'The Gardai?'

'No, he's English. My guess is that he's working for the insurers or something.'

'What's he doing here then?'

'Your father, guv'nor. The bloody vultures are gathering.'

Amy and Jack watched Fergus unsaddle and walk over to the weighing room.

'What did I tell you, Amy? That horse hasn't even had a race. I sweat more waiting for my bank statement. He wasn't trying, your lovely Mr Kildare.'

'Which isn't surprising after what he's gone through. I admire him for even having a go. Anyway, I suspect you're talking through your pocket.'

Jack saw no need to admit that he had only had a fiver on. 'I never complain about losing. Did you see Joe giving us a funny look? He's probably remembered me from our meeting at the pub.'

'Wasn't that a bit silly then, coming here and being recognised?'

'Why? I want them to know that the insurers are still interested. I can't very well send in a visiting card, can I?'

'I suppose not. Cheer up. Let's go and collect.'

Jack fumbled around in his pocket and produced a betting slip. He had no intention of telling Amy that it represented his wager on Tongue in Cheek and that he didn't have a penny on the winner. 'I'll collect mine in a moment,' he said. 'There's a bit of a queue over there at my bookie's. Let me come and help you carry your winnings.'

He followed Amy over to a bookie on the far corner of the enclosure. Liam Hartley looked far from pleased with the world. He grabbed her ticket and handed it to his clerk. Jack's eyes nearly fell out of his head as Hartley started counting out Amy's winnings from a fat wad of ready money.

'That makes four hundred and fifty, less tax,' he concluded, delivering the total as if he were reading his own epitaph. She smiled disarmingly and stuffed the money into her handbag.

'Brilliant. Come on, let's go and have a celebratory Guinness. Oh sorry, I forgot, you've still got to collect.'

'You go ahead and set them up. Make mine a large Jameson. I won't be a minute.'

He watched her walk off towards the bar and then waited five minutes before going to join her.

'Collected?' she asked, handing over his whisky. 'Did you get the eight to one as well?'

'Not quite. Mustn't grumble though.'

Chapter Seven

The four men who gathered at lunchtime in a private room at the Rutland Arms had not the slightest interest in the result of the one thirty at Tipperary although in normal circumstances each of them would have enjoyed having a large wager on a steamer like Hoolahan's Folly. For the previous few days their attention had been focused on the yearling sales being held by the auctioneers Messrs Tattersalls but it had been diverted by the news splashed across that morning's racing pages. The headlines of 'Stud owner murdered' and 'Irish breeder death mystery' had provoked a flurry of phone calls and a speedily arranged meeting of the surviving owners of the stallion Moondancer. Three of them now sat round a mahogany table in the middle of the room while the fourth, and easily the youngest, paced distractedly up and down. Over six foot tall and what one of his rich American women owners had described as dangerously good-

looking, Hugo Fitzwilliams was so lost in his thoughts
that he hadn't even bothered to remove the brown
trilby that made a forlorn attempt at covering his crop
of pitch-black hair.

'Hugo, for the Lord's sake, come and sit down.
You're making me nervous with all your walking.'
Eamon Fitzwilliams, the bloodstock agent, motioned
him towards the empty chair beside him.

'I prefer to keep moving, Dad. This couldn't have
come at a worse time. It's typical of bloody Patrick.'

'Do you mean, to get murdered or merely be discovered?' asked the middle-aged man sitting at the
head of the table, a glass of champagne in his right
hand and a copy of *Sporting Life* in front of him. He
took a sip of his drink. 'You really are a hard bastard,
Hugo, though that's probably why I like you training
for me. Sit down and relax. For all we know, Patrick
killed himself. All it says here is that he was found by
Fergus in the walled garden at Drumgarrick and that
the Gardai are investigating.'

'I suppose that's your definition of an Irish suicide,
eh Guy? Patrick manages to hit himself on the back of
the head and then bury himself four foot under-
ground below the asparagus.' Eamon Fitzwilliams
was less than pleased with the flippant approach being
adopted by Guy Pritchard. But he knew he had to be
careful. Pritchard was one of his best clients and in
the bloodstock business the only friends you had were
four-legged.

'And how did you know that, Eamon? There's no mention here of how he died. Unless of course you were there at the time.' Guy Pritchard was beginning to enjoy himself.

'I know because I telephoned the racing correspondent of the *Irish Times* in Dublin this morning and he filled me in with the latest news. The Gardai believe the body's been there since March, since Patrick disappeared. Apparently he'd been struck over the head from behind with a blunt instrument—'

'Guy's tongue possibly?'

Fitzwilliams ignored the jibe which came from the fourth member of the group '. . . and they're considering the theory that this is the work of the same people who killed Moondancer.'

Kieran Steele, the fourth man, rose from the table, walked over to the sideboard and poured himself a large whisky. A short dapper man, conservatively dressed in a Donegal tweed suit, it was only his greying hair that gave any indication that he was in his late fifties. A self-made millionaire, he was the youngest of the nine surviving children of a farm labourer in Tramore. Memories of his deprived childhood made him a hard and determined businessman; he had absolutely no intention of losing his wealth and position and returning to his roots. He demanded and expected unwavering loyalty from his employees and associates. Behind his back he was known as 'the Berlin wall' – you crossed him at your peril.

Having filled his glass almost to the brim and added the merest suspicion of water, he took a couple of generous swallows and turned to face his partners: 'Who's kidding who here? I for one have never bought that IRA rubbish and I don't believe that any of you lot have either. If we're honest, Moondancer's death was a relief to us all. He was useless as a sire and the only way we were ever going to see our investment back was from the insurers. That's why we insured, wasn't it? In the absence of the horse having an accident, it was necessary for him to meet with an untimely end and, hey presto, we collect. I've never asked which of you pulled the trigger and to be frank I don't care. What I want is very simple: for the insurers to pay up so I can collect my share.'

'I suppose you think I killed Moondancer,' Guy Pritchard commented lazily. His tone of voice gave no clue to his thoughts on the subject. He had learnt long ago while growing up in the East End of London never to show his true feelings. As far as he was concerned sleeves were for noses not hearts. Not that anyone hearing him talk would have guessed his background. Elocution lessons had seen to that.

'As I've already said,' answered Kieran Steele, 'it doesn't matter to me. Whoever killed Moondancer did us all a favour.'

'Perhaps you did it,' said Hugo Fitzwilliams from across the room where he was resting his back against the mantelpiece above the fire.

'That would make sense,' interjected Guy Pritchard who pursed his lips as if he had been about to smile and had then thought better of it.

'What the hell do you mean by that, Guy?' asked Steele angrily.

'Only that my brokers have been making one or two inquiries on my behalf into your financial position. They tell me that your companies made quite a large loss last year and I suspect that shutdown at your Dublin factory wouldn't have helped much. I reckon you could do with your million and a quarter from the horse.'

'Guy, if there's one thing I admire about you, it's your consistency. When I first met you I thought you were a disagreeable sod and I still do. I just tell myself that businessmen, like whores, can't choose their bedmates, provided of course the price is right. But isn't this a case of the pot calling the kettle black? Haven't you had one or two problems with your clubs in Soho, or shouldn't we talk about them in public?'

Guy Pritchard's initial silence showed that Steele had hit a raw nerve. Pritchard was always at pains to describe himself and be described in the press as a financier and private investor which, in one sense, was true. What he didn't want the world or his children to know was that he made his money out of hostess nightclubs, massage parlours and pornography. That's why he liked Hugo Fitzwilliams. When the young but brilliantly successful trainer had discovered his owner's secret, all he had done was to badger him for a few free blue movies. Pritchard wasn't prepared to let Steele's jibe go unanswered.

'I don't know what you're talking about. All my business interests are fine. If they weren't, I'm hardly likely to have been buying so heavily at this week's sales.'

Steele, who in contrast to his counterpart enjoyed showing his every emotion, contented himself with a wry smile. He knew as well as Guy Pritchard that ostentatious displays of wealth were often merely a ploy to deceive anxious creditors into believing all was well and possibly even giving more credit.

'Come on, you two,' said Eamon Fitzwilliams, anxious to avoid any further acrimony. 'Now's not the time for trading insults.' The bloodstock dealer had a vested interest in the continued financial wellbeing and unity of all the parties in the room. Steele and Pritchard both had several horses in training in his son's yard and although he didn't give a monkey's cuss if they didn't like each other, he didn't want open warfare between them. He tried to steer the conversation back to the purpose of their meeting. 'Isn't the real question, gentlemen, whether the discovery of Patrick's body is going to affect the payout on the insurance? Both Hugo and I have money at stake too, remember.'

'I don't see why it should,' said Pritchard. 'The case is fixed to be heard in February and our lawyers are convinced that the insurers are on the verge of settling. Even if Kieran's right and Moondancer wasn't shot by the IRA, there's no way the insurers could ever prove it was one of us and abort the policy. If anything, Patrick's death is an advantage. It means he can't suddenly turn up at the trial and embarrass us.'

'Guy, you say my boy's hard, but at times you're something else.' Eamon Fitzwilliams regretted the words as soon as he had uttered them.

'You can stop your posturing, Eamon. Show me a bloodstock agent who wouldn't syndicate his grandmother and I'll show you a liar. No one was more glad than you when Moondancer died and you were the first to say that Patrick would make a terrible witness in court.'

'All right, Guy. I won't pretend I was upset when the horse was killed. But at least remember Patrick Kildare was my friend, and someone has murdered him. You can't equate that with Moondancer. And what I don't want now is the Gardai trying to blame it on my son or me,' he paused unintentionally, 'or any of us.'

'I'm glad you added the last bit,' retorted Pritchard, helping himself to a smoked salmon sandwich from the silver tray hitherto untouched in front of him. He took an enormous mouthful and continued talking: 'None of us, I'm sure, need have any conscience as far as Patrick's death is concerned. We must help the police, or whatever they're called in Ireland, with their inquiries, and if they say it's the work of the IRA that's their business. For all I know they're probably right.'

'For once I agree with Guy,' said Kieran Steele, taking a sandwich from the tray himself. 'And what about you, Hugo? You've gone very quiet again. Dreaming of those gallops on the Curragh?'

'Something else has occurred to me,' replied the young Irishman in his gentle brogue. 'Now that Patrick's dead, presumably his beneficiaries inherit his share in the litigation?'

'Good point,' said Pritchard. 'In all the drama I had overlooked that aspect. He's probably left the house to Fergus – you know, all that romantic baloney of passing it from son to son and making impoverishment hereditary. As for the shares in Moondancer, I imagine they'll go to either Colette or Fergus. I hope it's Colette. Fergus is a bit too sentimental for my liking. He'll be more worried about catching his father's killer than collecting on the insurance.'

'I don't believe it matters too much,' said Steele. 'Patrick once told me that he was up to his neck to the Allied Irish. The bank will be as keen to get their hands on the readies as we are, provided of course they took the shares in the horse as security for any loan.'

'That must be right,' said Pritchard. 'Eamon, you

can do us all a favour. You know Colette best. Give her a call over the weekend when she's recovered from the shock and started thinking about the will, and use that Irish charm of yours to find out just who's inherited what. If she's got the shares, make sure she doesn't do anything to foul up any settlement.'

'This weekend? Don't you think that's a bit tasteless?'

'Taste? What's that got to do with it? Anyway, I'm sure Colette will welcome your particular shoulder to cry on.' Pritchard's dig was not lost on the others in the room. Fitzwilliams' response was to change the subject.

'Well, unless there's anything else, there are one or two nice yearlings coming up that I thought Hugo and I might go and inspect. That Dancing Brave colt might appeal to you, Guy.' After what Kieran Steele had said about Pritchard's financial position, Eamon Fitzwilliams couldn't resist the chance of goading him into another expensive purchase.

'If you say so, or even to Kieran perhaps?'

Steele suddenly felt the urge to teach Pritchard a lesson by outbidding him that evening at the sales ring but he realised that that was just what Pritchard was trying to push him into doing. The time had come to leave. 'I'll think about it. I'll be in touch with you later.'

Guy Pritchard watched him leave and then rose from his chair, walked round the table and put his hand on Eamon Fitzwilliams' shoulder. The bloodstock dealer later hoped that his client had not detected the shudder it sent through him.

'Don't forget to make that call to Colette, Eamon, will you?'

'Of course not, Guy.'

'And phone me at the Bedford Lodge if you like that Dancing Brave.'

'Sure thing. It won't be cheap, though.'

'The best never is.' Pritchard put on his dark blue cashmere overcoat, grabbed a last sandwich and, with a wave to Hugo Fitzwilliams, left the room.

Father and son were alone. Eamon doted on his son but like most fathers was fully aware of his flaws as well as his strengths. Hugo was ambitious and able, and determined to have his own way. The charm which he could turn on for any wealthy or potential owner masked a violent temper which flared all too readily if anyone put a foot out of line. That was unfortunate although not in itself dangerous. What was more worrying was his weakness for the opposite sex, a hereditary condition in the Fitzwilliams family. Already a father of two, Hugo was not averse to adultery or cuckoldry.

'Are you all right, son? You're looking a bit pale. There's not something you want to tell me, is there, now the other two are gone?' Eamon asked the question hoping that the answer would be 'no'.

'There is actually and you might as well know now.'

Eamon paused and waited for it. At times like this
he missed the counsel and support of his wife, Rhona,
who had been killed in a car accident five years
previously.

'It's Emma.'

'What about her?' Eamon knew that his son had
been having an affair for the past eighteen months or
more with Fergus Kildare's girlfriend, but he had
hoped that it would eventually blow itself out, provided of course Hugo's wife didn't find out in the
meantime.

'She's pregnant.' Hugo Fitzwilliams half laughed
as he said the crucial word.

'You silly bastard! What bloody timing. She'll have
to get rid of it.'

'Ah, but there's the crack. She's a good Catholic
girl.'

'It's a bit late to be that, isn't it?' Eamon glared at
his son. 'You ought to have been gelded, that's your
trouble.' With that he turned and stormed out of the
room.

Chapter Eight

Colette Kildare heard the sound of the horsebox returning but made no effort to leave her bed and find out how her son had got on. She was surprised, as well as irritated, that he had gone ahead and ridden the day after discovering his father's body. She knew how much he had loved him and what he must now be suffering, but there was little she could say or offer by way of comfort, even if she had felt inclined to do so. She had made a dreadful mistake in marrying Patrick Kildare, as she had realised within a few weeks of their marriage. By then it was too late to do anything about the arrival of their son who thereafter had become a symbol of her captivity. She had tried to love him, to be like other mothers, but the trouble was simple: he was his father's son, a Kildare through and through; he looked like his father, he talked and walked like his father, he even made the same facial expressions as his father. She laughed to herself. And, like his father, he was a rotten judge of women. Emma no more loved Fergus than she herself had loved Patrick. That sensual little bitch was just playing with Fergus. The poor fool must be blind not to realise that Hugo Fitzwilliams was where Emma's interest lay at the moment.

And of course there was one other damning similarity: both men lived for their horses. When at the age of nineteen she had agreed to become Patrick Kildare's second wife she had imagined that being the mistress of a large house and stud would more than offset the constant presence of those four-legged beasts. How naive and wrong she had been. Patrick's finances were as precarious as the slated roof of his house and his idea of a perfect spring evening was delivering a foal to one of his beloved brood mares.

After only two years of marriage, Patrick Kildare had realised that they were never going to have a loving or in any sense close relationship and had proposed a kind of pact: that they should stay together for Fergus's sake and that she would be free to have her own private life, provided it remained as such. She had agreed. At least that meant she would never have to suffer his enjoying her body again. She still shuddered at the memory of his left hand with its stump of a thumb and missing finger caressing her breasts.

From that day on they had enjoyed separate bedrooms and, in emotional terms, separate lives. She had considered leaving him on several occasions but she had no money of her own and who would support her? The lovers she took were never the sort that she would want to settle down with, even if any of them were free to do so. She was sufficiently honest to recognise that the only person she could ever really love was herself and that sex and infatuation were much more fun than marriage and commitment. After all, weren't trailers always better than the movies they advertised?

She had spent that afternoon in her bedroom planning the funeral service, which she had decided would not be family only after all, and trying on clothes. Despite her husband's increasing financial problems she had always enjoyed turning up at the bloodstock sales in Dublin and Newmarket, and after Moondancer's arrival at Deauville as well, wearing the latest fashions. The sole consolation about the breeding business was its innate virility. The competition and high stakes acted as wonderful aphrodisiacs and she had used these occasions to meet new men and have short yet passionate affairs. Patrick's disappearance had sadly but inevitably put an end to all that. She expected that the funeral would attract a large crowd from the racing world and now that she was officially a widow and free she wanted to launch herself on the social scene.

She had made one other decision. She would leave Drumgarrick for good by Christmas. The house was going to Fergus and he was welcome to it.

101

She lay back against the huge feather pillows, propped up against the headboard, as she did most afternoons when she retired upstairs to her bed, books and fantasies, and began re-reading her husband's will. Fergus didn't know that she had a copy but Patrick had given her one shortly after he had made it six years ago. He hadn't shown it to Fergus for fear of upsetting him, not that he had intended to betray his son. It was just that he was honouring the final part of his pact with his wife, namely that he would ensure that she would be provided for after his death. At that time he had expected to live for some time yet and had assumed that Moondancer would be a success, enabling him to pay off all his debts. He had therefore left the house and stud to Fergus and the shares in Moondancer to her.

Poor old Fergus, she reflected. He would have a terrible shock when he discovered that while Drumgarrick might be his in name, the real owners had a branch in the high street. Every single penny owed by her late husband was secured against the house and stud. The shares in Moondancer were blissfully unencumbered. Once the insurers had paid up, her portion would amount to over half a million punts. Together with the insurance policy on Patrick's life, she would be worth nine hundred thousand punts. That was enough for her to live off. She couldn't decide whether to buy a house in Dublin or move to London but there was no rush to make up her mind.

Colette slipped off the bed and, dressed only in a long satin dressing gown, walked over to the dressing table and sat down in front of it. She could hear movement downstairs, probably Fergus making himself some tea. It could only be about five thirty judging from the light outside. As she combed her hair she studied herself in the mirror. The face of a widow. She had aged remarkably well. There were no wrinkles. The hazel eyes she had inherited from her mother drew attention away from her less than perfect nose, and her rosebud lips gave her an insouciance which was deliciously misleading, as her admirers had quickly found out on closer acquaintance. Her skin was smooth to touch and even if she didn't have the high cheekbones possessed by every heroine of romantic fiction, she had the kind of looks which men obviously found attractive. She thought of all the hours she had spent here happily combing back her long black hair and experimenting with make-up, and wondered whether Fergus would let her take the dressing table with her. She would ask him tonight before he found out about the will.

She began to picture herself at the funeral. She had rejected all her present wardrobe for one reason or another and decided that she should use her husband's burial as an excuse to go out tomorrow and buy a new outfit, something which she could wear subsequently at cocktail parties or smart lunches with the right pieces of jewellery to give it colour. At the service she would content herself with a very simple sentimental piece. And underneath her new outfit she would wear nothing. The cool draught would be a stimulating reminder of the wind of change that lay ahead for her.

Downstairs the telephone was ringing yet again. All day she had steadfastly refused to answer it for fear of having to play the role of the desolate widow to sympathetic callers. It was far easier for her silence to be construed as mourning. Now he was home, Fergus could deal with it. She was finishing combing her hair when there was a knock on her door. She walked over and opened it.

'Sorry to disturb you,' said Fergus, 'but that was the Gardai on the line. They say they've been trying to contact us all day. They want to come over and take statements from both of us and wondered whether tomorrow would be convenient. I said I thought it would be okay but would call back later if you weren't ready yet.'

Colette was almost as tall as her son and as she looked at him she could see by the marks round his eyes that he had been crying. She felt curiously unmoved.

'No, that's fine,' she told him. 'They said they'd need signed statements from us.'

'We can expect them at around twelve o'clock and I suggest we deal with them in the drawing room again. The only other question is whether we should ask

Tommy Kirkpatrick to be present.' Kirkpatrick was the senior partner of the family's solicitors and had drafted Patrick's will. 'The trouble is, he may not be able to come at such short notice.'

Colette immediately grasped the opportunity.

'I think we ought to. Why don't you phone him at his office or, if he's left, at his home number. It's downstairs in the book. You could ask him to bring along your father's will and any other details about your father's estate.'

Colette was standing on the threshold of her bedroom and had only half opened the door to her son. She could see Fergus looking through the gap and noticing the various clothes she had been trying on strewn across the floor. She had no intention of offering any explanation.

'There's one small thing, Fergus, and I'm mentioning it because it's the last time I ever want to burden you with financial matters or discuss the house. Your father always told me that Drumgarrick would come to you, together with all its contents, and I accepted that as your right. It's just that I wondered whether I could keep my dressing table. It's not very valuable and over the years I've become very attached to it. It was a present from your father shortly after we married.' In fact it had belonged to Fergus's grandmother. 'Could I possibly keep it?'

Fergus was slightly surprised at his mother's sense of timing yet inwardly pleased if she really meant what she said. He had to admit to himself that he was also relieved that she seemed to have made up her mind to leave Drumgarrick. He would not shirk the responsibility of providing for her financially and once he had paid off the debts with the insurance money from the horse, he intended to take out a mortgage on the house and give her an annual income. That, together with the expected life insurance on his father, would, he hoped, satisfy her. Then if he and Joe could pull off the coup in January, all his problems would be solved.

He smiled at his mother. 'Of course, and if there's anything else of particular sentimental value, you must take it, if you're sure you want to move out. As far as I'm concerned, Drumgarrick is as much your home as mine.'

She shook her head. 'No, you must have your own life here. With Emma,' she added innocently.

Her son changed the subject. 'Perhaps tomorrow we can also discuss the funeral arrangements.'

'I've one or two suggestions to make. I don't think after all we should make it family only. It's up to you whether we have a wake. In the circumstances it would seem inappropriate but on the other hand your father would have wanted his friends to celebrate his life.'

'I'll think about it overnight,' replied Fergus, wondering how many more times he would be asked to speculate on what his father would have wanted. As far as he was concerned, only one such wish could be identified with any certainty: that his killer or killers be found and brought to justice.

Fergus left his mother and went downstairs to telephone Tommy Kirkpatrick. The solicitor who had acted for his father for over thirty years was more than happy to come over although Fergus thought he detected a certain nervous edge creep into his voice when he asked him to bring along the will.

'Are you sure now's the right time to be doing this?'

'Don't worry. I'm pretty certain I know what it says but my mother wants to get it over with.'

There was a slight pause before the solicitor replied. He had of course drafted the document and was well aware of what it would do to Fergus. He decided that, in the best tradition of bad news, it could be postponed until the following day.

'I'll be along by about eleven thirty,' he said. 'I want you to know how upset I am about all this. Your father was a good friend to me as well as being a loyal client and he will be sorely missed.'

Fergus thanked him for his thoughts and put down the receiver. He looked out of the kitchen window towards the barn at the other end of the courtyard. There were still people inside inspecting his father's car and he wondered when the hunt would start for the murder weapon. There was a lot of ground to search around the house and even if the Gardai had the manpower available he thought it highly unlikely that they would find anything. It had probably been disposed of long ago. No doubt they would start by digging up the rest of the asparagus bed. He thought of the brooch hidden away safely upstairs and wondered how it had come to be near his father's body. He had intended to return it to his mother and ask her when she had last seen it but something in her manner just now had put him off. If he was honest with himself, his attitude was ambivalent. He didn't want to believe that she could have had any part in his father's death – after all, what would she gain from it? – yet on the other hand something inside him, no doubt born of years of resentment at her failure to show him any kind of affection, made him believe her capable of at least planning it, if not actually doing the deed herself. No doubt she would be able to give a perfectly innocent explanation and he resolved to ask her the following day.

The telephone rang, interrupting his thoughts. It was Emma phoning from Newmarket.

'Darling, at last, I've been trying to get through all day. I'm so sorry about your father. It's dreadful. You must be feeling shattered.'

Fergus sensed that she was playing a role. Her voice lacked that indefinable quality of sincerity.

'I am. I can't believe anybody could have done this to him. How did you hear?'

'It's all over this morning's papers. Hugo and his father are in a terrible state. Do you want me to fly home tomorrow? I would have come today if I could have got hold of you.'

'I was out and Mother was refusing to answer the phone.'

'How is she?'

Fergus knew that Emma hated his mother and that any inquiry after her feelings was pure ritual.

'Bearing up. She's been trying on funeral clothes.'

'Typical. Where were you today?'

'At the races. I rode Tongue in Cheek at Tipperary.'

'You went to the races? I can't believe it!'

Fergus had never told Emma about the proposed coup. It was a secret between him and Joe; not even Tongue in Cheek had been let into it.

'Joe declared him behind my back as he needed a run and he refused to let anyone else ride him.'

'That's still no excuse.'

Fergus thought he could hear stifled laughter in the background.

'Are you alone, Emma?'

'Yes, the others are down at the sales. When's the funeral?'

'Provided the Gardai let it go ahead, it will be on Monday or Tuesday.'

'Can I tell the others?'

'What others?'

'You know, all the people here who knew your father. Hugo and Eamon had a meeting today with

Guy Pritchard and Kieran Steele and I know they'll want to come. Patrick was so popular.'

Fergus didn't much like any of them but he supposed it made sense for them to come. It would also provide an opportunity to discuss the litigation. He wanted that particular matter resolved as soon as possible so the bank could be paid off.

'Yes, go ahead and tell them.'

'When do you want me to come back?'

'Saturday will do fine. Honestly, there's nothing you can do here.'

'Are you sure you can cope?'

'Yes, don't worry. I'll see you on Saturday. Take care.' He put down the receiver. He was sure it was a man he had heard laughing as she talked to him and he had no difficulty imagining what Hugo Fitzwilliams' hands were doing at the time.

Jack and Amy left the bar at Tipperary about an hour after the last race. Amy had backed two more winners in the course of the afternoon and was feeling very pleased with herself and well disposed to the world at large. Her high spirits had attracted the attention of other racegoers; such is the camaraderie of the turf that after each race instant friendships are formed over large whiskies and water. As one punter after another regaled them with racing reminiscences and stories of coups that nearly were, Jack felt himself to be far less relaxed than his companion. His quietness was in part explained by the fact that every horse he backed appeared either to be a non-trier or burdened down by the responsibility of carrying his money; not one of them ever looked like troubling the judge. He was also beginning to worry about the next crucial steps in his investigations. It was all very well talking big in front of the lawyers but at the end of the day most of his work involved thorough and painstaking checking, often without anything to show for it. At least he knew what his immediate plan of action was to be. Provided Seamus's source in the Gardai had come up with the necessary information on the security measures in operation at Drumgarrick, the risk would be minimal. And if all went to plan, the visit might be very worthwhile. After that, the next item on the agenda was to try and talk to Joe again. He was sure from their one meeting in the pub that the stud groom knew more about Moondancer's death than he was letting on. Now that his employer had been found murdered there had to be a chance of his tongue becoming a little looser.

Most of the racegoers had gone home by the time Amy and Jack made their way to the car park. As they passed a telephone, Amy grabbed his arm.

'Hold on,' she said, 'I might as well call those people in Dublin to ensure my meeting's on tomorrow morning. I'm probably over the limit and it's a long way to drive if I'm not wanted.'

She returned five minutes later.

'It was lucky I called. The meeting's been postponed until late afternoon. The chap I wanted to see has been summoned to court to give evidence and there's nobody else in the office who can deal with me. I'll drive over tomorrow morning and fly home from Dublin on Sunday. That means I'm free this evening and unless you have something planned, how about helping me celebrate my victory over the Irish bookies? Come on, cheer up.'

Jack forced a smile to his face. He was due to meet Seamus that evening and didn't want Amy involved in tonight's visit to the Kildare home. She could see him hesitating.

'Is there a problem?'

'No problem. I'd love to have dinner, that's very sporting of you. I'm booked into a hotel about ten miles outside Drumgarrick and I'm sure they'll be able to put you up for the night as well. The food's meant to be pretty good.'

'Great. And tomorrow we can go our separate ways. Have you worked out your next step?'

'I thought I'd try and talk to Joe. I have this feeling he knows something and that maybe the discovery of the body will jog his memory.'

'Do you really think he'll talk to you? I mean, you're on the other side and surely he'd tell the Gardai first?'

'Not necessarily. Not everybody likes confiding to the appropriate authority. They tend to think they'll

112

get themselves into trouble for having withheld information, and you mustn't forget how independent the Irish people are. I accept it's a long shot but, as they say, if you don't run outsiders they can't win races.'

Amy followed Jack in her car to the hotel and managed to book a room on the floor above his. An hour and a half later, at eight o'clock, they were sitting on stools beside the bar of the Ardmore Arms having pre-dinner drinks. Judging from the black and white photographs of point to point races around the walls, the proprietor of the hotel had been a keen amateur rider himself in his youth. As Amy made light conversation, talking over their day, Jack kept looking anxiously at his watch. His repeated attempts to contact Seamus on the telephone from his room had met with no success and he had resorted to slipping the man at reception ten pounds to give Seamus a note when he arrived at eight thirty and to ensure that on no account did he come into the bar. At least the receptionist couldn't very well miss a short, ginger-haired man with gold-rimmed glasses wearing a beige duffel coat.

'Will you be seeing that nice Seamus Pink again?' asked Amy.

'I expect so, sometime,' Jack said vaguely. 'He's involved in one or two other claims I'm working on.' He picked up his drink. 'That's not his real name, you know.'

'I thought it was too good to be true. I've never heard of anyone called Pink before.'

113

'Oh no, he's always been called Pink. It's the Seamus bit he's adopted. He was christened Peter but didn't like it; made him sound like a character from children's television.'

Amy couldn't tell if Jack was having her on. Not that she cared. There was something about him that she found attractive. He appeared to have none of the characteristics one would expect of an allegedly hard-working and cynical investigator. He was transparently honest for a start, and she had been able to tell from his face during the race that he hadn't had a penny on Hoolahan's Folly. He had only started shouting the horse home when she did and, what's more, she had watched him place his bet before the off and it certainly wasn't with the bookmaker he had pointed out afterwards. He also appeared to be kind and thoughtful and, she suspected, genuinely protective. Lastly, he was quite good-looking. The scar on the side of his face gave him a certain machismo – although that wasn't exactly what she sought in a man.

'Why are you staring at me so oddly?' he asked, 'or has some devastating Adonis just walked into the bar? You have to watch out for these glib Irishmen, you know.' Jack turned round to see if anyone was there. He had tried to get the seat facing the door but Amy had beaten him to it.

'I was thinking about you, actually. Your face reminds me of somebody but I can't put my finger on it.'

'Harrison Ford perhaps?'

114

'A Ford yes, but with your battered face more like a model T. It'll come to me. Oh look, it's the lovely Mr Pink.'

Jack swivelled round to see Seamus coming into the bar with all the jauntiness of a man who has just won the national lottery. What was he doing in that dark blue duffel coat and cloth cap? And where the hell were his glasses? Jack put his finger to his mouth to try and warn him not to say anything but Seamus didn't notice. He was too intent on kissing Amy.

'Ah, this is a real treat. Jack never said that you would be here.'

'Nor vice versa. How very remiss of him.' Amy wagged a mocking finger in Jack's face. 'Now, what brings you here, Seamus, or is that a confidential matter?' Before he could answer, she went on: 'Whatever it is, I'll leave you to it. I want to get something from my room anyway.'

Amy rose from her stool, revealing an extremely shapely piece of thigh in the process.

'Seamus, are you going to join us for dinner?' she asked. 'I'm going to Dublin tomorrow and then back to London on Sunday. It's my treat, I've had rather a good day at the races.'

'I'd love—'

'What a pity you can't,' interjected Jack. 'You mentioned something earlier about going to see your widowed mother in Cahir.'

Seamus's expression suggested that his mother's

115

widowhood and place of residence were recent discoveries.

'Did I now? In that case I must reluctantly refuse. No doubt Jack will let me know when you're next over.'

'I'm sure he will,' said Jack impatiently.

Amy couldn't resist a broad grin. 'Is ten minutes long enough for your chat?' she asked.

'That should be ample,' answered Jack. They watched her leave and then Jack walked to the bottom of the stairs to check that she had gone. He also took the opportunity to glower at the man at reception who, with an inane grin on his face, held out the note to show that he was still waiting for Seamus's arrival. Jack resisted the temptation to go over and snatch his money back and instead returned to the bar.

'What's all this about my widowed mother?' asked Seamus, taking off his cap. 'Last time I saw her she was making tea for the man I always thought was her husband and my father.'

'I want you sober tonight, and I don't want Amy involved. If she had any idea what we've got planned for later this evening, she'd probably want to come with us. And that's definitely not on. By the way, what are you doing in that coat and hat and where the devil are your glasses?'

'Don't you think I look good, then? I've put the dark duffel on for later, the cap will keep the chill off my head, and I'm trying out my new contact lenses.

My widowed mother thinks that they really suit me.'

'Well, I don't. They've already cost me a tenner. How are we placed for tonight? Did you get the map?'

Seamus produced a sketch plan from his pocket.

'Flynn, my man in the Gardai, gave it to me earlier. He went up to the house this morning and did his best. On the whole it ties in with the one we did last year. He's marked the spot where the body was found and the stable where Moondancer was killed. I think it should be pretty reliable although he has the occasional trouble knowing his left from his right.'

'Have you got the bugs?'

'Right here.' Seamus opened up his duffel coat to reveal three small electronic bugs stuck to the inside pocket. 'All present and correct. These will work on a five-mile radius and the receiving kit is all set up in the back of the van. Have you decided where we should plant them?'

'I was hoping your man Flynn might be able to help us there. Does he know if Brogan is going to interview Fergus and his mother again and, if so, whether it will be at the house or down at the station?'

'You're in luck. Brogan is going up there tomorrow at midday and if it's like last time they'll see him in the drawing room. From my point of view it's a good place to plant one as I can reach it through those big french windows, coming across the lawn.'

'Well, that's the first bug taken care of. I think we only need one more and that should preferably be by

117

the busiest phone. Did Flynn say anything about that?'

'No, he never saw one in use although apparently there's an extension in the kitchen which you can see through the window from the courtyard.'

'That'll do. It should at least give us some idea of what their plans are and tell us who they talk to. What about the dog? All these places have dogs.'

'I know, but this seems to be the exception. There was no sign of one when I did my research last year and Flynn says he neither heard nor saw one today. I'll soak my hanky in chloroform in case.'

'And the Gardai?'

'There's one man on night duty at the entrance to the walled garden on the west side, but the last thing he'll expect is anyone to be wanting to clamber inside and have a look, particularly now the body's been taken away. We can get in over the wall from the paddock on the other side. There's also a patrol car which drives up to the house on the hour. By my calculations, if we aim to be on the top of the hill which overlooks the study by five to two we can watch the car come and go through the night binoculars and be in and out again by two fifty.'

'Perfect. And what time and where are we going to meet?'

'I've drawn you a little map. It's about five miles from here and easy to find. Shall we say half past one?'

'Agreed. Look out, here she comes.' He took the note and shoved it into his jacket pocket. 'Thank you, Seamus, that should be very useful. I think we might have to consider meeting that claim.'

'I'm sorry,' Amy said, 'have I interrupted you?'

'No,' said Jack, 'we were just finishing. Seamus is already late for his mother.'

Seamus got up and held out his hand. 'Goodbye, Amy, and I pray we meet again.'

'Me too, Seamus.'

Ten minutes later Jack and Amy had ordered dinner and were sitting in the small restaurant which led off from the bar. The conversation was friendly and relaxed. Jack felt on good form, stimulated by the prospect of the night's work ahead. After holding court for an hour he persuaded Amy to tell him something about her university days and then gently probed her about her love life.

'Is there a Mister Right at the moment?' he plucked up the courage to ask as they had their coffee.

'No, there's a Mister All Right who makes me laugh and with whom I have a good time but I'm in no mood for settling down. I have a career, you know. And you? I presume your life style doesn't lend itself to steady relationships, or is there as we talk a thoroughly decent girl curled up in front of the television at your flat, pining for her loved one?'

'Not unless the landlords have re-let the place. Girls

in my experience don't like absentee boyfriends who cancel dates at late notice and who tend to drink too much when they do keep them. I'm a very secretive person and that tends to go down badly in open society. My mother says I became like that – repressed, she calls it – when my father died.'

'When was that?'

'When I was ten. He was a journalist who drowned out in Piraeus while investigating the disappearance of a tanker and its valuable cargo of oil.'

'How ghastly.'

'It was all very suspicious and the British consul thought it might be murder but the Greek police didn't want to know.'

'Didn't that make you very bitter?'

'It did for a long time. I was old enough to understand his loss but too young to come to terms with it. It left me with a deep sense of anger about injustice and the need for retribution and I suppose that partly explains my increasing enthusiasm for this case. Although Fergus may not see it this way, I actually want to see his father revenged.'

'Not forgetting the insurers, I hope.'

'Not forgetting the insurers, no. Don't worry, I won't let my paymasters down. And your parents?'

'I'm glad to say they're both alive and well. At least they were two hours ago when I phoned them. My father's retired from running the farm and spends a large part of his time going to the local race meetings.

There's plenty of them in the West Country at this time of the year.'

'And your mother?'

'She goes with him. Backs winners on the tote for a couple of pounds a time while he, who professes to know the form book backwards, seems to have a continuing run of misfortune.'

'So you've inherited your mother's luck?'

'And my father's love for a plunge. I suppose I like the thrill of having more money on than I can really afford and there's no greater joy than collecting from a bookie.' Jack could think of one but kept his mouth firmly shut. 'That's the one reason I would hate a tote monopoly. You can't build up any feelings against them.'

'I've never considered it in those terms. More coffee?' he asked, signalling to the waitress.

'How about one more Irish and then bed?'

He thought for a moment that she had made him an offer he couldn't refuse.

'Our own,' Amy added pointedly, relieving him of his dilemma.

At ten thirty they said goodnight on the stairs and went to their respective rooms. Jack passed the time by memorising the directions Seamus had given him and trying without much success to do the crossword in the copy of the *Irish Times* he had picked up downstairs.

At long last the time came to leave. Having put on

his sneakers, black pullover and dark trousers, he quietly opened the door and tiptoed downstairs. There was no night porter and save for a single red light in the bar the hotel was in darkness. In his pocket was a night key which he had borrowed earlier from that oaf in reception. He let himself out of the front door and as noiselessly as possible walked round to the back where his car was parked. He opened the unlocked driver's door – he was very slack with hired cars – and looked to make sure no lights had come on in the hotel. None had. He kept his headlights off until he was out of the hotel car park, then set off down the Drumgarrick road, following Seamus's directions for Bregawn. After half a mile he drove over a cattle grid and then took a sharp left up a dirt track. Two hundred yards on he stopped and turned out the lights. He now had to wait for Seamus. The waiting increased his tension about the work ahead, though he was confident that all would go smoothly to plan. Seamus was extremely efficient, almost clinical on such occasions. What they were doing was strictly illegal but not, he reassured himself, in the least bit immoral. Sometimes it was necessary to use underhand means to get at the truth. His clients of course knew nothing about his methods of collecting evidence. If he was caught, he alone would take the rap.

Jack looked at his watch. Seamus wasn't due for another five minutes. He had a sudden craving for a cigarette but decided it was better to remain in complete darkness. He turned on the radio and after a bout of station searching came across one playing 'Strangers in the Night'. He began to hum the tune.

'Who are you waiting for?'

The crisp voice, immediately behind his head, made Jack jerk forward in terror. Instinctively he ducked, and his forehead cracked into the steering wheel. Then, as his brain rapidly put a face to the voice, his fear turned to anger. He looked round.

'What the bloody hell do you think you're doing?' he shouted.

'I'm sorry,' said Amy, genuinely apologetic. 'I didn't mean to give you such a fright. I was asking you the same thing really, only a little more politely.'

At that moment Seamus repeated his trick of arriving at the most inopportune of moments. He parked his van in front of Jack's car and cut his lights.

'This is a funny place for you and Seamus to come and settle insurance claims,' Amy remarked. 'Or do you both talk to the goblins before making any final decisions?'

Seamus walked over and knocked on the driver's window. Still cursing under his breath, Jack wound it down.

'Everything all ri—Ah, I see you've brought the intrepid Amy with you.'

'I haven't,' answered Jack, 'and she isn't coming any further.'

123

'I hope you're not thinking of leaving me here in the middle of nowhere while you two drive off on your own? The answer to that is no way. I'm staying with you.'

Jack got out of the car. He wanted to talk down at her rather than crick his neck trying to turn round and assert himself. 'No, I'm not that heartless. Here, take the keys to the car and the night key to the hotel and go back to bed. Seamus will give you the directions. We have a little business to do and it's a definite case of two's company and three's a crowd.'

'Is it?' she retorted. 'I suspected you earlier and I positively distrust you now. That's why I asked the man on the desk if you had already asked for the night key. He thought we were together and told me you had. By the way, he gave me this note to hand back to you and asked me to pass on the message that there was no sign of the man in the beige duffel.'

Jack cursed the receptionist. 'You still can't come, Amy. Your clients have hired me to do a job and it's not part of the deal that a solicitor rides along to play nanny. Take it from me, you're much better off out of this.'

'Because I'm a woman?'

'It's nothing to do with that. It would make no difference if you were a man and the President of the Law Society. Please don't argue.'

Amy opened her door and joined them on the grass verge. She too knew the psychological value of standing up and facing your opponent.

124

'Seamus,' she said in a voice which was all sweetness and light, 'do you have any objection to my
coming along?'

Seamus put his hands behind his back like an
embarrassed school child.

'It's not his decision. It's mine,' said Jack.

'That's decided then. I'm coming. I'm here to
represent your employers, and in the exercise of my
responsibilities I'm instructing you to take me with
you.'

'No,' answered Jack firmly.

'Right.'

Before they realised what she was doing she had
skipped over to Seamus's van, taken the ignition key
out and, together with the set which Jack had already
given her, shoved them down the front of her blouse.

'Now, am I coming or not?'

'Nothing would give me greater pleasure than to
stick my hand down the front of your blouse, but now
is not the time. You can tag along if you must, but on
your head be it. Now, we'd better get moving and
please, Amy, on this occasion do as you're told.'

'No heroics, I promise,' she answered. 'Brownie's
honour.'

Only when they were seated three abreast on the
front seat of Seamus's van did Amy produce the ignition key from its hiding place.

'Where are we going?' she asked as they drove back
and onto the main road.

'Drumgarrick Stud,' replied Jack.

'What? Are you crazy?'

'No, eccentric possibly. Seamus here has it all nicely worked out, and what better time than the present to visit the scene of the crime.'

They arrived at their reconnaissance point on the top of the hill shortly before two o'clock. They stopped the car beside the road and from their position overlooking the stud two miles below them Seamus was able to watch the comings and goings of the Gardai patrol vehicle through his night binoculars. Its lights appeared just after the hour, going up the drive, and disappeared after going down again five minutes later. The trio got back into the van and having driven down a narrow road for about four minutes Seamus braked sharply and then reversed twenty yards or so up a dirt track. The surrounding trees and bushes meant they couldn't be seen from the road even if, as was highly unlikely, anyone drove up there at that time of night.

'Right,' said Jack as soon as the engine was turned off. 'We're in your hands, Seamus.'

'And there's no safer place. Jack, you and I will go across the field down at the bottom of this road and make our way as far as that oak tree in the middle. You can wait behind it while I enter the house via the drawing room.' Seamus had enough sense not to say anything in front of Amy about the purpose of his visit. 'When I come back we'll go round to the walled garden from the east side.'

'Fine. Okay, Amy,' said Jack turning to her, 'you wait here. We'll be back in about half an hour or so. If we're not here by two thirty, say a quick prayer and go on home.'

'No way. I'm coming with you. I'm afraid of the dark on my own.'

Jack looked at her in exasperation. He had foreseen this and was too worked up to have another fight.

'I can't be bothered to argue with you any more. You can come as far as the oak tree but for God's sake stay low and keep behind me at all times.'

There was a crescent-shaped moon but the dark, rain-filled clouds meant that it was virtually pitch black as a nimble-footed Seamus led them across the field to the tree. They waited there and listened. Seamus said nothing, merely tapped Jack lightly on the jacket to indicate he was off. They could barely make out his silhouette as he moved rapidly yet silently towards the drawing room. It seemed like an eternity before he returned, breathing heavily.

'Done it,' he whispered to Jack. Amy desperately wanted to know what but realised that now wasn't the moment to ask. Being an accessory to breaking and entering was a rare albeit exciting sensation and it brought back memories of her childhood days when she and her brother used to spend the late summer evenings camping and occasionally stealing the apples from the orchard of the neighbouring fruit farmer. She would find out later what Seamus had been up to.

'Now to the walled garden,' said Jack.

'Can I come?' whispered Amy.

'No. There's a big wall to climb. Two make a lot less noise than three.'

She decided not to push her luck. 'I'll wait here then. Good luck.'

She could hear Jack heave a sigh of relief and then they were gone, scuttling across the field and into darkness. With the moon temporarily asserting itself through the clouds, they used the chimneys of the house as barely discernible landmarks and reached the east side of the walled garden within ten minutes. Seamus produced a rope from round his waist, with a mountaineering hook on one end that he'd covered in rubber to muffle it, and threw it up onto the top of the wall. At the first attempt it held and within seconds he had scaled the wall and was over. Jack lacked his nimbleness but his strong forearms provided suffi- cient leverage for him to reach the top quickly. He knelt down, undid the hook and threw the rope down to his waiting accomplice. Seamus had obviously memorised Flynn's plan and he led Jack slowly yet deftly round the edge of the vegetable garden, the muted light from a pocket torch picking out the ground ahead of them, until they reached the spot where stakes now marked out Patrick Kildare's burial place.

There was not much to see, just mounds of earth, piled to one side. Jack wasn't expecting to find anything different but a morbid sense of curiosity and a desire to understand what Fergus must have felt had driven him to come to this spot. There was no point in hanging around. He shuddered at the thought of man's inhumanity to man and beckoned to Seamus to go back. Five minutes later they were on the other side of the wall again. They had gone about a hundred yards when Seamus pointed out the stable and covering yard which had belonged to Moondancer.

'Come on,' said Jack, 'let's go and have a peep. I'd like to see how they managed to get in and shoot him.'

They crept up slowly towards the stable. The night was still and quiet and although for a brief second Jack thought he had made out the growl of a dog, he swiftly reassured himself. If there was a dog in the house or yard they would have heard it by now.

They reached the stable and as Seamus turned on his torch Jack pulled open the top door.

The jab of cold metal against his nose told him he was staring at the two barrels of a shotgun.

'Don't move or I'll shoot. And that goes for you too,' the gunman added in the direction of Seamus. 'Throw the torch down on the ground and put your hands up.'

They did as they were told.

Fergus was trying to stay in command of the situation. Being unable to sleep, he had decided to go and see if Tongue in Cheek had eaten up after his race.

Drummond had come along with him and it was his growling which had told him that somebody was outside moving around.

He moved over to the edge of the box and turned on the light which he had left off so as not to upset Tongue in Cheek. He recognised the taller of the men immediately from the racecourse. It was that same chap who had been asking Joe those questions last year about Moondancer. He just hoped that they did not try and run for it. Tongue in Cheek began snorting behind him at the sudden intrusion on his privacy.

'It's all right, boy,' he said. 'Settle down.' He couldn't let go of the gun to stroke the horse or coax him away.

Jack couldn't believe his eyes. He had never thought that the box might have another occupant and as for there being no dog, the huge beast – he thought it was a Doberman – was giving him anything but friendly looks. He wondered how they were ever going to get out of this one and wished he was with Amy behind that tree.

Fergus pushed open the bottom part of the stable door with his right hand and told them to come in. He indicated they should sit down on the straw in the nearside corner while he stood over them, the shotgun held firmly in his hand and pointed in their direction.

'Are you going to tell me what you're doing here or should I call the Gardai straight away?'

Jack decided to come clean, or at least partly so.

'I'm sorry. It's not what you think. I know we have no right to be here. My name's Jack Hendred and I'm investigating Moondancer's death on behalf of the insurers, and before you jump to conclusions about my presence you ought to know that my clients have no idea I'm here tonight. If they find out all hell will break loose.'

'And him?' Fergus pointed the barrels at Seamus.

'He works for me, but all this is my idea.'

Fergus was inclined to believe what he was hearing. Hendred's story tied in with what Joe had told him and judging by his appearance, the short round-faced man in the duffel coat couldn't have said boo to a goose.

'You still haven't answered my question. What's brought you here tonight?'

'I wanted to see the stable where Moondancer was killed, that's all.'

'I don't believe you.'

'It's the truth.'

'Okay, then you'll have no objection to emptying your pockets. Stand up, each of you in turn. You first.'

Jack got up and pulled out the insides of his pockets. He had nothing on him. As far as he knew his car keys were still stuffed down Amy's cleavage. Lucky car keys, he thought. He sat down and it was Seamus's turn. This is it, Jack winced to himself.

Seamus began by emptying his trouser pockets, which yielded only a fifty pence coin, and then followed with the side pockets of his duffel coat. All he had there was a five pound note, a filthy yellow handkerchief smelling of chloroform and a credit card. Jack assumed he had used the card to force the lock of the windows of the drawing room.

Fergus took it and read it. 'So your name's Dermot Maloney.'

Jack had to stop himself from laughing. Nice one, Pink.

'And now the inside pocket of your duffel coat.'

Jack crossed his fingers and hoped that Seamus had not brought with him the third bug he had revealed at the restaurant. Seamus flashed open the coat. Jack breathed a sigh of relief. He hadn't.

'What's this then?' Fergus had noticed the rope tied round Seamus's waist. 'I thought you said you only wanted to see the stable. Have you come to do some burglary as well?'

Jack immediately offered him a bit more of the truth. 'I wanted to see where you found your father's body. You might as well know that I believe Moondancer's death had nothing to do with the IRA and that your father's murder is in some way linked to Moondancer's. I felt like visiting the scene of the crime.'

'Why should I believe you?'

'Because it's the truth. Don't you suspect there's a connection too?'

Fergus hesitated. It was that very link which had kept him from sleeping. He was no longer certain what to do next.

'I'm going to have to tell the Gardai about this,' he said after a pause of a couple of minutes. 'You could have destroyed vital evidence in there.'

Jack was about to launch on a speech about how they were both on the same side even though their motives were different when the sound of footsteps could be heard outside. Drummond sprang to his feet and started barking.

'Stay there and don't move,' said Fergus as he edged out of the stable.

Two seconds later he pulled in the surprised and shaken figure of Amy. Jack covered his face with his hands and groaned.

'A friend of yours?' asked Fergus. It was in fact a rhetorical question as he recognised the girl from the racecourse. Amy lifted her eyes to the sky and volunteered to sit down beside the others. She couldn't very well say it was the wrong stable.

'And who are you?' asked Fergus.

'Please don't point that gun at me,' she replied, holding out her arm to fend it away. 'It might go off and then where would we all be? It would certainly frighten your horse.'

Her directness took Fergus off guard. He was feeling extremely nervous as it was and was beginning to wish he could think of a way of getting rid of all these intruders without any loss of face. None of them looked in the least bit dishonest or violent and there had to be a distinct possibility that Hendred was telling the truth. He pointed the gun downwards at the floor.

'All right, but if one of you moves I'll set Drummond onto you.' Little did they know that Drummond's bark was considerably worse than his bite, particularly when it came to women, and there was every chance that if Amy stretched out a hand he would lick it.

'You're Fergus Kildare, aren't you?' she said. 'I'm very sorry about your father.'

'And your name?'

'I'm Amy Frost. I'm working for the solicitors acting for the insurers in the Moondancer case.'

'Isn't it somewhat improper for a lawyer to behave like this? What would your principals say?'

'They wouldn't be very pleased, that's if you felt obliged to tell them.' Amy deliberately chose not to make a direct emotional appeal. She knew she could say goodbye to her job at Messrs Arthurs if they found out about this indiscretion but there were always other jobs for good solicitors.

'And why shouldn't I?' responded Fergus. 'As a result of my father's death I naturally have a vested interest in seeing the claim successful. Why should I help the other side? You've made us all wait nearly two years for settlement and just about bankrupted this place in the process.'

'I can't argue with the logic of that. All I do know is

that we believe your father's death is linked to the stallion's, and if that is indeed true, surely you, as his son, want it proved?'

'Your friend Mr Hendred has already tried to make that point.'

Jack nodded unintentionally. He had deliberately kept quiet during the present exchange; he could see that Amy, with her candour and artlessness, was making a real impression. Fergus was wavering.

'I want to think about this overnight. You can all go now, but I warn you that in the morning I will almost certainly report this matter to the Gardai. You can leave that rope here. Now please leave.'

Fergus watched them get up and walk outside. Tongue in Cheek was standing looking at them over his shoulder and beside his master sat Drummond, giving his best impression of a Doberman trained to kill.

Jack, Seamus and Amy hurried away for a speedy return to the Ardmore Arms. When they were out of sight, Fergus opened the shotgun. Both barrels were empty. They hadn't been that night it was fired into Moondancer's head.

Chapter Nine

Superintendent Brogan insisted on seeing Fergus and his mother separately. Colette Kildare arrived downstairs shortly after the officer's arrival and her pallid complexion and drawn eyes gave the clear impression of a woman who had spent a sleepless and tearful night grieving for her murdered husband. In fact, as Fergus half-suspected, she had slept like a lamb and had occupied the morning by preparing herself for the police visit. Choosing the right outfit alone had taken over an hour. She had heard Tommy Kirkpatrick, the family solicitor, arrive as arranged at eleven thirty but she had no intention of letting him announce the contents of the will that soon. It might provoke Fergus into revealing the state of his parents' marriage and the last thing she wanted was tedious questioning about whether she had loved her husband.

She spent a relatively painless thirty minutes with Brogan in the drawing room and emerged looking suitably distressed after the trauma of recounting, yet again, the last occasion she saw her husband alive.

Fergus's interview lasted a little longer. As with his mother, Tommy Kirkpatrick was in discreet and silent attendance to ensure that nothing improper was asked. Brogan sat opposite Fergus, asking questions, while his answers were written down by a young Gard who seemed to be having difficulty keeping up. Brogan referred Fergus to statements he had made to the Gardai both after Moondancer had been shot and later after his father had disappeared. Fergus was asked to go over again what had happened on the night that Moondancer had been shot.

'Must I?' he answered. 'I've told the Gardai all this once.'

'Please tell me again, sir,' Brogan said respectfully. 'If there is a link between the horse's death and your father's murder then logic says that I have to start again at the beginning. Please remember I wasn't involved in any of these earlier inquiries. I know this is painful for you but some clue might emerge, something we've all overlooked. You do understand, don't you?'

Fergus disliked recalling that particular time but realised he had no alternative.

'It was the weekend of the fifteenth of January. My father had asked me to come down from Trinity for the weekend as he was having a meeting of the syndicate which owned Moondancer. That consisted –' the young Gard dropped his pen and Fergus paused while he picked it up – 'of my father, Hugo Fitzwilliams the trainer, his father Eamon the bloodstock dealer, and two businessmen, Kieran Steele and the Englishman Guy Pritchard. At the time very few mares – I think it was only six – had been booked in to Moondancer for the coming covering season, and even then half were on a foal-sharing basis.' He could see the superintendent was lost. 'Foal sharing is when the owner of the mare doesn't pay a nomination fee but instead shares the sale price of the resulting foal with the owner of the stallion. We had already reduced Moondancer's nomination fee to three thousand Irish, which was a far cry from the forty thousand he started at four years previously. On top of that, my father had received a number of phone calls from someone claiming to be the IRA threatening that unless we made a one hundred thousand punt donation to the cause they would kill the horse. My father told the Gardai about those calls a week or so before the killing.'

'It was the Monday before, to be precise.'

'Anyway, that Saturday the syndicate had their meeting and it was agreed that under no circumstances would we yield to any demand from the IRA. In fact, both Steele and Pritchard thought they were just silly hoaxes. Eamon Fitzwilliams was instructed to try and sell Moondancer abroad, Japan or Italy or somewhere. It was reluctantly recognised that if we got half a million for him we would be doing well. You can imagine the mood was not exactly a happy one when we sat down to dinner that night as all the shareholders were nursing massive losses, or at least the prospect of them. My father was probably the worst hit as he had sunk everything into buying his shares and doing up the stud. To his credit, he and Eamon were determined to cheer everyone up and we all laid into the alcohol at dinner.'

'Was anybody else present?'

'Yes, my mother and my girlfriend Emma.'

'Is she around at the moment?'

'She's arriving back from England on Saturday if you want to see her. Shall I go on? We got to bed in the early hours of the morning and the next thing I knew I was being woken by Joe, our stud groom, saying that Moondancer had been shot. I raced down to his stable and found him lying in the corner, his head blown away.'

'Had you heard anything suspicious during the night?'

'I was out for the count, I'm afraid. We had polished off at least three bottles of cognac between us.'

'Were there any guns about the house?'

'I've a shotgun and of course my father had one as well. We used to do a bit of rough shooting; this place is plagued by rabbits.'

'Where were the guns kept?'

'In a cupboard in the gun room.'

'Locked up?'

'Yes.'

'And did you check to see if it was locked after the discovery of the dead horse?'

'I did.'

'Why was that? You had no reason to believe it was the work of one of your own party, had you?'

'I checked to reassure myself.'

'And were you reassured?'

Fergus gave the same answer he had given when first interviewed eighteen months ago by the local Gardai.

'Yes.'

'And did you look at the guns to see if either of them had been fired recently?'

'I did, for the same reason, reassurance.'

'And were you reassured?'

Fergus again kept to his original story. 'I was. Neither had been fired.'

Seemingly satisfied with these answers, Brogan then asked Fergus about his whereabouts on the weekend his father disappeared.

'I was phoned by my father on the Thursday night to say he was going down to Sligo to see a hunter which was for sale. He had often done that in the past, buying and selling horses, and I was glad that he was showing a bit of his old form. He had been very depressed after the Moondancer business even though he was expecting the insurance money. I couldn't go

141

with him as I was riding in a point to point, and Joe was coming over to help me. If you want, I can give you the names of plenty of people who saw me there.'

'I suppose your girlfriend can confirm it?'

'Emma? No, she didn't come with me. She had some other plans, I can't remember what, you'll have to ask her.'

'Now finally, I asked your mother if she could think of anyone who had a grudge against your father, anyone who could have done this terrible thing to him.'

Fergus shook his head. 'And did she suggest anybody?'

'She's convinced that this is a revenge killing by the IRA because your father and the others wouldn't pay up over Moondancer.'

Fergus made no comment. Instead he studied Brogan's expression as the man rose to his feet and went and stood in front of the fire, obscuring its flame with his massive physique. He had an unnerving habit of wrinkling his nose as if he could smell something unpleasant. Perhaps it was his way of scenting a clue.

'And do you agree with her, Superintendent?'

'At the moment I don't have a view. I prefer to deal in fact rather than speculation. Let's just say it's a possibility.' He put away his own notes and proffered Fergus a hand. 'Thank you very much, Mr Kildare. I assume you won't be leaving here and if you do you'll keep us informed of your whereabouts?'

'Of course. There's one other thing. We, my mother and I, would like to bury my father as soon as possible. Is there any chance that his body can be released?'

'The body is, you understand, still undergoing a post mortem. I'm told that will be finished tomorrow and, provided the coroner agrees, I've no objection to a burial. It is a burial and not a cremation?'

'Does it make a difference?'

'Well, you can always exhume a body.'

'It'll be a burial.'

'That should be all right then. I'll contact you to confirm if it can go ahead and you can make the necessary arrangements through your undertakers. If you'll excuse me, I want to go and have a word with your stud groom.'

'Is he expecting you?' Fergus asked.

'It's all arranged. He says he'll be in Moondancer's old stable.'

'With Tongue in Cheek?'

'I'm sorry?'

'That's the name of Joe's favourite horse, and mine for that matter.'

Brogan wrinkled his nose. He must have been the only person in Ireland who loathed horses; he could think of nothing more uncongenial than to have to carry out his investigations in the company of a horse.

Fergus showed the two Gardai out, gesturing to Kirkpatrick to stay behind.

'Have you got the will, Tommy?' he asked when he was back in the drawing room.

'Yes, right here.' The solicitor opened his briefcase.

At that moment Colette came into the room.

'Ah, Colette,' said Kirkpatrick. 'Fergus said you wanted me to bring over the will and the other relevant documents. Would you like me to leave you both here in peace while you read them? I brought a couple of spare copies with me. There's no rush and I could pop out and walk round the yard and then explain any problems.' Kirkpatrick was hoping she would agree. He had never taken to Colette and had counselled her late husband against altering his will in her favour and leaving his son burdened with debt. Patrick had laughed it off at the time. 'Don't be silly, Tommy,' he had said, putting his arm round the lawyer's shoulder, 'by the time I die, and that won't be for many years yet, Moondancer will be the greatest sire in Europe and we'll all be rich.'

Colette ignored Kirkpatrick's suggestion and walked over to the drinks cabinet in the corner.

'Would anyone else like a sherry? That aspirin has upset me terribly.'

Kirkpatrick glanced anxiously at Fergus.

'Go on, Tommy, have one.' Fergus joined his mother at the drinks cabinet and poured out two more sherries.

'I know,' said Colette, throwing herself down on the sofa nearest the fire, 'why don't you read the will out, Tommy? I'm so tense I couldn't read it if I tried, let alone understand it, and you can then explain it to us. Though I doubt if it will contain any surprises. We all know that Patrick doted on his son and who can blame him for that?'

'Reading it out loud would be most unusual,' replied the solicitor, taking off his glasses and cleaning them nervously with a handkerchief. 'That kind of thing is best left to Agatha Christie thrillers.'

'But Patrick loved thrillers. Go on, Tommy, do it for Patrick, he would have wanted it this way.'

Kirkpatrick eyed Fergus for a reaction.

'Why not?' he said, sitting down in an armchair opposite his mother.

The solicitor, a small almost shrivelled seventy-year-old who had come to dislike his fellow man after a lifetime in law, stood by the fire and put his glasses on. What he would have given to be standing on the bank of the Liffey with his fishing rod in his hand. In a clear yet weary voice he began.

'I Patrick Mungo Kildare of Drumgarrick House, Drumgarrick in the County of Limerick, stud owner and breeder, hereby revoke all my testamentary dispositions heretobefore made by me and declare this to be my last will and testament.

'I appoint Tommy Stephen Kirkpatrick and Fergus Kildare to be the executors and trustees of this my will.

'I devise and bequeath to my beloved son Fergus all

145

the land and estate known as Drumgarrick House, subject to such mortgages or charges as there may exist thereon, together with all the livestock and machinery.

'I devise and bequeath to my wife Colette' – Fergus noticed his father's omission of the term 'beloved' – 'my shares in the stallion "Moondancer" subject to any charge or encumbrance thereon. Subject thereto I devise and bequeath the residue of my estate (which I expect will be very little) to my son Fergus to whom I wish every future happiness and joy.'

'Thank you, Tommy,' said Colette. 'It was no different to what I expected. Could you just explain the reference to charges and encumbrances. I can't follow all this legal mumbo jumbo. Are there any?'

Kirkpatrick half suspected that she knew the answer to her own question and wished again that he was many miles from this house with its depressing and ghoulish atmosphere.

'Yes, Colette, I'm afraid it's not quite as cut and dried as it sounds.'

He produced from the same brown envelope from which he had extracted the will two other legal-looking documents.

'This,' he directed his words towards Fergus as he held up one of them, 'is a legal charge in favour of the Allied Irish Bank and secured against Drumgarrick. The amount outstanding against the charge is,' he paused as he saw Fergus's nervous and anxious expression, 'six hundred thousand punts.'

'Drumgarrick? I don't understand,' said Fergus. 'You don't mean that I have to pay all that money off before the house is mine?'

'Yes, I'm sorry, Fergus. Your father's financial position was such that he had to borrow heavily to do the repairs to the stud and to buy his shares in Moondancer.'

'But surely all that was secured against the horse? I mean, that's what I always understood to be the position.'

'What about the shares? I assume that they are also charged to the bank?' asked Colette. From the tone of her voice no one would have guessed that her heart was pounding with the excitement of the impending revelation.

'No, Colette. You take the Moondancer shares, or in other words the equivalent interest in the insurance claim, free of any encumbrance.'

The colour drained from Fergus's face. He couldn't believe what he was hearing. He was ruined at one stroke and his mother was rich. He would have to sell the house, land and the horses to pay off the debts. There was no way he could meet the interest payments; they would be astronomical. His father couldn't have done this to him. There had to be a mistake.

'Are you sure that was my father's last will,

Tommy?' he managed to ask. 'When is it dated?'

'Unless there is another homemade one lying about the place. He certainly didn't take my advice about any subsequent will. He made this one just over six years ago, about six months after Moondancer took up his duties here. Out of fairness to your father, I should make it clear that at the time of making it he genuinely believed that Moondancer would be a great success and all the debts on the house paid off.'

Fergus glanced over at his mother. Beneath the dispassionate expression he knew she was enjoying her triumph. The slight quivering of her bottom lip was the surest sign that she was elated. Anger brought some colour back into his cheeks. So be it, he reasoned to himself, but he would deny her this victory; how, he had not the faintest idea.

'Is that all?' he asked the solicitor.

'No, there's one other thing. This other document is a life insurance policy taken out by your father. On his death the sum of two hundred and fifty thousand punts becomes payable to his . . .' he paused. Fergus breathed a sigh of relief. He had forgotten about the life policy. His father had no doubt left him a decent sum towards paying off the debts. '. . . wife, Colette Kildare.'

This time Fergus caught his mother smiling. He clenched his hands on the armchair and with a supreme act of self-control got up and shook the solicitor's hand. 'Thank you, Tommy,' he said. 'It was

148

very good of you to come here today at such short notice. Just one last thing. The life policy. When did my father take it out?'

Kirkpatrick looked at the date typed on the back of the policy. 'One year ago. On the twenty-eighth of December.'

'Three weeks before he was murdered,' said Fergus.

'You cow!' exclaimed Jack. One mile away from Drumgarrick he was squatting beside Seamus in the back of the van listening in to the latest developments taking place in the drawing room. Seamus had planted the bug behind one of the few remaining pictures in the house, a large and well-executed oil of the Limerick Hunt in full flight at the turn of the century. It hung above the mantelpiece and thus proved an ideal medium for transmitting all conversation. Judging from the dust which had come off in Seamus's hand as he positioned the bug, there was no danger of it being discovered by either the family or the cleaning lady.

Seamus had picked him up from the hotel at ten and they had driven straight to the spot where they were now parked. Jack was particularly keen to listen in to Superintendent Brogan's interview with Fergus, scheduled for twelve o'clock. If the heir to Drumgarrick was going to report their visit during the night, surely that would be the ideal time to do so.

Jack was far more worried than Amy about the prospect. She had appeared distinctly unconcerned and had left in the early morning for Dublin. Her attitude was that life is too short to worry about matters over which you have no control. As a philosophy, it was one which Jack himself embraced, only on this occasion he was embarrassed at the explaining he would have to do to his clients back in London. He had promised to telephone Amy that evening with an update. The trouble was that she did not know anything about the bugs they had planted and he still felt a mixture of reluctance and embarrassment in admitting the full extent of his illegal activities.

From the outside, Seamus's dark green, two hundredweight van appeared no different to those driven by countless tradesmen and handymen. Inside, however, considerable time and money had been spent turning it into a highly efficient centre for receiving, monitoring and recording everything picked up by sensitive and well-placed listening devices. Seamus loved playing with gadgets and nothing gave him more pleasure than being hired to do surveillance work of this sort. He had set up two pairs of headphones in the van and there was a separate recording machine for each bug. As yet the one in the kitchen, by the telephone, had only picked up a brief conversation between Fergus and his girlfriend Emma from which it appeared she was no longer arriving back on Saturday night as planned but was flying over by private plane from Newmarket on the Sunday. The one in the drawing room was far more active.

They had begun by listening in to Colette's interview but from her softly spoken voice it was hard to conjure up any real image of the woman or the depth of her grief. Fergus had been a good deal more emotional in answering the questions put to him and had confirmed who had been staying in the house when Moondancer was killed. Even more importantly he had made no mention of their visit during the night. Then came the reading of the will. Seamus had whistled out loud when he heard about the shares and Fergus's ruin and when the timing of the life insurance policy emerged, Jack had let out his exclamation of anger directed at Colette. As soon as it was clear that the meeting had broken up they took off their headphones. Seamus rewound and marked the tape, while Jack rubbed his hands in disbelief.

'That woman is incredible. I can hear her now asking that solicitor all those questions as if she had no idea what he was on about. She was stringing them along, the pair of them. I'll bet you a tenner she wrote the will herself and killed both the horse and the old man.' Seamus had never seen him so worked up.

'Jack, calm down. It's only a case. It wasn't your own father in that asparagus bed. Think about it for a moment. If it was her, how could she have done it alone?'

'It's not difficult hitting someone from behind,

Seamus. I've met her and she's nearly as tall as he was and anyway she could easily have cracked him over the head while he had his breakfast. Snap, crackle and pop, you're dead. The pathologist will be able to confirm the angle of trajectory.'

'And the asparagus bed? How did she get him there? Or are you supposing he had his breakfast in the walled garden?'

'Put him on a wheelbarrow or a horse. I don't know. I haven't thought it through. I do know that if you have all day, you can move a body single-handed from A to B. It's not uphill or anything.'

'Much more likely that someone helped her. Who would you suggest?'

Jack considered the question and shrugged his shoulders. For all his inquiries over the last year he had learnt surprisingly little about the members of the syndicate. He knew their public profiles from reading newspaper cuttings but no one had ever been able to give him any worthwhile insight into the personalities within. Those men had two things in common: they all loved horses and money, and when it came to Moondancer it appeared that for at least one of them the latter was more important. His own instinct told him that Patrick Kildare was of a different breed of man: caring, compassionate and out of his depth in the world of high rollers where everything is judged by the bottom line. And it was that difference which probably explained why he had to die.

The key to it all, Jack concluded, was his widow. He thought back to his conversation with Fergus in the stable. It was possible after the reading of the will that the son's attitude might have undergone a sudden and understandable change. For a start, he would no longer have any interest in the Moondancer litigation, and there certainly didn't appear to be the usual kind of bond between son and mother. If he had chosen not to report them to the Gardai it was just possible he would consider working with them. It had to be worth finding out. Jack remembered the funeral was to be on Monday or Tuesday. It would be tactless to make an approach before then, but why not afterwards?

In the meantime, there was still plenty to do. It was agreed that Seamus would spend the weekend in the van listening and recording any conversations and that he would deliver the tapes each evening to Jack at his hotel. Jack would make further inquiries about the private lives of the surviving members of the syndicate and discover if possible which if any of them was having an affair with Colette Kildare.

His thoughts turned to Amy. When they had eventually got to bed that morning he had been unable to sleep. All he could think about was her unshakable *joie de vivre* and his unshakable lust for her body.

As soon as Tommy Kirkpatrick had gone Fergus made for the sanctity and solitude of his room and paced up and down cursing his mother and directing the odd plaintive remark to the heavens, asking his father how he could have done this to him. Eventually he calmed down and decided that he would from now on concentrate his energies on discovering his father's killer and pulling off that coup with Tongue in Cheek. That way honour and fortune could be restored to Drumgarrick.

His anger and suspicions were firmly and exclusively directed towards his mother. The terms of the will and the timing of the insurance policy provided her with the clearest of motives – assuming she had known about them, and Fergus was now convinced she had. If he was right about that, then the discovery of the brooch by Joe in his father's grave was no coincidence. She was obviously worried that she had dropped it there when burying her husband and that was why she had insisted on being alone when he showed her where he had discovered the body. He still had not told her that he had the brooch; he had hidden it under a loose floorboard which he had used as a secret store when a child. He remembered how Emma had laughed at him when he told her about it and of the treasure trove he used to keep there. In fact the only thing it had hidden over the past few years was his own key to the gun room. The other key had been kept by his father.

Emotionally drained by his father's disappearance and now his death, cuckolded for the last few months if not longer by Emma, Fergus sorely felt the need for someone to talk to. He thought of last night's intruders. He hadn't taken to that chap Hendred – the scar down his face unnerved him and he was a shade too self-righteous – but Amy Frost was quite different. He had believed her when she said that she wanted to catch his father's killer. He had originally intended to report her and her colleagues to the Gardai that morning, but something in Brogan's manner – indifference masquerading as concern – had put him off. Now there seemed little point. He had no further interest in the insurance litigation since his mother now owned the Moondancer shares.

With sudden resolve Fergus checked that his mother had gone up to her room, then went downstairs to the kitchen and telephoned the solicitors in London who were acting for them in the Moondancer case. They were surprised at his request for the names of the insurer's solicitors but eventually came up with a name and a London telephone number. Fergus soon discovered that the switchboard of Messrs Arthurs tended to be a little sleepy on a Friday afternoon and it was only by a stroke of luck that he caught Amy's secretary as she was slipping off early for a weekend in the country. Somewhat reluctantly she provided Fergus with Amy's hotel number in Dublin. Three hours later, shortly after seven o'clock, he managed to track her down.

'Is there anything I can do to help?' was her first question.

Fergus hesitated, faced with the response he had hoped for but not anticipated.

'Are you still there?' she asked.

'I'm still here. It's just that that's not an easy question to answer over the phone.'

'Then why not tell me to my face? I really meant it the other night when I said that Jack and I wanted to help you.'

'Jack, I mean Mr Hendred, he's with you at the hotel then?'

'No, he's off pursuing his investigations elsewhere. He's determined to get at the truth, you know.'

'He can keep his Moondancer money. All I want to discover is who killed my father.'

'And you'd like me to help you?'

'Yes,' Fergus said simply. He felt embarrassed. He just wanted to talk to her, that was really why he'd phoned, but maybe she could help.

'Why don't we meet for a chat? You never know, sometimes a complete stranger can throw fresh light on a problem and even provide a little support.'

'I'd like that. When do you suggest? The funeral's going to be on Monday, provided they release the body over the weekend, and I've got a hell of a lot of organising to do.'

'How about Monday night then? Do you think you could escape for a couple of hours? It would probably do you good.'

'But where can we meet? Not Drumgarrick.'

'Not Drumgarrick, no. I spotted a hotel called Killiney House or something on the Tipperary Road about twenty miles from you. Do you know it?'

'Yes, it's pretty good. I've had the odd drink there over the years on the way back from the races. Will you stay there or what?'

'I'll book a room for the night and meet you there for dinner. Shall we say about seven thirty? Leave a message if you can't come or are held up.'

'Thank you. And one other thing.'

'Yes?' Amy had already guessed the request.

'Please come alone.'

Chapter Ten

'Thank you, Eamon. It'll be much easier dealing with Colette than Fergus. Until this afternoon then.' Guy Pritchard handed the telephone to his chauffeur, Carl, a square-shouldered former nightclub bouncer who had been quarried rather than born, and told him to turn on the radio so he could catch the weather forecast.

The news from Eamon had come as no real surprise although he had to admire Colette Kildare's style at suggesting a meeting of the Moondancer syndicate on the very evening of her husband's funeral. He personally had never had much time for the dead – what was it the Bible said about letting the dead bury the dead? – and it was good to know that she was in as much a hurry as he was to lay her hands on the money. She had invited them all to spend that night at Drumgarrick, and who knows? He might even get lucky. Colette might not be in the first flush of youth but she had class and there was still something about her that he found very sexy.

He often looked back on the first time he'd had her. It was at the Goff yearling sales in Dublin and Patrick was trying to sell one of the first crop of Moondancer, a filly he had bred himself from one of the brood mares he kept at Drumgarrick. Normally you would expect there to be great interest in a filly by a first-season stallion – not as much as in a colt, of course – but the animal had inherited the characteristics which were to be Moondancer's undoing: a really poor conformation and she moved so ungainly that no decent judge of horseflesh would give any worthwhile sum for her. She had been led out unsold and the plan to put her into training had subsequently come to nothing. Poor old Patrick had drowned his sorrows that evening by going out on a bender with Eamon, and Colette had revived hers by mouth to mouth resuscitation with one of his partners. Pritchard thought he was experienced in bed but she knew more tricks than a circus dog and had taken him to heights of satisfaction hitherto unknown. It would be nice to think he was the only one in the syndicate to have played at stud with her, but he doubted it somehow. Eamon could not be trusted within a yard of a good-looking woman and he had seen that gleam in Kieran Steele's eye one evening during the Newmarket sales.

Eamon he could forgive but Steele never. The mere

160

thought exacerbated the anger which Guy felt towards him. Steele had overstepped the mark on Wednesday with that jibe about his financial position, made all the more unacceptable because it was true. He could not afford to have someone like that bad-mouthing him behind his back, particularly when he knew the real source of his income. After all, he had a family and social position to protect. Once the litigation was over, Steele would have outlived his usefulness.

Pritchard leant forward and poured himself a glass of champagne from the mahogany drinks cabinet built into the Rolls. This was the life he had earned and nothing and nobody was going to take it away from him. He told Carl to put his foot down and head straight for home where he would have a quick lunch, pick up his suitcase and make for the airport.

Kieran Steele's private plane, an eight-seater Cessna, left Stansted at two thirty and was due to arrive at Shannon approximately four and a half hours later. Two Mercedes would be waiting at the airport to ferry him and his passengers to Drumgarrick and then the next day, Monday, they would pay their last respects to Patrick Kildare.

Respect was probably putting it a bit high in Steele's case. From very early on he had recognised that it had been an error of judgment to stand Moondancer at Drumgarrick; Patrick was quite simply out of his depth. Running a proper stud required commercial acumen allied to an ability to persuade the owners of high-class brood mares to send them to be serviced by the resident stallion. Patrick possessed neither quality. His experience had been confined to breeding from a handful of moderate mares at nomination fees in their low thousands and amusing himself in his spare time by training the odd hurdler or chaser. He simply was not interested in financial matters, even though he had sunk his whole fortune into Moondancer, and not even the threat of ruin could change his basic character. It was not surprising that the venture had failed loudly and expensively and if there was one thing Steele could not forgive, it was someone costing him large sums of money.

When he had said he was glad that Moondancer had died, he meant every word of it. He felt neither pleased nor sad about Patrick's death. Its only significance was that the discovery of his body came at an awkward time in relation to the insurance claim as it necessitated the involvement of the Gardai, and that in turn might give false hope to the insurers. The news that Colette had inherited the shares was reassuring; she had the financial drive that her late husband so palpably lacked. Not for her any nightly promenade down to a horse's stable to whisper sweet nothings in his ear while stroking his mane.

Standing in front of the cockpit door he surveyed his human cargo, a motley collection if ever there was one. Sitting together and, if he wasn't mistaken, holding hands, were Hugo Fitzwilliams and that girl Emma. He could understand his trainer's interest in this particular filly. She was almost Amazonian in build and, with her long red hair and lipstick to match, decidedly raunchy. She laughed easily and loudly and, he expected, was very good in bed. In conversation she had a habit of fixing you firmly in the eye as if to say 'I dare you to try it!' One day he would.

In the seat immediately behind her Eamon Fitz-williams was going through his sales catalogues marking up purchasers' names and prices. There was no doubting his shrewdness and dedication as a judge of bloodstock. He took infinite care and patience in selecting horses for his clients and was very particular not to allow bloodline to triumph over conformation and movement. Moondancer had been one of his rare failures. His only problem was a desire for self-enrichment which almost bordered on the pathological. He was never content just to receive a commission from his principal; he demanded, and invariably received, one from the vendor as well. His buyer's and seller's 'premium' was how he liked to describe them, as if he was a one-man auction house. Of course the commission from the vendor was normally kept secret from his client, otherwise – shame of shames – he might think that Eamon had bid the price up for his own advantage. He had even tried to do it once on a yearling he had bought for Kieran. A few well-chosen words about the future of his manhood had persuaded him never to do it again.

Kieran wondered whether Eamon had ever attempted the same trick on Pritchard. The Englishman was seated on the other side of the narrow aisle reading the *Mail on Sunday* and appeared as calm and relaxed as ever. It was a front, of course. Kieran had made it a rule of business to know everything he possibly could about the people he associated with, every detail of their personal lives, every weakness or peccadillo which might come in handy if relations broke down or negotiations for some reason became necessary. Pritchard's composure would soon fall apart if he ever glimpsed the contents of the yellow folder nestling in Kieran's briefcase. They ranged from a detailed analysis of the network of companies set up by Pritchard to hide his involvement in gambling and vice clubs to his insider dealings on the London stock market. The most recent addition to the file was a video film of Pritchard paying a visit earlier that week to a flat in Notting Hill Gate and leaving hastily, pulling off a face-stocking and running as if his life depended on it. The inquiry agent employed by Kieran had checked up on the flat and discovered it was occupied by an insurance investigator who was no doubt looking into a recent spate of arson at certain over-insured properties in Soho. Kieran wondered what that investigator would give to find out who really owned them and, even better, who the arsonist was. As soon as the Moondancer affair was settled, he might just give the investigator a nudge in the right direction.

Kieran walked to his seat at the rear of the plane and sat down. Within minutes he was asleep, a man at peace with himself.

Emma ran forward to embrace Fergus. He kissed her on the cheek and unwound her arms from his shoulders. He felt decidedly cold towards her and acutely embarrassed at the presence of the four men standing beside the cars which had brought them from the airport. There was a moment's silence before Eamon Fitzwilliams proffered his hand.

'I'm so dreadfully sorry, Fergus, this is a most terrible thing. We can't believe it.' The others nodded in accord.

Fergus mumbled a few words and gestured at their cases. 'I'm sorry if I seem a bit surprised, but my mother never told me you were coming all together like this, and Emma didn't mention it on the phone on Friday either.'

'I'm afraid that's my fault,' replied Eamon, setting himself up as the group's spokesman. 'I telephoned your mother yesterday to pass on my commiserations and she suggested that we come and stay the night – you know, with the funeral being tomorrow. As Kieran, Hugo and I were flying over anyway with

Eamon we merely diverted from Dublin to Shannon.'

'Well, you're all here now. I'm afraid I don't know what sleeping or eating arrangements my mother's made. As you can imagine, things are a little chaotic here.'

They followed him into the house and had reached the hall when his mother came down the stairs. She stretched out a hand to the group, each of whom somewhat dramatically embraced her. It was, thought Fergus, pure Hollywood. Having accepted their condolences she asked Fergus and Emma to show them to their respective rooms and announced that dinner would not be for a couple of hours. She suggested that they all meet in the drawing room half an hour before, at seven thirty.

Having billeted the three men, Emma and Fergus went to their bedroom. As soon as he had closed the door she gave him a long kiss on the lips.

'Poor you. You must be feeling wretched. I really am terribly sorry for you.'

'I feel far more sorry for my father. I still can't believe all this has happened.'

'Have the Gardai said anything? Do they suspect anybody?'

'If they do, they haven't said anything to me about it yet. Obviously they're considering it's a revenge job by the IRA after the Moondancer business, but who knows? They interviewed my mother and me on Friday and then saw Joe afterwards.'

166

'How's he taken it all? He worshipped your father.'

'I think he's very badly hit. He went off for the weekend after the interview and I haven't had a chance to talk to him. I'll see him this evening.'

'And how is Tongue in Cheek? Recovered from Thursday's run?'

'He's fine. I took him out for a long ride this morning across the moors. He's getting better by the day.'

'Good. At least you'll have Drumgarrick to comfort you in the years ahead, I suppose.'

Fergus noted the 'you' and not 'us'. As far as he was aware, Emma had no idea of the terms of his father's will or the insurance policy and for the moment he decided to leave it that way.

'Emma?'

'Yes?' She turned round from the wardrobe where she was putting away her dresses.

He had suddenly felt the urge to challenge her about her relationship with Hugo Fitzwilliams but that glint in her eye as she turned deterred him.

'Oh nothing, I was just wondering why my mother asked Eamon and everybody else to come and stay. It's not that I dislike them' – in fact he did – 'but they aren't my first choice of company the night before we bury my father.'

'Aren't you being a little unfair? They were your

father's business partners and stood by him when things went wrong.'

Fergus wasn't too sure he shared that view but there was no point in arguing.

Emma crossed the room and stood very close to him. She began stroking his hair. 'Don't you think you ought to relax?'

He felt her hand go down to the top of his trousers and begin to undo his belt. He had already made up his mind not to sleep with her that night, let alone make love with her, but his body was responding to her touch. Brute instinct took over; perversely, he wanted to indulge himself as if to punish her. He allowed her to undress him and then half-dragged, half-carried her to the bed and pushed her down on it. He tore open her shirt, letting loose the firm breasts, bra-less as ever. Emma was surprised, even slightly frightened by his sudden strength and determination. Perhaps, she thought, his father's death had changed the boy into a man? Since this was probably going to be one of their last times together she decided she might as well enjoy herself. Hugo would understand. After all, he still slept with his wife. But not for long, she would see to that.

Fergus bent forward and sucked at her breasts until the nipples were hard and erect. Then he dropped one hand down and pulled up her skirt underneath him. She was naked except for her suspenders and stockings and he immediately wondered whether she and her lover had joined the mile-high club on the way over from England. Emma began to try to move on top of him and gain some control, but he pinned her down with both his arms and thrust himself inside her. There was no point in fighting him so she moved her body in rhythm with his. Suddenly he stopped and roughly pushed her over onto her stomach before entering her again from behind. She responded enthusiastically, preferring to ignore the obvious anger which was driving him on. Soon she could feel him coming and his groans of satisfaction were quickly followed by her own cries of ecstasy.

Fergus pushed her forward, away from him, and rolled over onto his back. He stared up at the ceiling, cursing his weakness and vowing that this was positively the last time he would betray himself. Emma was utterly relaxed beside him, her eyes closed, one hand resting across her stomach, the other between her thighs. He needed to talk but he had nothing to say.

He waited until she had dropped off to sleep and then went to the bathroom before dressing. With a bit of luck Joe would already be down with Tongue in Cheek. He crept out of the bedroom and went down the stairs.

Jack parked his hired car in front of Seamus's van and went and knocked on the rear doors. He hoped that his assistant's day had been more productive than his own, than his whole weekend for that matter. His attempts to discover further details about the private lives and financial status of the partners had uncovered very little, though he did discover through reading the latest set of filed accounts of Kieran Steele's business group that most of his companies were losing money and were heavily borrowed. If Steele had given any personal guarantees, his share of Moondancer, worth a million and a quarter pounds, would certainly come in useful.

Jack hadn't seen Seamus since Friday morning when they'd listened to the reading of the will. He'd driven back to his hotel late that night and listened to the rest of the day's recordings which Seamus had left there for him. There was hardly anything of interest until he played the tape which Seamus had cheekily highlighted by drawing two hearts with an arrow through them on it. The sound of Fergus talking to Amy made him angry and, although he wouldn't want to admit it, jealous. He knew that he ought to be relieved that Fergus clearly no longer intended to report them to the Gardai and was now seeking their co-operation, but he resented Amy being so openly sympathetic and agreeing to secret liaisons.

The next morning, Saturday, he had telephoned her in Dublin and waited for her to tell him about the call and her proposed rendezvous. She made no reference to Fergus, merely remarking that she had decided for work reasons to stay on in Ireland a little longer and would meet him for an update probably on Tuesday. She would ring him later to confirm exactly when and where. Jack had to go along with the pretence. He had no intention of telling her about the bugs which Seamus had planted at his instigation in the house.

Seamus greeted him with a warm smile as he climbed into the van and sat down on the mattress which covered the floor. The Irishman was glad to see him; he'd had another tedious day when nothing of interest had occurred – Saturday's tapes had been mostly blank. All Seamus had to tell Jack was that Emma had arrived with a number of men, precisely who he couldn't say, and that they were going to meet at seven thirty in the drawing room for drinks before dinner. At least they could eavesdrop on the conversation there.

Jack glanced at his watch. It had just gone half past six.

'It doesn't appear as if Fergus is going to report us,' he remarked, accepting a glass of some dark and highly alcoholic substance which Seamus had poured from his pocket flask.

'Not judging from that phone call. Did you like my little drawing?' he winked at Jack.

Jack made as if to cuff him across the face. Seamus laughed and continued: 'Have you talked to her since?'

Jack nodded.

171

'And don't tell me, she didn't say a word about it.'

'Got it in one. And nor did I. I can't wait to see her face when I stroll into the Killiney Hotel tomorrow night. "Please come alone." What a bloody nerve.'

'Personally, I don't blame him. I wouldn't mind a candlelit dinner with Amy and judging by the way you act when she's around, nor would you.'

'Rubbish. My interest in her is purely professional. She alone decides how long this investigation goes on for, so I have to be nice to her. It's as simple as that.'

Seamus raised his eyebrows in disbelief.

'By the way,' said Jack, pretending not to have noticed, 'in all the excitement on Thursday night I forgot to ask you who this Dermot Maloney fellow is and what you were doing with his credit card.'

'Ah, that's a long story. Let's just say that I found the card by accident, as it were, and always keep it with me in case.'

'In case you have to give a name in an emergency. You had me worried in that stable. I thought for a moment when you opened your duffel coat we were going to see the third bug. What's the matter?'

A broad grin had come over Seamus's face.

'You've reminded me. I did have it with me. As you got up to empty your pockets I slipped it under the straw up against the wall. We could listen to it now and hear that horse eating his dinner.'

He slid over to his receiving equipment and after fiddling for a second or two put on the headphones.

'Hey, listen to this! Either he's the first horse to master the English language or Fergus is in there talking to somebody.'

Jack put on the second set of headphones and immediately recognised Fergus's voice. The other man had to be Joe. Judging from slurping sounds in the background, Tongue in Cheek was tucking into his feed. Fergus was telling Joe how well Tongue in Cheek had gone in his morning work.

'The more I ride him, the better he seems to get.'

'No sign of a broken blood vessel either,' said Joe.

'The next stop is Dundalk and then I think I'll take him over to Eamon Kyle's gallops and try him against one of his.' There was a pause, and then Fergus went on: 'Things couldn't be much worse, Joe. You might as well know that I've inherited the house all right but the old man was badly in debt and, well, unless we can pull off this coup, I'm ruined. I'll have to sell up, brood mares and all.'

'And your mother, what will she be doing now?'

'She won't be staying on. I don't think Emma will either, for that matter. It's going to be just you and me up here for a bit.'

'And the Gardai,' remarked Joe in a voice of unalloyed disdain.

'And the Gardai. Did that fellow Brogan come and see you?'

'He did but I didn't have much to tell him for all his questioning.'

173

'Did you mention about the brooch?'

Jack's back straightened as he became more attentive. This was the first time they had heard about a brooch.

'None of their business, is it? I was away the weekend your father disappeared so I told them I couldn't help them.'

'That doesn't mean they won't bother you again.' There was a lull in the conversation during which Jack and Seamus could hear Tongue in Cheek moving about in the stable.

'Joe.'

'Yes, guv'nor?'

'Do you mind if I ask you something about Moondancer's death? You don't have to answer.'

'You can always try me.'

'Do you think the IRA was really behind it?'

There was another pause. Jack could picture Joe stroking Tongue in Cheek while he thought about his answer.

'Not in a million years.'

'So who do you think did it?'

'It's not for me to have theories. You ought to know this though, now your father's gone. About a week before Moondancer was killed I answered the phone inside the house. Whoever was calling thought I was the guv'nor and started making threats about what would happen to the horse if he didn't pay a ransom.'

174

'And so? Surely that supports the IRA theory?'

'It was the voice.'

'What about it?'

'I recognised it.' Joe suddenly stopped talking. 'Hey, I think there's somebody outside.'

At that moment Tongue in Cheek became agitated and all Jack could pick out was the sound of Joe's and Fergus's voices trying to calm him down.

'If there was anybody, he's gone now,' said Fergus as soon as it was quiet again. 'You were about to say, Joe . . .' But before Joe had time to reply a woman's voice could be heard.

'Fergus, are you there?'

'Yes, Emma.'

'I've been looking for you everywhere. Your mother wants you.'

'I'll be there in a minute.'

'No, she wants you straightaway,' said Emma, her voice clearer now as she presumably leant over the stable's bottom door. 'She'd like to talk to you before dinner about the funeral arrangements.'

'I'll catch up with you later, Joe.'

Jack could hear Fergus leaving the box and only wished he could leap into his car, drive up to Drumgarrick and ask Joe then and there to identify that voice.

They learnt nothing that night. The conversation in the drawing room before dinner was mainly devoted to reminiscences about Patrick and the stud, and since neither Jack nor Seamus had ever heard Hugo or Eamon Fitzwilliams or Kieran Steele talk before, it was impossible to make out who was saying what. The only voice they could identify by a fairly easy process of elimination – since its owner wasn't Irish – was that of Guy Pritchard. He said relatively little anyway, making only a passing reference to his recent purchases at the Newmarket sales. It was hard to believe that among their number was the killer of Patrick Kildare.

Back in his hotel room Jack set about working out a fresh plan of action. His efforts the previous day to talk to Joe had made it abundantly clear that the groom had no intention of confiding anything to Jack. Joe had cut him dead in the bar of the village pub when he had tried, admittedly somewhat awkwardly, to make conversation, and the landlord had indicated that Jack would be advised not to linger over his pint of Guinness. What mattered now was winning the full co-operation of Fergus and through him discovering about the brooch and, even more importantly, whose voice it was Joe had recognised. Why Patrick had had to die was still something Jack didn't understand. Perhaps he had discovered the identity of the horse's killer and was not prepared to go through with a bogus insurance claim. By all accounts he was a man of honour and would put honesty and self-respect before self-interest.

Nothing, Jack accepted, could be done until after the funeral but then he would have to move quickly. Although Amy would not be best pleased, he would have to interrupt their little tête-à-tête, confront Fergus, and persuade him that co-operation was now essential.

Chapter Eleven

Fergus slept fitfully and woke up at six o'clock. There was still a lot to arrange before the funeral at four o'clock that afternoon and he had no idea just how many people would be likely to attend. There was bound to be a big turn-out from the village and he expected that a lot of people from the racing and the point-to-point worlds would come. Although no official notice had been placed in the papers, the *Sporting Life* and *Racing Post* were going to carry an announcement and word of mouth was usually the best source of information in these parts anyway. His mother had told him that she wanted him to organise drinks at the house afterwards – there was not going to be a proper wake but she wanted her husband to be seen off in some sort of style. Fergus had not argued. He would pay his own respects to his father in his own way and today was merely a necessary ordeal which he had to endure as best he could. He found himself

179

looking forward to seeing Amy Frost that night and talking to someone who was a stranger to his family and its past.

In the event, two hundred and fifty people crowded into the tiny church of the village of Drumgarrick that afternoon and most of them came back to the house afterwards. After much deliberation, Colette had finally decided to wear a black coat over a beautifully cut black suit. She had covered her face with a veil. Fergus stood beside her throughout the service and then at the graveside. To the outside world they had played the role of the united family. This, Fergus had resolved, was to be their last public appearance and he wanted to imbue it at least with some dignity. The presence of uniformed Gardai among the congregation provided a stark and cruel reminder of the circumstances which had brought them here.

The mourners crammed into the drawing room of the house and spilled out into the dining room, hall and sitting room. Helpers had come from the village to serve drinks and snacks and Fergus soon found himself cornered by old friends of his father and locals wanting to share their memories and convey their own sense of loss. He was determined to be patient and civil and when at times he felt he could face no more he reminded himself that this was an essential part of the cathartic process, not just for him but for all who knew and liked his father. He had become separated from Emma and his mother at an early stage, although he regarded that as more of a blessing than anything else. Now the only person he really wanted to see was Joe. In the rush of the morning's organisation he hadn't been able to get him on his own and was still desperate to find out whose voice it was he had recognised. He had seen him in church, indeed he had been one of the pallbearers at Fergus's insistence and despite his mother's objections, but not since. Perhaps he had escaped back home or was down with Tongue in Cheek. Fergus was waiting for a suitable opportunity to escape and go and seek him out when Emma grabbed him.

'There you are. I've been looking for you everywhere. People keep asking after your mother and she can't be found either. Mark you, it's not surprising in the crush. I never knew your father was so popular.'

'Except with one person, of course,' said Fergus drily.

'I don't get you.'

'Think why we're here, Emma.'

Paradoxically her face brightened up as she understood him. 'At least I'm glad you're getting on with the Moondancer case. I think you and Colette are very brave to call a meeting of the syndicate so quickly.'

'What meeting?'

'Come on, Fergus, you know, the one tonight, the one your mother fixed up over the phone with Eamon on Saturday. You don't think Pritchard came over here just to say goodbye to your father. He wouldn't get out of bed unless there was something in it for him.'

Any remaining doubts he may have had about his mother now vanished. All he wanted to do was go upstairs to his room, retrieve the brooch from its hiding place, find Joe and go to the Gardai. But first he was due to meet Amy Frost. He made an excuse to Emma about talking to some friends of his father who had come down from the North and rushed up to his room. Having collected the brooch he walked briskly to the top of the stairs and then stopped. His mother's room was off to the left and the door was slightly ajar. He could hear movement. He tiptoed over to listen and gently pushed open the door a little.

At the other end of the room, on the double bed, sat his mother with her back to him, her black skirt pulled up above her waist, her naked thighs wrapped round the object of her lust. Fergus strained in vain to put a face to the fingers whose nails dug deep into her back. As her gasps of pleasure reached a crescendo and her thighs clenched in orgasm, he had a sudden urge to declare his presence. But what could he say? Instead, he ran down the stairs to his car, cursing her. The thought of his own mother having sex with one of her guests on the day of his father's funeral sickened him. He'd make certain she paid for what she'd done.

Fergus arrived at the Killiney Hotel at six forty-five, three-quarters of an hour before his appointed rendez-vous with Amy. He decided to wait in the bar rather than see if she was already in her room and disturb her. He was still dazed and hurt by what he had witnessed in his mother's bedroom. He would lay the full story before Amy, and then the next day he would go to see Superintendent Brogan. He didn't know or care where he would spend the night although it certainly wouldn't be under the same roof as his mother. He was on his third whisky and feeling increasingly emotional when Amy arrived. She was taller and more attractive than the image of her he carried in his mind and he could have sworn her hair was much lighter, almost blonde. At their last and only meeting, however, he had hardly been concentrating on her appearance. Fergus got up from his chair as Amy spotted him. She walked towards him, smiling.

'Would you like a drink?' he asked, signalling the barman to come over to the table he had chosen in the corner for privacy.

'Good idea. A gin and tonic, please, with ice and lemon.'

'What time did you get to the hotel?'

'I left Dublin soon after two and did a bit of sightseeing en route. This is a very beautiful country – all those ruined castles. I got here about two hours ago in the end. And how about your day? Or shouldn't I ask? You look like you've really been through it.'

'It's not been one I'd care to repeat, not that it's possible. The funeral went as well as it could, given the circumstances. I couldn't believe how many people turned up. In a way that made me very proud of him. But since then, well, there's been a . . .' he hesitated. Did he really want to confide in someone he had only just met? Amy's receptive and understanding expression encouraged him to go on. '. . . a dramatic development. My mother has a lover and I'm convinced that together they killed the horse and my father.'

'Hold on, Fergus. One step at a time. What makes you think that? Surely you can't believe that your own mother—'

'You think I'd make this kind of thing up?'

'I don't think anything. Until you give me the details, I can hardly venture an opinion. But it just seems difficult to believe. Why don't you start at the beginning?'

Fergus nodded. 'Okay then.'

'What evidence do you have to connect your mother or her lover to the shooting of Moondancer?' Amy asked.

'The gun. Moondancer was shot in the early hours of Sunday morning after my father had allegedly received a number of threats from the IRA threatening to kill the horse if the syndicate didn't pay up a large sum of money. If it was really the IRA behind those calls, they didn't know anything about breeding. As far as the owners of Moondancer were concerned, nothing would have pleased them more than the death threat being carried out, followed by a large claim on the insurance. On that Saturday, all the owners had gathered at Drumgarrick at my father's suggestion to consider the demands. The one thing which was agreed by everybody that evening was that IRA or no IRA, Moondancer had no future as a stallion standing in Ireland or probably anywhere else in the Western hemisphere. When Joe, our stud groom, woke me in the morning to tell me that someone had blasted Moondancer's head off, the first thing I did was check the gun room downstairs. Only two people, my father and myself, had keys.'

'Where were they kept?' asked Amy.

'I kept mine hidden under one of the floorboards of my room, and my father kept his in a secret compartment in his desk in the study.'

'Why the secrecy?'

'My grandmother's butler blew his brains out after running up some heavy betting debts on a hurdler trained by my grandfather and ever since then the rule of the house has been to keep the gun room locked and the number of keys down to a minimum and well-hidden. The tragedy was that the horse won next time out at thirty-three to one.'

'And did anybody else know about that?'

'The horse winning?'

'Come on, be serious. Where the keys were kept.'

'My mother knew where my father's key was but not mine, or at least not as far as I know. I unlocked the gun room and the cupboard where the two guns, mine and my father's, were kept. The barrels should both have been clean as I had cleaned them myself that very afternoon. My father and I had been doing a bit of rough shooting, you see. Anyway, one gun was as I had left it but the other had obviously been fired recently. Whoever had used it had made a clumsy attempt at cleaning it because they left smudges over the barrel.'

'And whose gun was that?'

'My father's.'

'So what did you do?'

'That's not quite the end of the story. Later in the day I went to find my father in his study and there he was, closing the secret compartment where his key was kept. His back was turned to me, so I made a speedy exit.'

'So you assumed he had done it?'

'It all pointed that way and if he had I couldn't really blame him. He had sunk everything into standing that horse at Drumgarrick and I reckoned that he could not bear the prospect of financial ruin – not so much for his own sake but for mine. There was no way I could give him away so I returned to the gun room, cleaned the barrels properly and kept my mouth shut.'

'But did you never think of challenging him about it?'

'That was in January. About three weeks later when it appeared that everybody had swallowed the

IRA theory I brought the subject up – fairly clumsily, I must admit. He had been very depressed and I was worried that he felt guilty about what he had done. You have to realise, he loved horses and in normal circumstances would have put Moondancer – failure though he might have been as a sire – above any money.'

'Honourable but expensive.'

'That was the way he was. I waited for an opportune moment and made it clear that if he had done it I understood and he wasn't to blame himself.'

'And did he give any reaction?'

'That's what puzzled me. He just said he didn't want to see me hurt.'

'That's rather strange. What do you think he meant by that?'

'I didn't understand it at the time. It could have been a veiled way of saying he did do it but didn't want to bring dishonour on the family by admitting it. But I now think I know what he meant – that he knew who had done it and was covering up.'

'In which case that could only mean your mother?'

'Exactly. Although he was aware of my feelings, or rather lack of them, towards her he would hardly want to see her and therefore the family name publicly disgraced.'

'And do you think he told your mother that he knew her secret and she in turn realised that he was beginning to have doubts about going on with the insurance claim?'

'It makes sense. Or maybe she guessed that he knew and was afraid that he would abandon the case. In any event, his death would be her fortune.'

'You're ahead of me. Slow down. I thought your father had no money.'

'I'm sorry, for some reason I assumed you knew everything. Under the terms of my father's will I inherit the house and my mother inherits the shares in the horse. The house is so weighed down by mortgages that I'm surprised it's still standing. The shares, on the other hand, are as free as the air. In addition, she also receives a large amount of money under my father's life policy, which was taken out only three weeks before he was murdered.'

'When did you discover all this?'

'On Friday morning before I phoned you.'

'So your mother had plenty of motive, you say.'

'I do.'

'But what's this about a lover and how do you link them to your father's murder? You need evidence which will stand up in a court of law, not guesswork, however educated.'

Fergus stretched out the index finger of his right hand. 'Firstly, she could never have done it alone, she hasn't got the stomach for physical violence. And secondly,' he held out his middle finger, 'this afternoon I caught her making love – if you could put it that high – with one of her fellow shareholders in Moondancer – at least, I'm almost certain it was one of them. Thirdly,' another finger shot out, 'look at this.' His other hand went into his jacket pocket and came out holding some tissue paper. Fergus laid it on the table in front of them and Amy watched as he unwrapped it. 'There!' He handed her the brooch. 'It's my mother's, those are her initials. Joe found it in exactly the same spot where I found the body, while I called for the Gardai.'

'Circumstantial evidence at best,' Amy said gently.

'As soon as I told my mother that I had discovered the body she insisted on seeing my father's remains on her own.'

'That's perfectly understandable. A kind of final communion.'

Fergus was becoming a little impatient with Amy playing the role of devil's advocate. 'Please just let me finish. When she came out of the walled garden her skirt had dirt on it and her hands were muddy, just as if she had been crawling on the ground looking for something.'

'The brooch?'

'Exactly. She must have been frightened that she had dropped it when she buried my father. It just happened that Joe got there first. I bet she now thinks she must have lost it elsewhere. I can't wait to see her face when this is produced in court.'

'If you're right about all this – and I'm not saying you aren't – there's an awful lot that's going to be difficult to prove.'

'That's not all,' Fergus went on. 'Last night Joe told me that he had answered one of those so-called telephone calls from the IRA and that the caller had mistaken him for my father.'

'And so?'

'He recognised the voice.'

Amy leant forward in anticipation. The devil's advocate had become counsel for the prosecution. 'Well, whose was it?'

'He didn't tell me. He was just about to when Emma arrived – we were in Moondancer's old stable.'

'You'd better find out pretty damn quick who Joe recognised. Is he on the phone?'

'Yes, of course. The twentieth century has also arrived in Ireland, you know.'

'Then go over there and give him a call.'

A couple of minutes later Fergus returned shaking his head. 'I've talked to Moira, his wife. She said that he's not back yet from the wake and she reckons he's gone on to the bar to have a few pints by way of drowning his sorrows.'

'When does she expect him back?'

'Knowing Joe, once he's on a bender it could be any hour of the night. I'll see him first thing in the morning though. He hasn't missed a day in thirty years. Don't worry, he won't have for—'

'Hello, this is a surprise,' Amy interrupted.

Fergus looked up to see the grinning face of Jack Hendred.

Amy made no attempt to hide her displeasure. 'What are you doing here?' she asked, her tone hard.

Jack waggled his finger against his nose. 'Let's say a little bird told me. And since I'm sure you would want me to share in any information Mr Kildare here might wish to impart, I thought I'd join you.'

Fergus immediately made to get up and leave but Amy put her hand firmly on his shoulder and pushed him back into his chair.

'Don't get angry, please. I never told Jack about this meeting, I promise you. He'll explain to me later why and how he found out about it and I warn you now, Jack,' she added, shifting her gaze to him, 'the explanation had better be good.'

Jack was momentarily taken aback by the hostility in her eyes and voice, and by the disconcerting way she somehow managed to smile and glower at the same time.

'Do you mind then?' he asked, pulling up a chair and directing his question at a point on the table somewhere between the two of them.

'Yes, but as you're here you might as well stay,' sighed Amy. 'I'm certainly not going to ask Fergus to repeat what he's been telling me, but it seems to me he has pretty good grounds for alleging that Moon-dancer's death and his father's murder were, how can I say it, an inside job.' She looked at Fergus for approval. She knew she would have to tell Jack

191

everything but she didn't want to forfeit Fergus's confidence in her at such a critical time.

He responded by touching her arm with his right hand. 'It's all right, Amy. I believe you when you say you didn't tell him we were meeting. When I've gone you can tell him everything I've told you and he can make what he wants of it. If I'm right, there won't be any need for him to hang around Drumgarrick much longer. I'm sure he has lots of other business in London to attend to.'

Jack was beginning to feel about as welcome as a bounced cheque. 'Plenty,' he replied, 'but you can rest assured that I won't be leaving Ireland until this case is sorted out. Isn't that right, Amy?'

Determined not to be forced to take sides between the two men, Amy hedged: 'Well, naturally as far as the insurers are concerned they will give Fergus any assistance he may need but of course once it has become clear that we can no longer play a positive role, then we will withdraw. But until then—'

'Until then I would very much like to keep in contact with you, Amy,' said Fergus. 'I have a feeling this is all about to turn very nasty and I might be in need of some good advice.' He rose to leave and on this occasion Amy made no attempt to stop him. 'If you don't mind, I'd better be pushing on. I think I'll drive down to the bar in Drumgarrick village and see if Joe's there. Can I call you tomorrow?'

'By all means,' answered Amy. 'And if you want

someone to come down with you to see Brogan, I'm very happy to do it.'

'Thanks.' Fergus offered his hand to Jack. 'No doubt we'll be meeting again soon. Give my regards to Mr Maloney.'

Jack shook his hand. He wondered whether Mr Maloney had heard anything of interest since he had left him listening in to the mourners getting steadily more drunk in the drawing room at Drumgarrick.

Fergus reached the bar in the village at half past ten. It was crowded with locals, many of whom had been to the funeral and who raised a glass in his direction as he looked around for Joe. There was no sign of him. He eventually caught the landlord's attention. 'Have you seen Joe?' The landlord's eyes were glassy; he'd obviously been making his own contribution to the prosperity of the brewing industry. Having made his own quick survey of the bar he shook his head and shouted out the same question to his customers. There was a universal shaking of heads and someone in the corner suggested Fergus tried Joe's home. That, thought Fergus, was the least likely place Joe would be, and in any event he had no desire to risk the sharp end of Moira's tongue if he disturbed her sleep. He decided he had no option but to wait until the morning.

He drove out to Drumgarrick, parked his car at the bottom of the drive and walked across the fields to the front of the house towards Tongue in Cheek's stable where he intended to spend the night. The curtains were drawn in the dining room but the lights were on; the syndicate meeting was presumably still in progress, his mother no doubt holding court. The King is dead; long live the Queen.

Fergus carefully and quietly opened the door of the stable and crept inside. Tongue in Cheek was lying down but stood up straightaway and began to whicker. Fergus could see and smell that the stable hadn't been mucked out for some time. If Joe hadn't done evening stables then he really must have been on a bender, and if that was the case, Tongue in Cheek wouldn't have been fed either. The horse began nuzzling against his jacket pocket.

'Okay, I'll go and get you something,' Fergus said, patting the horse on the neck. He unclipped the water bucket from the hook on the wall and put it under the tap while he went to the feed room and prepared a bucket of food.

A few minutes later Tongue in Cheek began calling as he heard Fergus returning with his long-overdue supper. He started to snatch the feed from the bucket as soon as it was within reach.

'Poor old lad, you were starving,' Fergus said as he emptied the bucket into the manger. He went back for the water and then stood and watched Tongue in Cheek bolting his food for a few minutes. Finally he shut the door and made his way to the tack room where he settled down under a couple of blankets. It didn't take him long to drop off and soon he was deep in his dreams.

Distorted images of the events of the last few days gave way to the impression that his father was in the tack room with him chatting away as in the old days and telling him everything would be all right. He could see his father's face and hear his voice so clearly that the immediate past seemed like a nightmare. Now he was introducing Amy to his father, knowing how well they would get on, and then he and Amy were in bed together and he was holding on to her for dear life, afraid she would leave him.

For some reason Fergus suddenly awoke and remembered that he hadn't given Tongue in Cheek any hay. He looked at his watch. He felt as if he'd been asleep for ever and yet it was still only three o'clock. He rolled out from under the blankets and made his way over to the barn. The moon was out and as he walked he looked across to the house. It was in complete darkness.

He collected a couple of wads of hay from a half-open bale and took them back to Tongue in Cheek's box. The horse was standing with his back to the door, his head hung down, sleeping, but awoke and turned round as soon as Fergus pulled back the bolt. Fergus walked quietly past him to the rack in the corner. As he reached up to throw the hay in, his left foot hit something under the straw and he stumbled forward against the wall. He bent to uncover what it was, brushing the straw aside. Suddenly he jumped backwards, frightening Tongue in Cheek. There between the wall and the door lay a lifeless body. Fergus stooped down and pulled away more straw to reveal the hideously contorted face of his one remaining friend.

There would be no betting coup for Joe.

Chapter Twelve

Seamus realised he was beginning to tire of spending his life in the back of his van as he climbed into it that Tuesday morning. Two and a half hours of eaves-dropping the previous afternoon had put him off wakes for life. People really did talk an immense amount of rubbish when they were drunk, unless of course you happened to be drunk with them. He hadn't bothered to deliver the tapes to Jack at his hotel as they contained absolutely nothing of interest. He now felt that the surveillance part of their investi-gation had served its purpose and that if Jack did manage to win the co-operation of Fergus, then a more open approach should be put into action.

Seamus turned on the receivers to pick up the bugs in the kitchen and the drawing room; as he suspected, there was nothing going on. Jack would be joining him in about ten minutes and would at least be able to cheer him up with an account of how his imitation of a gooseberry had gone down with Amy. Seamus chuckled to himself. If Amy had been ugly as sin he somehow doubted that Jack would have been so enthusiastic about bursting in on her rendezvous with Fergus.

Bored with hearing nothing, save for the tick of the kitchen clock and the grunts of that wretched dog eating away at the furniture, he tuned in to the bug he had concealed in Tongue in Cheek's stable. A conversation between Joe and Fergus about how well the horse was working would be better than that damned gnawing sound. He was somewhat surprised when the first voice he heard was unmistakably that of Superintendent Brogan.

'Show me, please, Mr Kildare, the exact position of the body when you say you discovered it.'

'It was just as you see it now.'

'And what were you doing sleeping in the tack room?'

'For reasons which I'll explain later, I preferred to sleep here rather than in the house.'

'Is that a usual practice on your part?'

'No, I wouldn't call it usual. I've done it a few times before when I couldn't sleep and a couple of times when Tongue in Cheek was unwell.'

'And you say you found the body when you were putting the hay in the rack.'

'For God's sake,' shouted Seamus at the receiver, 'say whose body it is!'

'What did you do then?' went on Brogan.

'I stared in disbelief for a few seconds and then ran up to the house and used the telephone in the study to call you.'

'Why did you use the study? Isn't there a nearer phone, in the kitchen?'

'Yes, but I didn't want my call to be overheard.'

'Is that because you suspected someone in the house?'

There was a long pause and all Seamus could make out was the sound of Tongue in Cheek moving about.

'Superintendent, do you mind if we go down to the barracks? There's something I want to tell you.'

Seamus could hear the sound of them leaving and at that moment Jack climbed into the van.

'Top of the morning, number one assistant,' he said, throwing him a bacon sandwich. 'Are you all right? You look like you've seen a ghost!'

'Not quite,' answered Seamus. 'Something worse. There's been a murder at the house, a dead body in the stable. I've just heard Brogan interviewing Fergus and they've gone off together to the barracks. I think Fergus is about to confess.'

'I don't believe you. Whose body?'

'The buggers didn't say; kept on referring to the corpse as "him". Who do you think it could be?'

'One of the house guests maybe, but I don't see why. I bet you it's Joe. Shit. According to Amy, last night Fergus still hadn't got the name of that caller out of him and unless he managed to contact him last night, we'll never bloody know. This is just what we needed. Rewind the tape quickly and I'll take it with me. I'd better go and phone Amy.'

'And tell her about the bugging?'

'I don't see any other option. Did you gather when all this happened?'

'No, only that Fergus claims to have slept in the tack room and discovered the body when he went to give the horse some hay.'

'Brogan will enjoy that. I think you'd better stay here and keep listening and I'll go and make that call. Meet me at the hotel at lunchtime and make sure you leave all the recorders running.'

Jack stopped at the nearest telephone box and called Amy. She had just finished her breakfast and, as she walked up the stairs to her bedroom, was planning to make contact with her office to rearrange her week's appointments. After what Fergus had told her the night before, she really felt that she could be of some assistance to him and, she had to remind herself, her own clients if his accusations against his mother and her lover proved well-founded. At the moment all he had was circumstantial evidence coupled with an ample motive. She doubted whether that would be enough in a court of law, even with Joe's evidence, and that was on the assumption that the voice Joe had recognised belonged to Colette. As she opened the door, the telephone was ringing and she grabbed it, expecting to hear the voice of her secretary in London.

'Hello, Amy. Thank God. I thought you weren't there. It's Jack.'

'If you're phoning to apologise again for your behaviour last night, forget it. If we don't hear from Fergus today it'll be your fault for upsetting him.'

'There's been a murder at Drumgarrick.'

'Not Fergus?' The alarm in her voice took Jack by surprise.

'He's the one person we can rule out. He's down at the police station, or barracks, as they call them, at his own request, with Brogan.'

'But when? I mean, how do you know all this?'

'All I know is what Seamus has told me.' Jack recounted his conversation with Seamus, concluding with the opinion that Joe was the victim.

'If you're right, it can only mean that he was killed to stop him identifying that voice. How did Seamus find all this out?'

'He was listening in.'

'What do you mean, listening in?'

'The night we visited Drumgarrick we planted one or two bugs about the place.'

'Bloody hell! Whereabouts?'

'In the drawing room and beside the phone in the kitchen, and—'

'So that was how you knew about my meeting with Fergus? You sneaky little toad, Hendred. And you've probably overheard a good few other conversations at the house which you haven't seen fit to report to me. Jack, why didn't you tell me?'

'I can explain.'

'It'd better be good.'

'I did it for you.'

'Is that really your best effort?'

'What we have done is against the law and if you or the clients were involved then it might be held against you. By not telling you I have spared you any liability or potential embarrassment.'

'Oh, I see, you're motivated by altruism, not chauvinism. You still haven't explained how you came to be listening to a conversation in the stable.'

'That particular bug wasn't part of our original plan. Seamus planted one there the night Fergus caught us.'

'A stroke of luck, it now seems. Am I to assume that Mr Pink has been spending the last few days in some remote spot not far from Drumgarrick listening in to, and recording, all the goings on up in the house?'

'Nearly all. We've kept the tapes, so you can listen to any of them you want.'

'And I presume you've checked back over yesterday to see if the tape has picked up the murder being committed, assuming Joe, or whoever it was, was in fact killed in the stable?'

'Not yet,' said Jack. In the rush to call Amy he had in fact overlooked this obvious step. 'Why not meet me at my hotel at one o'clock and I'll bring with me all yesterday's tapes and we can listen together. I'll put Seamus on to checking up with his friend in the Gardai as to what's happening to Fergus and whether we're right about Joe.'

'Agreed. And Jack, one last thing?'

'Yes?'

'No more secrets, or you'll be going back to London.'

Jack and Amy arrived almost together at his hotel and immediately went up to his room for privacy. Jack had brought with him a cassette recorder and the stable tapes covering the period between two in the afternoon and midnight when Seamus had abandoned recording for the night. As was his practice, he had timed and then marked each tape.

'Where do you think we should start?' asked Jack.

'If we assume it happened after the funeral, and I seem to recall Fergus saying Joe had been one of the pallbearers, we might as well begin at about four forty-five.'

Jack separated the three tapes running from four thirty to seven thirty and began playing. The first tape lasted for an hour and consisted solely of Tongue in Cheek munching and moving about his stable. Impatient as they both felt, they had to listen to it all in case of missing anything.

Jack put on the second tape. For the first fifteen minutes there was silence save for the breathing of

Tongue in Cheek and then suddenly they could make out the voice of Joe as he came into the stable. He was talking away to his favourite horse as if he was having a conversation with a fellow human. For a few seconds the tape went silent and they could make out Joe walking round the stable. He then started chatting away again and appeared to be patting Tongue in Cheek. This was followed by someone entering the stable, who clearly took Joe by surprise.

'Oh' – it was Joe's voice – 'if you're looking for Master Fergus . . . You b—' He never finished the sentence. A single sharp scream of pain, which sent Tongue in Cheek racing round his stable, was followed by a chilling silence. Then came what sounded like the body being dragged across the floor, the rustling of straw and finally the door of the stable being closed.

'The poor bastard,' said Jack, turning off the tape. 'That scream is terrifying.'

Amy nodded silently.

'He was killed at ten to six by my reckoning,' Jack went on, 'provided Seamus's watch was accurate.'

'He obviously recognised his attacker. You could tell that by his greeting. Do you think his last word was going to be bitch?'

'It was certainly b . . . something. Hold on, I'll replay it.' Jack replayed the whole of the short murderous encounter.

Amy spoke first: 'He definitely says "you b . . ."'

but it's not clear whether the second letter is an i or an a. Bitch or bastard. You'll have to hand this over at once, it's crucial evidence.'

Jack looked less than enthusiastic.

'What's the matter?' asked Amy. 'You've got to. You can't withhold it.'

'I know. Stop being so self-righteous. I'll go with Seamus as soon as he gets here. They'll want all the tapes and any copies, and that's only the beginning. They'll do us for breaking and entering and God knows how many other offences as well. And in case you're worried, I'll make it clear that no one else knows about this.'

'You don't have to lie for me. Tell them the truth, all of it. I'm worried about Fergus, they might be charging him right now.'

Jack seized on Amy's preoccupation with Fergus's welfare. 'How can you be so sure he's innocent?' he asked her, without giving much thought to what he was saying.

'What do you mean by that?'

'Don't get annoyed. What time did you meet him last night?'

'We arranged to meet at seven thirty and he was in the bar waiting for me when I came downstairs. I don't have any idea how long he had been there.'

'But as far as you know he would have been at Drumgarrick until, let's say, six thirty?'

'Presumably. He said last night that he had gone

back to the house for the wake and he only left after he caught his mother in bed with whoever.'

'And we only have his word for that. Didn't it strike you as a rather fanciful notion? His own mother, and on the day his father was buried? He could easily have killed Joe and come over to see you.'

Amy's cheeks were flushed with anger. 'Your brain's fogging up, Jack. Either that or you've got cotton wool in your ears. You heard the tape, the first thing Joe says is, "If you're looking for Master Fergus". Fergus would hardly be looking for himself – even if he is Irish.'

There was a knock on the door which turned out to be Seamus.

'I thought you were never going to get here,' said Jack, glad of the interruption. Amy was getting to him, in more ways than one. 'What's the news?'

'Hello, Amy. My apologies. As you thought, it was Joe, stabbed in the heart and died almost instantly. The Gardai are searching the grounds for the murder weapon which was probably a carving knife or something of that sort.'

'That reduces the suspect list to about two hundred. Anyone could have picked one up in the kitchen,' said Jack.

Seamus ignored him and continued. 'Fergus is still with Brogan. None of the others are allowed to leave the house and the Gardai have already started compiling a list of all those who attended the funeral and went on to the house afterwards.'

'Who was staying at the house last night?' asked Amy.

'Mrs Kildare, Kieran Steele, Hugo and Eamon Fitz-williams, Guy Pritchard and, of course, Fergus's girl friend, Emma.'

'Are they all there still?' inquired Jack.

'All but Guy Pritchard. He apparently left at the crack of dawn to catch a flight back to England.'

'And very conveniently out of the jurisdiction of the Gardai,' commented Jack. 'I think I'll make a call to a friend of mine in London and ask him to keep an eye on Pritchard for us. Before I do, have a listen to this bit of tape.' He played Seamus the crucial tape. 'We can't make out what he was trying to say at the end.'

Seamus listened intently and then shook his head. 'Could be bitch or bastard or anything beginning with a b. With the equipment they have these days they'll be able to tell you if there's anything there.'

'You realise we'll have to hand over the tapes. I'm really sorry to have got you into this mess.'

'Don't go worrying yourself. If we play this right we might just get a bigger welcome than the prodigal son. After all, where would the Gardai be without us? We're going to save them huge pathology fees in pin-pointing the time of death, and that's just for starters. It was lucky that I decided not to use voice-activated bugs. It's impossible to judge time with those.'

Amy perked up at Seamus's philosophical approach. 'That's fighting talk, Seamus,' she said and grinned at him. 'The worst they can do is hang you. You'd better make that call to London, Jack, and then go and see Superintendent Brogan. He's in for a big surprise.'

The Gardai had been swarming all over Drumgarrick since Fergus's phone call had alerted Brogan to the latest tragedy. The hunt for the murder weapon was on in earnest, with every available constable being drafted in to help look. The preliminary view of the pathologist who had examined Joe's body in the stable was that he had been killed by a knife with a sharp blade, possibly a carving knife. Once the grounds had been searched, the hunt began in the house and the first place to be searched was the kitchen. Four knives had been taken away in a plastic bag for forensic examination in the knowledge that if any of them did reveal any traces of human blood it would be possible, thanks to the DNA identification process, to say positively whether it was Joe's. Unfortunately, the Gardai were not the only interested parties. One murder in a sleepy village might be worth a couple of columns on the front pages of the national press but two within a week was regarded as a positive epidemic and at least five officers were fully occupied in preventing the press gaining access to the grounds.

The search soon moved from the kitchen to the

upstairs bedrooms and before leaving to take Fergus down to the barracks, Brogan had given clear instructions that all the remaining occupants of the house were to await his return in the drawing room. The atmosphere was remarkably relaxed considering that someone they all knew lay dead only a few hundred yards away. Colette, who had somehow managed to make herself up perfectly in the five minutes she had been given to come downstairs, seemed wholly unperturbed by Joe's demise. She had never made any secret of her dislike of the man and would have regarded it as the height of hypocrisy to be seen or heard mourning his parting. She was more concerned with planning how she would deal with that supercilious policeman when he came to interview her. She doubted that he would show her any additional consideration because of her recent tragic loss, and she resolved to say as little as possible. A touch of bewilderment and hurt at the events of the past week would be the order of the day.

Colette's only other concern was her son. She had learnt from one of the Gardai that he had gone down to the barracks with Brogan at his own request and it was worrying her more than she cared to admit. Since the reading of the will and the disclosure of her interest in the life insurance policy, Fergus had studiously avoided her and his conduct at the funeral and the wake afterwards had bordered on the insulting. She didn't like to dwell on what he might be saying about

her to Brogan. Like his father, Fergus was a senti-
mentalist and sentimentalists were anathema to her.

As she watched Kieran Steele and Eamon Fitzwilliams discussing bloodlines over by the window
with Emma hanging on their every word, and Hugo
Fitzwilliams reading the form book, she could not
discern the slightest trace of anything but glorious
self-interest and utter indifference to Joe's fate. Only
Guy Pritchard was missing and he had been lucky
enough to leave the house before the body was discovered. A taxi had picked him up at six and by now he
was no doubt safely ensconced in one of his favourite
restaurants having lunch. A smile crossed her face. It
was a pity he didn't time his love-making as well.

Sandwiches and coffee – she had no idea where
they came from – were brought in at lunchtime and
when by four thirty they had still not been given any
indication of when Brogan intended to see them, signs
of anger and frustration were beginning to show.
Eamon was the first to vent his feelings, directing his
remarks at the assembled company in general.

'What I want to know,' he announced, 'is why
we're being cooped up here? They don't seriously
think one of us would kill a stable lad, do they?'

'Eamon, I never knew you were such a snob,'
exclaimed Kieran, feigning astonishment. 'Poor old
Joe was the stud groom here and in his youth a very
able jump jockey, until a couple of falls put an end to
his career. The fact that they happened after the pub

and not on the racecourse is neither here nor there. What's more interesting is why someone thought it was necessary to stick a knife into him at all.'

'How do you know he was stabbed?' asked Eamon, eyeing him suspiciously.

'Let's just say an informed guess. I might be quite wrong. Did anyone hear a shot in the night, for instance?' There was no response, which Kieran took to mean they hadn't. 'Although that doesn't prove he wasn't shot. After all, no one heard a shot the night Moondancer was killed. I suppose with the stable door closed and given the distance from the house, the noise might not carry. Maybe poor old Joe was garrotted or struck from behind with a blunt instrument, like this.' He picked up a bronze of a racehorse from one of the side tables and made as if he was about to strike Eamon.

'It's not funny,' replied the bloodstock agent, moving quickly away.

'It wasn't meant to be. I wouldn't be at all surprised if the Gardai think one of us here or dear old Guy is the murderer, and the reason we're being kept hanging around is to make us sweat. No doubt they've been giving all our rooms a thorough going over.'

'Even our personal possessions?' asked Emma, who remembered that she had left the result of her pregnancy test in her handbag.

'Nothing's personal at a time like this. What they're after is any trace of blood on bits of clothing or in the sink where the murderer has washed his,' he paused for effect, 'or her hands.'

'You're really enjoying all this, aren't you, Kieran?' said Hugo. 'You might have some respect for Colette's feelings, and Emma's for that matter.'

'Feelings? I hardly think they come into this any more. If Colette were in a state of shock and tormented by grief she would hardly have called a syndicate meeting for the evening after Patrick's funeral. And as for Emma, I'm sorry if I disappoint you, Hugo, but I don't think sensitivity would be high on my list of her many and undoubted attributes.'

Colette ignored Kieran's remarks and if anyone expected a fiery response from Emma they were disappointed. She was enjoying this display of vitriol between the two men and was curious to find out exactly which of her attributes were on Steele's list. That would have to await a more suitable and less public occasion.

'What I want to know is where the hell Fergus is,' remarked Eamon, attempting as ever to play the role of peacemaker when his interests were directly or indirectly threatened. 'He's behaved bloody strangely towards us since we arrived on Sunday. And I don't put it all down to the horror of discovering Patrick's body. If you ask me, he suspects one or possibly all of us of being behind Moondancer's death and his father's murder. I don't believe the Gardai will place much credence on any accusations he may make, but what about the insurers? What if he were to concoct some story about us plotting to kill the horse to claim on the policy?'

'Don't worry,' said Kieran, 'the insurers are still going to pay up. These deaths are merely a temporary nuisance – that is, unless someone wants to confess to something we don't know about?' He looked around the room as if to invite such a confession. 'Of course, none of us can speak for Guy.'

Just then a Gard put his head round the door. 'Excuse me, but which one of you is Mr Steele?'

Kieran held up his hand.

'Would you come with me please, sir? Superintendent Brogan would like a few words with you.'

Kieran had been gone about twenty minutes when the same officer reappeared and asked Eamon to follow him. Hugo was the next to be summoned after a similar interval, leaving Emma and Colette alone together. Since Emma's return on Sunday the two women had exchanged only a few words and the present opportunity to be more intimate was not taken up by either of them. They had little to say to each other at the best of times. Colette was conscious of Emma's dislike of her, and characteristically was indifferent to the younger woman's feelings towards her. They did have one thing in common, however, and that was a healthy appetite for men. Colette could well understand Emma's interest in Hugo Fitzwilliams. He was extremely handsome, particularly when roused, and radiated virility. Like his father, he had bedroom eyes and Colette had first noticed them radiating that message in her direction about a year previously. Eamon had been an energetic and enthusiastic lover but was beginning to show his age. They say that when that happens to a stallion, you should send your mare to be serviced by his best-looking son. And how right they were, thought Colette wistfully to herself.

She was glad when she was finally alone in the drawing room. If Brogan was trying to frighten or put pressure on her by seeing her last, he was guilty of a serious misjudgment. Over the years, she had developed the ability to hide her true emotions and to play whatever role was called for at the time.

Emma had been gone for over half an hour when Colette's turn arrived. She followed the Gard into her late husband's study to find Brogan standing beside the fireplace. In his hand he held a framed photograph of Patrick in his hunting kit. He put it back on the mantelpiece and beckoned her to sit down.

'I'm very sorry to have kept you waiting for so long, Mrs Kildare.' The Gard who had shown her into the study closed the door and sat down by the window. 'This officer will take a full note of our conversation,' Brogan told her.

Colette's only reaction was to take a handkerchief from her handbag.

'I won't beat about the bush,' continued Brogan. 'Yesterday afternoon Joe Slattery was murdered and

214

this morning his body was discovered by your son. He had been stabbed. We believe that the knife used to kill him came from the kitchen of this house. Fortunately,' and at this point Brogan reached into his pocket to produce Seamus's tape of the fatal encounter, 'we have been able to pinpoint the precise time of death.' He watched in vain for a reaction; Colette remained impassive and evidently unflustered. 'Could you tell me exactly what you were doing yesterday at five forty-five?'

'Of course. I was here, with all the other mourners who had returned here after my husband's funeral.'

'Are you able to remember who you might have been talking to at that time or who might have seen you then?'

'Superintendent, please. Last week I find out that my husband has been murdered and that the months of waiting for him to return have been in vain.' She slowed down to ensure that the officer recording the interview was able to take a complete note. 'And now you're asking me to account for my movements at the wake. I hope you'll understand when I say that time was the last thing on my mind at such an occasion. I talked to lots of different people, as you might expect. You must ask them.'

'Of course, and I've already been doing that. Did the discovery of your husband's body come as a terrible shock to you?'

'Yes. Although he had been missing for a long time,

215

I had never given up hope that he might return. I've read about people getting amnesia and turning up years later and that kind of thing. Yes, it was a terrible blow. I certainly never conceived that he might have been murdered.'

'Did you go into the walled garden often, or was that more your husband's territory?'

'I went there very rarely. He loved pottering about there, when he wasn't with his horses.'

'Did your husband once give you a brooch, with your initials on it?'

'Yes, it was an anniversary present. I've been unable to find it since he disappeared. I—'

Before she could finish Brogan produced the brooch from his other pocket.

'Would this be it?'

'Yes, that's it, the bottom part of the K has snapped off. I had given it to him to take to be repaired the week before his disappearance. Where did you find it?'

Her answer caught the superintendent unawares. 'It was found by Joe in the soil where your husband had been buried. Does that really come as a surprise to you, Mrs Kildare?'

'I don't understand.' Colette appeared genuinely perplexed by the question.

'You see, your son has said that after he told you of his discovery of the body, you immediately went to your husband's grave, insisting that you were left there on your own. When you emerged ten minutes later there was soil on your skirt and hands as if you had been looking for something – like this perhaps?' Again Brogan held out the brooch in the palm of his hand.

'If you're trying to suggest that I dropped the brooch there and therefore had something to do with my husband's death, you ought to be ashamed of yourself. I loved my husband, Superintendent, and I like to think he loved me. I can see my son has been poisoning your mind against me. You have to understand that Fergus has never loved me, like any normal son would love his mother, and since learning of his father's wishes as to his estate, that dislike has turned to hatred. It's all very sad.' She dabbed a tear from her eye with the handkerchief.

'But do you deny that there was soil on your skirt?' Brogan's voice displayed a note of frustration as he sensed that Colette was outmanoeuvring him.

'Of course I don't. I wanted ten minutes to be alone with my husband for the last time, to pay him my respects. To do that properly I knelt beside him just like any decent Christian would, and my hands and skirt got muddy in the process.'

'You referred to your husband's estate a moment ago. I understand that you have inherited his shares in Moondancer absolutely and unencumbered.'

'Did Fergus tell you that too? My husband wanted to give me security should anything happen to him.

You have to understand that when he bought Moondancer and invested all that money, he really believed
that he would be a great success as a stallion and that
he would leave both Fergus and myself well provided
for. Sadly, Moondancer was a failure, and Fergus will
have to suffer the consequences.'

'And the life policy? Your husband took that out
only three weeks before his death, and made you the
sole beneficiary. Were you aware of that?'

'Until last Friday when our solicitor told us about it
I had no idea of its existence. I can only assume that
Patrick thought there might be a problem claiming
the insurance on Moondancer and wanted to provide
for me in some other form. He was over seventy, you
know, and had been feeling his age, particularly after
Moondancer was killed.'

Brogan tried a different approach.

'Moondancer was killed with a shotgun kept in this
house. You knew where your husband kept his shotgun, didn't you?'

'Of course I did. In the gun room along with
Fergus's.'

'And you knew that only two people, your husband
and Fergus, had a key to that room?'

She nodded.

'You also knew where your husband kept his key,
didn't you?'

She shook her head. 'I never asked him and he
never told me.'

218

'Are you seriously expecting me to believe that, Mrs Kildare?'

'It's the truth. For all I know he could have changed its hiding place regularly. Since I'm not one of those women who shoots, I didn't regard it as my business.'

Brogan walked over to the desk and put his hand into the right-hand drawer. A concealed compartment sprang open from beneath it. Moving with uncharacteristic delicacy he took a handkerchief out of his top pocket and used it to lift out a small, well-worn key.

'Are you saying you've never seen this before?'

'Never.'

'And this?'

With a sudden movement he produced a carving knife, its handle already wrapped in polythene. Colette's eye widened with shock.

'We found this hidden here this afternoon. Yesterday it was buried in the stomach of Joe Slattery. And on the handle, Mrs Kildare, are your fingerprints.'

The constable taking notes just failed to catch her as she fell to the floor.

Chapter Thirteen

Amy had been waiting in her hotel room all afternoon for news and when by eight o'clock she had received no word from either Jack or Fergus, she began to feel distinctly uneasy. It was highly likely that Seamus's optimism as to the kind of reception they would be given by the Gardai was misplaced, and that he and Jack were now behind bars down at the barracks. However useful the tape-recording of the murder might be, the Gardai would scarcely be attracted to a couple of private investigators interfering with their inquiries.

She had resigned herself to the wrath of her senior partner as soon as he discovered from his hospital bed what had happened. A lot of the firm's business came from insurance work and its reputation would suffer once the truth about some of Jack's methods of collecting evidence emerged. Her more conservative and high-minded partners would clamour for Jack's dismissal, advise the immediate settlement of the litigation and expect her to disassociate herself entirely from his conduct. She would succumb to none of that. Anyway, her own position was, as she reminded herself, the least of their problems.

Tired of waiting upstairs she had decided to go down to the bar and have a large reviver, when the telephone rang. It was Fergus, calling from Drumgarrick.

'Amy? I was worried you might have left. Have you heard the news?' He sounded out of breath and agitated.

'About Joe's murder? Fergus, I'm so sorry. I know how fond you were of him.'

'That's not all. They've arrested my mother, this afternoon.'

'What, for killing Joe?'

'And on suspicion of killing my father as well. I told Brogan everything this morning – well, nearly everything. I explained why I thought that one of the guns from the gun room had been used to kill Moondancer and when I told him about the secret compartment in my father's desk he went up to the house, and guess what? He found a knife, a carver, hidden there. They're almost positive it was the murder weapon.'

'But how can they link it to your mother?'

'Because only she and I knew of the drawer's existence. But more damning than that, there are some fingerprints on the handle and they match prints taken from her bedroom.'

'Fergus, I can't believe your mother is up to knifing anybody. Surely she can establish that she was in the house when Joe was killed?'

'But no one knows what time precisely Joe was killed.'

Amy realised that Fergus was unaware of the bugs which had been planted and the existence of the tape. 'That's where you're wrong. Jack and Seamus have told them.'

'I'm sorry, I don't follow. And who the hell is Seamus?'

Amy hesitated but decided he would have to be told sometime.

'You know Seamus as Mr Maloney, the short round-faced man in the duffel coat. He and Jack were planting bugs in the house that night you caught them in Tongue in Cheek's box.'

The line went quiet. When Fergus at last spoke, he sounded hostile and aggressive. 'Were you in on this?'

'No. I only learnt about it myself this morning.'

'It still doesn't explain how they know about the murder.'

'Seamus had a spare bug on him when you caught them and he hid it in the straw.'

'How much have they heard? Do they know about the will?'

'They have a tape of everything which was said in the drawing room and in the kitchen over the last five days. That's how Jack knew that we were meeting last night.' Amy was sure she heard him mutter 'bastard' under his breath.

The revelation made Fergus feel distinctly unclean – as if someone had been privy to his most private thoughts, and laughing at them. It confirmed his view of Jack as shifty and untrustworthy, and he was hurt that Amy appeared to be taking his side, or at least not openly condemning his behaviour.

'Are you still there?' she asked, after giving him time to cool down.

'Yes, I'm still here.' He sounded only a little less angry. 'I hope they've handed all those tapes over to the Gardai.'

'Yes, they have, but I haven't heard from them since they went down there and I'm worried. Please try and understand, Fergus; they're both on your side and Jack was only doing his best to try and discover the truth about Moondancer. In one sense, we should be grateful to him and Seamus for coming up with a tape of Joe's murder.'

'And have you heard it? Does it prove it was my mother?'

Amy thought she could detect the first sign of uncertainty in his voice as if he was torn between his own feelings towards his mother and the stark realisation of what it meant to find out that your own parent has committed such a terrible wrong.

'It doesn't prove it either way,' she answered. 'It was pretty obvious that Joe recognised the killer; just before he was killed he referred to you as "Master Fergus" as if he was on familiar yet respectful terms with whoever had come into the stable.'

'Master Fergus? That's how Joe always referred to me when he was talking to my parents. It could only have been my mother.'

Amy didn't know how to respond. After all, he was still Colette's son and surely in his heart he would rather she was innocent. Amy decided to concentrate on his present needs: 'Are you on your own or are the others still there?'

'Everyone's gone. All the men left as soon as they got the all-clear from Brogan. Only Emma was here when I returned. I told her I needed a few days to sort myself out, on my own.'

'How did she take it?'

'She was very decent. She said that she realised how I must be feeling and that she would go and stay with some friends for a while. She knows our relationship is finished but, to be quite honest, it's not the kind of thing I want to discuss with her at the moment. And what are your plans?'

'I'm waiting for Jack and Seamus to get in touch. I thought that this was them when you called.'

'Oh.' Fergus sounded put out again.

'Are you sure you're going to be all right on your own there?'

'Don't worry, the place is swarming with Gardai and, without Joe, there's a hell of a lot of work to be done. The lad who helps out with the brood mares is all right provided he's watched over. I'm going to have my time cut out keeping the place going. I simply can't afford any extra help. I hope at least the lad remembered to feed Tongue in Cheek. I'm just going down to check.'

'And Joe's wife? Have you heard how she's taking the news?'

'I'm told she's in a terrible state. I only wish I was in a position to offer some financial support, but as things stand at the moment, I'm broke and will probably have to sell a couple of the mares to pay the bills as it is.'

'I suppose your only hope is if your mother is convicted of your father's murder. Then everything will pass to you.'

Amy immediately regretted her remark.

'Great minds obviously think alike. Brogan made the very same comment.'

Amy could well imagine what counsel for Colette would be suggesting to Fergus in the witness box. She changed the subject. 'Is there anything I can do for you? I'm very happy to come over tomorrow with some food and cook a meal and keep you company.'

'Would you? That would be terrific. If you want, you can stay the night. This house is full of bedrooms, you can take your pick.'

Amy usually turned down that kind of invitation. But she was bored with staying in the hotel and the advantage of a short stay at Drumgarrick was that, apart from helping Fergus, she could see the place properly at first hand.

'I'd love to. What time shall I come over?'

'About ten thirty? By then I'll have seen to the horses and I'll be able to introduce you to the other love of my life.'

Amy chose not to ask who the first one was. 'Good, I'll see you then. Take care.'

She put the receiver down and reflected on the day's events. As yet the Gardai hadn't charged Colette and she could see them having great difficulty in proving beyond reasonable doubt that she had in fact killed her husband. They looked like being on safer territory with Joe's murder, that is unless she had an alibi for what she was doing at five forty-five. She thought of how Fergus had caught her making love to somebody. He had never said what time that was, and she wondered whether he had mentioned it to the Gardai. Even then, the all-important question remained unanswered: just who had she been in bed with?

Amy went downstairs to the bar and was on her second gin and tonic when Jack came bounding in.

'Am I glad to see you,' she said, standing up to greet him. 'I was beginning to fear that you and Seamus would be spending the night behind bars.'

'We very nearly did. Brogan wasn't very impressed when we handed over the tapes. It's only thanks to some wily talking by Seamus's solicitor that we've been allowed out on bail. I'm not very popular in Ireland right now, so I'm flying back to London tomorrow. Brogan approves, he wants me off his patch, and there's nothing more I can do here anyway. Seamus will keep me in touch with any developments this end. At the moment it looks like the Gardai are going to throw the book at us unless the solicitor can persuade them that our evidence will be so important at the trial that now will not be the time for Brogan to make fresh enemies.'

'You mean at Colette's trial?'

'You've heard she's been arrested then?'

'Yes. Fergus phoned me about half an hour ago. He didn't know about the tapes and when I told him about Joe referring to "Master Fergus", he felt that proved his mother must have done it.'

'He's really got it in for her, hasn't he? I wouldn't want to be in his shoes at the moment. He does realise he'll be one of the main witnesses at the trial, that is if they do go ahead and charge her?'

'And will they?'

'Your guess is as good as mine. My relationship with Brogan hasn't quite reached the stage of confidant. In fact, the man's a bit of a pig and even if he doesn't do us for some crime or another, he's certain to make life very difficult for old Seamus in the future.'

'Poor old Seamus. Where is he? Gone to see his widowed mother perhaps?'

Jack was glad that she hadn't lost her sense of humour. Having endured an extremely uncomfortable five hours at the barracks, he was keen to unwind and hoped that Amy would assist him.

'Can I get you another?' he asked, pointing to her empty glass.

'Why not? I suppose we can celebrate your freedom and that this might now mean that the insurers won't have to pay out.'

'Don't kid yourself. As things stand, nothing's changed. If Colette stands trial she won't be charged with any offences concerning Moondancer's death, although many Irishmen would think that the law has its priorities wrong. It's only if they can pin Patrick's death on her and then link it to Moondancer's death that we're in with a chance, and even then you mustn't forget that at the time she wasn't one of the horse's owners. So, strictly, the policy remains good, and we'll have to pay up.'

'Unless, of course, Fergus is right and she has a lover.'

'And that lover is one of the owners. That gives us four candidates, three if you count out Hugo Fitzwilliams.'

'Why him?' asked Amy, who had a sufficiently cynical mind to exclude nobody from the presumption of guilt.

'Because if I remember correctly, you told me last night that he was having an affair with Emma,

229

and anyway, he's years younger than Colette.'

'Ever heard of "toy boys"?' she said, giving him a thoroughly wicked grin.

'I'm not younger than you, by any chance, am I?' he replied, nonchalantly putting his hand on hers on the table.

She gently removed it. 'No, you're older, and not necessarily wiser.'

The next morning Amy left early to shop in Tipperary before going on to the house. The papers were full of the murder and, according to one of them, charges were expected early that day. She was stopped by the Gardai at the beginning of the driveway to the house, but fortunately Fergus had had the good sense to notify them of her impending arrival. Even so he was summoned down to identify her. He joined her in the car for the half-mile drive back to the house and directed her to park in the courtyard at the back. He was wearing a yellow shirt and short-sleeved pullover, and a fairly dirty pair of jodhpurs that looked and smelt as if he had been mucking out in them. Coming from a farming background, Amy took no notice. As she lifted her case out of the boot, Drummond appeared and, putting his front feet on her shoulders, started licking her face.

'Not much of a guard dog, is he?' said Amy, turning her head to avoid the dog's affection.

Fergus grinned at her, remembering her first

encounter with the Doberman in the stable. 'He'd lose a fight with a rabbit.' He pushed Drummond off and took her case into the kitchen.

He was under strict instructions from the Gardai that they were only to use the kitchen, his bedroom and the one opposite, as the other rooms were still being checked for fingerprints and any other clues they might yield. With such limited space at their disposal he decided to take Amy on a tour of the stables and an inspection of his bloodstock. He first showed her the remaining brood mares, all but one of whom had been home-bred. Two had recently been tested in foal and as a result the second instalment of the nomination fee had become payable on the first of October. Fergus admitted to her that he had no idea where the money would come from.

'And now,' he said, 'last but by no means least, let's go and see Tongue in Cheek.' He whistled to Drummond who ran on ahead of them.

In spite of all the drama that had taken place inside his home, Tongue in Cheek looked remarkably fit and relaxed. Fergus put a head collar on him, led him out of the stable and stood him proudly before Amy.

'Isn't he magnificent? This is some racehorse, I tell you, and what's more he hasn't finished improving yet.'

'You must have been disappointed then by the way he ran last week, although I suppose it was a pretty competitive race.'

'He needed that run. He hadn't been on a race-course in ages,' answered Fergus, stroking the horse's nose.

'Is that what Joe thought, or is he one of those frustrating animals that leaves all their best races behind on the gallops? Catches pigeons at home and the punters catch a cold on the track?'

Fergus shook his head. 'Not this one. There's no reason why you shouldn't know as it doesn't matter any more. Tongue in Cheek wasn't off last week. That was merely the first stage of our master plan. With Joe dead I've decided to abandon it.'

'Why? Go on, tell me about it.'

'You know something about horses and racing, do you?' Fergus asked, already certain she did.

'It runs in my blood,' Amy replied.

Fergus outlined to her the details of their scheme to land a huge betting coup in the Ladbroke hurdle in the New Year. Amy listened with increasing interest and could already feel the urge to put her own betting boots on.

'So,' concluded Fergus, 'that was the way we were going to save the house and raise a few thousand in readies to keep us going. Joe had been dreaming of a chance like this for years and now, just when we've found the right horse, bang goes the crack.'

'Rubbish,' said Amy. 'You owe it to Joe and yourself to go through with it. If anything, you need the money more than ever now. Even if your mother is charged and tried, I reckon it's three to one against a conviction and that leaves you right back where you started.'

'It's no good,' Fergus said gloomily. 'I owe the bank so much money I've got nothing to bet with.'

'I might lend you some. I can never resist a good bet.'

Fergus smiled at her, but shook his head. 'No, I could never accept, because if it goes wrong how could I ever pay you back?'

'Stop being so gallant. We have to make sure that it doesn't go wrong. From now on it's us against the bookmakers.'

Fergus heard the 'us' and felt like hugging Amy. The dark cloud of loneliness and depression that had enveloped him lately began to lift.

'I could see if there's any furniture left to sell. With a bit of luck I might raise about five thousand,' he said.

'That'll do to begin with. The main thing is to keep to Joe's plan. When did you say the Dundalk race was?'

'A week on Saturday.'

'Good. You concentrate on training him for the next ten days and I'll come over on the Friday night to keep you company and drive you to the races. I can be travelling head lad-cum-assistant trainer. Is it agreed?'

Amy's enthusiasm was infectious. Fergus didn't

question this sudden and somewhat incongruous shift in his relationship with the solicitor acting for Moondancer's insurers; he simply welcomed it.

'Why not?' he agreed. 'It'll give me something to keep my mind on over the weeks ahead and, who knows, we might even do it.'

'There's no might about it,' replied Amy. 'We'll do it.'

They spent the afternoon walking round the land which surrounded the house and talking about Fergus's childhood and university days. Amy deliberately steered the conversation away from anything remotely morbid and by the time they had finished nattering it was past six o'clock. Amy wanted to have a bath before cooking dinner and Fergus showed her up to her bedroom. It was opposite his own and had its own bathroom adjoining.

'I'm afraid it's not been cleaned since its last occupant left, but I did at least change the sheets this morning. Mrs Magee, our daily, didn't turn up – I can't say I blame her – so I don't know what state the bathroom was left in.'

Amy unpacked and ran a bath. It was a vast Edwardian cast-iron affair standing on four clubbed feet and when she turned on the hot tap it let forth a stream of brown water. After a couple of minutes a more normal colour was disgorged. At least it was boiling hot and she settled down to a long leisurely soak. The bath was so large that her toes couldn't touch the taps and she allowed her mind to flirt with the idea that it could accommodate two bathers with remarkable ease.

She was lounging with her head back against the end of the bath when she spotted what looked like a folder or file stuck behind the massive old-fashioned mahogany loo about six feet to her right. Her curiosity aroused, she washed herself quickly and having wrapped a large, slightly damp towel round herself went over and pulled it out.

It was a yellow folder with no name or identifying feature on the front. Amy opened it, not knowing what to expect. It contained a number of typed reports prepared, judging by the name and address at the top of the first page, by an inquiry agent in London. Each report was headed 'Subject: Guy Pritchard' and contained a blow by blow account of his movements over the past four months. At the back of the folder was a separate report, on much finer paper, marked 'private and confidential' and prepared by an eminent firm of City accountants. Amy read its contents avidly through to the end. It set out in minute detail Pritchard's financial background and revealed how, through a web of overseas trusts and nominee companies, he controlled a large empire in vice and illegal gambling. It concluded that owing to a number of imprudent investments and the attention of the Inland Revenue, his financial position was perilous and that a spate of recent fires at his Soho premises were being treated as possible arsons by the insurance companies against whom substantial claims had been lodged.

Amy moved from the bathroom and onto her bed to read the inquiry agent's reports in detail. Two in particular caught her attention. The first, dated July of that year, recorded how the inquiry agent had followed Pritchard late one evening to a property in Soho and how fifteen minutes later he had left by the rear entrance. A few minutes later the property was ablaze. The second, dated only the previous Friday, referred to how the agent had followed Pritchard early one afternoon, three days before that, to a flat in Notting Hill Gate and how twenty minutes after entering the block, he had come running out, removing a stocking from his face as he went. She was about to turn over the page to read the conclusion of the report when there was a knock on the door.

'Yes?'

'I'm sorry to disturb you,' said Fergus, 'but I've got Kieran Steele on the phone downstairs saying he left an important business file behind. He needs it urgently and is sending a driver down tonight to pick it up. He stayed in your room. Can I come in and get it?'

'Hold on a minute. I've just got out of the bath. Did he say where he left it exactly?'

'Yes, for some reason he put it behind the loo.'

'I'll have a look and if it's there I'll bring it down in a minute.'

236

Amy now knew to whom the file belonged but unless she had some sudden stroke of inspiration she had lost her opportunity to copy out its contents. She turned over the final page and read the single paragraph out loud to herself: 'Following the subject's departure I made inquiries as to the occupants of the various flats in the block and concluded that he had visited the flat of a private detective presently engaged in investigating a number of suspected arsons in Soho.'

Amy let out a gasp when she read the last sentence: 'His name is Jack Hendred.'

Chapter Fourteen

Amy returned to London the next day, promising Fergus she would be back in time for the Dundalk race. She took with her from Drumgarrick the name of the inquiry agent who was following Guy Pritchard and a hastily scribbled résumé of both his latest report and that prepared by the accountants. She hoped that they would provide enough for Jack to go on and in a brief and enigmatic telephone call from Drumgarrick, she had arranged to meet him for lunch in London on Friday to hand over 'something of interest'.

Pritchard's visit to Jack's flat had of course been the same afternoon that they had flown to Shannon and probably explained the marks on Jack's face. If that was the case, Pritchard clearly wasn't the man he pretended to be. Amy wondered if he was capable of committing murder.

She took a cab from Heathrow to the offices of

Messrs Arthurs in Lincoln's Inn and successfully slipped into her own room without being noticed. She had no wish to answer questions about the case from anybody just now. Her secretary smuggled her in some sandwiches for lunch and she managed to work throughout the day without being disturbed. Shortly after five the phone on her desk rang.

'I thought we agreed no calls. Oh, it's you. How did you persuade Venetia to put you through?'

'I told her that I was calling from Scotland Yard and that if she didn't connect me I would have her for interfering with the course of justice. She suddenly became very nervous and here I am,' answered Jack.

'You sod! You must have given her the fright of her life.'

'She'll survive. I've tried three times already this afternoon using my own name and I was beginning to despair. Trying to wash your hands of me now I'm on bail? Embarrassed about what your partners will say when they hear what you've allowed to go on in the client's name?'

'How did you guess? I was just dictating my report saying we ought to sack you and settle the case in full. My clients aren't interested in murders, you know, only paying out as little as possible to claimants.'

The silence made her think he believed her. 'Jack?'

'Yes, I'm still here. I'm quietly cursing myself for not telling Brogan that the bugging was your idea and that you told me you were allowed to do this kind of thing under English law. It's probably a bit late now but I might still catch him at the barracks . . .'

'All right, I'll throw away the report.' She picked up a couple of sheets of blank paper and tore them up beside the receiver. 'Hear that?'

'Music to my ears. We've had a little bit more information from Seamus's man inside the Gardai, although he swears this is positively the last time he can help. Colette will be charged tomorrow with the murders of both Joe and Patrick. Apparently she's playing her cards very close to her chest, refusing to answer any more questions or make a statement. All she says is she's innocent and that's an end to it. The Gardai are going to oppose any application for bail.'

'Do they know where and when the trial will be?'

'Hopefully in Dublin before Christmas.'

'So soon?'

'They think that will give them enough time to collect all the evidence and pursue any further inquiries. They're continuing their search for the weapon used to kill Patrick – over fifty men are combing the land around the house.'

'They'll be lucky.'

'I agree. The case against Colette is very circumstantial and a lot will hinge on whether Fergus is believed. Anyway, that doesn't solve our problem. Unless we can link one of the original owners to the horse's death, the claim remains valid. The irony is that Colette could be convicted and still recover her share of the insurance money.'

'That can't be right. Under English law a murderer cannot inherit or benefit from the estate of his or her victim. The shares will pass to Fergus and after what he's gone through, you wouldn't begrudge him that, would you?'

'I might, particularly if I thought he knew more about this than he was letting on. I know that you feel sorry for him, Amy, but hasn't it occurred to you that he has a habit of withholding vital information until an opportune moment arrives to produce it, like a magician taking a rabbit out of a hat?'

That thought had indeed occurred to Amy, but she had persuaded herself to reject it. She preferred to believe that Fergus's actions were inspired by honourable and, in the circumstances, perfectly understandable motives. 'Your trouble is you earn your living by being a cynic, Jack Hendred. Well, whatever you may feel, I like Fergus and I intend to go on helping him. In fact, I'm going to stay with him again the weekend after this and be there when Tongue in Cheek runs.'

'Bully for you. I don't advise you to spend the night in that stable, though, you never know what might happen to you. When it comes to giving evidence, Tongue in Cheek is particularly well-named.'

Amy managed a laugh. 'On that sombre note I'll say goodbye and see you tomorrow for lunch, same place as last time. I'll cheer you up with some news on Pritchard.'

'Won't you tell me now? I'm lonely and depressed and—'

'No dice,' Amy interrupted. 'I'll see you tomorrow.'

Over lunch the next day Jack was astonished when Amy produced the notes linking Pritchard to the arsons in Soho which he was investigating. Amy gave him a few moments to recover before asking him about Pritchard's visit to his flat: 'Does it perhaps explain why your face looked so awful on that flight to Shannon?'

Jack tried to make light of it. 'A close encounter with a piece of rope, that's all.'

'And was the rope anywhere near your throat, by any chance?'

Jack subconsciously stroked his Adam's apple. 'Possibly. Mr Pritchard is capable of some very ungentlemanly conduct towards his fellow men. Does Fergus think he was the man he saw *in flagrante delicto* with his mother?'

'I didn't mention the contents of Steele's file to him. I just handed it over for him to give to Steele's driver. I thought he had enough to worry about.'

'Talking about Colette and Mister X, it appears that Fergus chose not to tell Brogan about it when he went down to the barracks. Bit strange, isn't it?'

'Perhaps he thought it was something he'd prefer the world didn't know. It's certainly not something I would want to broadcast if I were him. Try and be a little sympathetic.'

'All right. But won't he have to tell the court about it?'

'Not necessarily and I have no intention of finding out what evidence he's going to give. From now on I'm being very wary of doing or saying anything relating to the trial which might be misconstrued. Sometimes I think you forget I'm a solicitor of the Supreme Court.'

He gave her his most intense and caring look. 'Please say that again. It sounds so damn magnificent . . .'

'Watch it. Here's the waiter. You can order some more wine.'

Jack left after arranging to take Amy out for dinner the following week. For the moment he had ruled out returning to Ireland where he was very much *persona non grata*. Instead, he would set about fixing Pritchard. Amy had given him enough to do just that and he thought the time had come for him to pay a visit to one of his chums in the Serious Crime Squad at Scotland Yard. Pritchard was going to find his fingers badly burned for having dared to play with fire.

A week later Amy kept her promise and flew over to Shannon and then drove to Drumgarrick. Fergus had been starved of company since her departure, with only the loyalty and affection of Drummond to keep his spirits from breaking. He wanted to talk about the case but Amy insisted on changing the subject.

'And how's our horse? Ready to do battle tomorrow?'

'All the way. I've put a lot of work into him in the past week and what really worries me now is that he may be too damn fit. I'm not totally confident I'll be able to stop him. Joe's plan was that we should run well, but not too well. It's a big enough field but I'm no expert at pulling racehorses.'

'What's the rule about horses running on their merits?'

'He will, only it'll be at Leopardstown and not Dundalk tomorrow. As Joe would say, that's the crack.'

'I can't wait. What weight are you carrying?'

'Eleven stone. I won't have any problem doing the weight. I've been running to keep fit and, to be honest, I've been off my food. I'll still need to shed a few more pounds before the Ladbroke.'

Amy looked at him. He had aged since she last saw him, his face was pinched and spare. 'Are you sure this is sensible?'

'There's no choice. I hope we get ten five in the handicap and there's no way I'm going to give away a pound of that. If we were beaten by a short head I'd never forgive myself.'

Amy admired his determination. He picked at his food over dinner and was content to retire early to bed. She guessed that just having someone else, an ally, under the same roof was some kind of comfort to him and hoped for once he would be able to have a proper night's rest.

Amy slept well and came down to the kitchen to find Fergus's head buried in the *Racing Post*. He was so caught up in whatever he was reading that he failed to notice her arrival.

'Try Tongue in Cheek in the second,' she said. 'It's an absolute certainty. I know the connections and they're going to have their money down.'

'Don't,' he answered, without looking up. 'I could hardly sleep all night I'm that nervous, and what's worse, I've just seen who's standing as one of the stewards today.'

'Someone you know?'

'Mick O'Connell, a friend of my father's. He's got eyes like an alley cat and since he's a fan of my riding, he's bound to keep a paternal eye on me during the race. That, and the fact that they make us third favourite in the betting, is all I needed.'

If Fergus was like this now, Amy thought his likely condition before the Leopardstown race didn't bear thinking about. They would probably have to lift him on to the horse and strap him into the saddle.

'Relax. How many other runners are there?'

'Twenty.'

'There are bound to be a few non-triers among them. I reckon Mick O'Connell's bins are more likely to be trained on one of the less trusted members of the racing fraternity than a poor old amateur like yourself. Now where's my breakfast?'

Fergus grinned and handed her the paper to read. 'You're the expert. Pick out a couple of winners to pay for the day.'

An hour later, after loading Tongue in Cheek into the rickety old horsebox, they were on their way to Dundalk with Fergus behind the wheel and Amy beside him, ready to act as travelling head lad, a role she had last played for her brother at the local point to points.

Joe had chosen Dundalk as part of his master plan because, like Tipperary, it was a sharp track and would not suit Tongue in Cheek with his big long stride. After the way he had run last time, Fergus reckoned they'd need all the help they could get. The Kilmallock Handicap Hurdle was due off at two thirty and having changed into the Kildare colours of purple jacket, yellow cap and purple spots – a little too eye-catching for what he had in mind – Fergus was on his way to the paddock as soon as the bell sounded for jockeys out. Amy was parading Tongue in Cheek with all the pride of a mother with a newborn baby, and she gave Fergus a knowing wink as he caught her eye.

For what seemed an eternity he stood nervously and awkwardly on his own in the middle of the ring while around him animated owners and trainers were giving last-minute instructions to their jockeys. He played self-consciously with his whip and tried to tell himself to calm down and remember that he owed it to Joe not to make a hash of it. As he watched the other horses walk round, he couldn't help but notice that Tongue in Cheek made them all look ordinary. That only made him feel worse. Seeking a distraction, he glanced up at the odds board and had the fright of his life. Tongue in Cheek was two to one favourite. He felt a sudden sinking feeling in the pit of his stomach. Everyone would be watching him now.

The bell rang for the jockeys to mount and he walked dejectedly over towards Amy, who had somehow managed to find herself on the far side of the ring.

He was barely three yards away when he felt a tap on his shoulder. He wheeled round as if he had been caught with his hand in the till.

'Fergus, how good to see you here.' It was Mick O'Connell, beaming from ear to ear, his steward's badge glistening ominously on the lapel of his overcoat. 'I'm so sorry about all your problems. I'm sure it's a ghastly mistake about your mother.'

Fergus could only nod and mutter, 'Thank you.' Now was hardly the time to tell O'Connell that he was talking to the chief witness for the prosecution.

The steward leaned forward and in a half-whispered confidential tone inquired, 'Are you off then?'

248

Fergus felt numb with panic. O'Connell had been renowned for his tilts at the ring before he joined the ranks of the establishment. Either old habits died hard or he was merely showing a fatherly interest in the young jockey's chances. Suspecting the former, Fergus pretended it was the latter.

'I'll be doing my damned best, sir, but with no Joe to train him, I'm terrified he may need the race.'

O'Connell winked at him and gave him a playful punch in the stomach.

'I hope you've told the horse that. He looks pretty good to me.'

Fergus touched his cap and walked the last few yards to Amy.

'Are you all right?' she asked.

'You're joking. That was Mick O'Connell. Have you seen the betting?'

Amy turned towards the odds board. 'Favourite? But why, Fergus?'

'Don't ask me. Just promise me one thing.'

'What?'

'You'll bury me in my riding silks after the lynching.' He pulled back Tongue in Cheek's rug and then tightened the girths.

'Damn it!' he cursed as the buckle snapped on the second girth. 'Amy, walk him round while I run and get another one.'

By the time he returned from the weighing room, all the other horses had gone and Tongue in Cheek was prancing round the paddock like a stallion, with his tail sticking up in the air. Not surprisingly he refused to stand still for little more than a second at a time but eventually Fergus managed to do everything up and Amy legged him into the saddle. Once he was aboard, the horse settled down and Amy led him straight across the paddock and onto the course.

'Good luck!' she cried as Tongue in Cheek pulled to be free and Fergus let him set off down the course.

The ground was officially described as good to soft but there had been a heavy storm during the morning and with Tongue in Cheek's easy action it felt much more like soft underfoot. The plan that Fergus and Joe had worked out was exactly the same as at Tipperary, except they wouldn't risk being left at the start and this time Tongue in Cheek would be carrying two stone extra. Doing this was easier than Fergus had imagined. After weighing out he just went over to the saddling box and switched weight cloths.

As Fergus reached the two-mile start on the far side of the course, he apologised to the starter for being late and asked for his girths to be checked. There were plenty of front runners in the race and if Fergus had done his job properly, Tongue in Cheek ought to run out of puff somewhere near the second last hurdle. All he would then have to do would be to wave his stick around and appear to be trying.

The starter's assistant finished tightening his girths as the starter climbed onto his rostrum and called the runners into line. Fergus manoeuvred Tongue in Cheek up against the rail and as the starter let them go, they raced away down the far side of the course. For the first mile Tongue in Cheek never saw more than eighteen inches of any hurdle but jumped superbly, just flicking the tops as he went. Once they had completed a circuit and began racing downhill on the far side, the field began to string out, and Tongue in Cheek started to pull for his head. Fergus gave him a quick sharp pull in the mouth and aimed him straight up the backside of the horse in front. Tongue in Cheek stumbled for a split second as he suddenly found himself with nowhere to stretch his legs, but much to Fergus's consternation he quickly recovered and began to pull again. As Fergus was desperately deciding what to do next the jockey on the horse in front turned round and gave him an earful: 'What the hell are you up to? Can't you bloody steer?' Fergus shouted 'Sorry' as he pulled Tongue in Cheek to the right and let him run as fast as he wanted for the next three furlongs.

The horse was humping thirteen stone on his back in ground he hated and yet he still felt as fresh as paint. They had just jumped the second last, with Fergus wondering what on earth to do, when Tongue in Cheek suddenly stopped pulling. Fergus breathed a huge sigh of relief and for the final quarter-mile went through the motions of riding a finish without actually doing anything. As they passed the post, there were at least half a dozen horses in front of him but he had still been beaten less than fifteen lengths.

He cantered back to where Amy was waiting and jumped off immediately.

'How did it look?' he asked, fearing that he had made a complete hash of it.

'I'm no professional,' she replied, 'but if I were a steward I'd take your licence away.'

At that moment someone spoke behind them and Fergus froze as the words sank in: 'Mr Kildare, the stewards would like to see you as soon as you've weighed in.'

He turned round, blushing with guilt, to face the stipendiary steward. He had blown it.

'They want to know why you didn't check your girths properly before weighing out.'

Fergus could not believe his luck and to the stipe's surprise thanked him profusely. As soon as the steward had gone he switched the weight cloths back again and went to weigh in. At the inquiry he made up some excuse about having borrowed a pair of girths because his own hadn't been long enough. A sympathetic Mick O'Connell let him off with a knowing wink and a warning.

The journey back from Dundalk was made in a considerably more relaxed mood than the one there, and that night Fergus and Amy celebrated together over the last two remaining bottles of champagne in the Drumgarrick cellars. It was well past midnight when Amy suggested it was time for bed. As they reached the top of the stairs Fergus put his hand on her shoulder and turned her round to face him.

'You're very beautiful, you know,' he said, taking her left hand.

'And you're very drunk,' she replied, kissing him on the cheek.

'Is this a brush-off? Am I treading on someone else's territory?'

'Who do you have in mind?'

'Jack Hendred. I thought there might be something going on between you two.'

She laughed. 'Well, that's the first I've heard of it. They always say the woman's the last to know!' And with that she released her hand from his grasp and went into her room.

Chapter Fifteen

Amy had never been so nervous before a trial and, unlike Fergus and Jack, she was not even being called to give evidence. She had only spoken to Fergus twice on the phone since the Dundalk race and it was clear that he was extremely depressed with the way the Gardai had pursued their investigations since his mother's arrest. The attempts to locate the weapon which had been used to kill his father had yielded no success and, even more seriously, Brogan appeared to accept that since Steele, Pritchard and the Fitzwilliams, father and son, had alibis for the precise time that Joe had been killed, there were no grounds for suspecting that any of them might be Colette's accomplice. The superintendent's attitude was that it was going to be hard enough securing a conviction against Colette without confusing the jury with conspiracy theories.

Although Fergus was in no doubt about his

mother's guilt he still felt a sense of betrayal of his family name in giving evidence against her. Amy had done her best to point out that he was merely doing his duty, like any other citizen in a democratic society, and when that had gone down like a burst balloon, she had persuaded him that even more importantly he owed it to his father to see his murder avenged. Fergus's dilemma arose partly out of his conviction that his mother had not acted alone. He bitterly regretted not having told Brogan that he had caught her making love in her bedroom after the funeral. He was afraid that if he told him now it would be treated as a late invention on his part to bolster the case against her.

Amy arrived at the modern courthouse in good time to claim a seat with a clear view of the proceedings. With its undertones of greed, black-mail and sex, the case was bound to prove irre-sistible to the press and the public, and, sure enough, there were already a number of spectators gathered and a great many journalists – one tabloid had already dubbed Colette 'The mistress of the stud'.

At the front of the court, in the rows reserved for them, the various counsel were busy arranging their papers and making themselves generally comfort-able. Standing with his back to her and intending to occupy the seat nearest the jury box was the man hired to defend Colette, Finbar Curley. Rumoured to be the most expensive and sought-after advocate in Ireland, he appeared from behind to be anything but imposing in build. The fee he had asked and obtained in this case was the talk of the Irish Bar, although Colette could scarcely be blamed for going for the best. The price would seem cheap if she was saved from having to spend the rest of her life in a prison cell. At the moment all Amy could make out was that, judging by the few curls which sneaked out from below his wig, he had carrot-red hair. He was said to be a Limerick man, born and bred, and Amy just wished he would turn round so she could obtain a good look at his face.

His opponent was more visible. Rory Kelleher had been born in the North and had made a name for himself as a fierce and uncompromising prosecutor. He was much taller and more slender than Curley and, Amy guessed, had a far more aesthetic appearance. She had made a number of inquiries about him and the general response had been that he was very able but with a slight tendency to overdo the moral righteousness in his conduct of a case and in his closing speech. To err might be human but to forgive was not Kelleher's policy. Curley, by contrast, was known to reduce the stuffy atmosphere of a court to the homely intimacy of the sitting room where sin could be regarded as a necessary expression of the human condition and where moral judgments were best left to others. Kelleher had a fair complexion and darting eyes which constantly took in everything going on around him. She certainly wouldn't want to be cross-examined by him.

The increase in activity near the bench and the excited chatter around her indicated that the case would soon begin; Colette would be brought up into the dock at any moment. Amy was impatient to see how the last two months in gaol had affected her and craned her neck over the elderly woman in front to gain a better view. A few moments later Colette appeared, flanked by two women prison officers. She entered the dock as if she were about to receive an Oscar. Dressed in a simple black woollen dress, wearing a minimum of make-up and with her hair neatly pinned back, she conveyed an unmistakable aura of style and composure. That did not mean to say she appeared haughty; her whole bearing was rather that of a woman of dignity. She looked impassively round the court as if to demonstrate that she had nothing to fear and then turned to face the bench and await the arrival of the judge.

At the call for silence from the court usher, the Honourable Mr Justice Quayle strode into court. Nearer seventy than sixty, he possessed a gentle, compassionate face, wrinkled profusely by age and many law books. His face belied his true character. Vincent Quayle had been unpopular at the Bar when practising as senior counsel and his elevation to the bench had not seen any change in his unfailing ability to antagonise all and sundry. He disapproved of wine, women and song, although not necessarily in that order, and some wag had once asked if he was really Irish. He had earned the nickname Molotov, the only kind of cocktail he could recognise.

Amy again willed Curley to turn round and this time he duly obliged in order to talk to his junior counsel. She fell for him straightaway. His face was covered with freckles and his cheeks were the colour of a sunrise. He reminded her of a grown-up and even more cuddly version of Seamus Pink. She began to worry about what he would do to Fergus in cross-examination.

The jury was sworn in. After three peremptory challenges by Curley, the twelve consisted of eight men and four women; of the men, all but two were in dark suits and ties. One, a nervous-looking individual in his late twenties with gold-rimmed glasses and a disconcerting twitch, was even wearing a stiff collar and could have passed as a bank clerk from the 1930s. The women were represented by a young girl barely out of her teens who was staring enthusiastically in wide-eyed amazement at her surroundings; a colourfully dressed woman in her early forties who might just as easily have been going to a wedding; another of roughly the same age in a sensible tweed suit; and finally a stouter more matronly figure whose hair had been newly permed and who was already giving Colette distinct glances of disapproval. It was all so frightening, reflected Amy. Who could ever know what would influence their thinking, which gesture or reaction by Colette would be taken as a sign of guilt, which as a sign of innocence?

Asked whether she pleaded guilty to the two charges against her, Colette answered firmly 'Not guilty' and with a nod of approval from the judge, counsel for the prosecution rose to his feet. In a quiet, controlled voice and a Northern Irish accent, he began his opening speech:

'Members of the jury, in this trial I appear on behalf of the prosecution and my learned friend Mr Finbar Curley appears with Stephen Johnson on behalf of the accused, Colette Kildare. It is the prosecution case that sometime in March of last year Mrs Kildare murdered her husband Patrick and then buried him in the walled garden of their home, Drumgarrick House, in County Limerick; and that following the discovery of his body by her son on the third of October, only two months ago, she proceeded to murder a potential witness to her guilt, one Joe Slattery, a stud groom who had served the Kildare family faithfully for over thirty years. A murder, I should add, which took place on the very afternoon of her husband's funeral. Before I come to the details of these sordid crimes and the evidence upon which the prosecution relies, it might help if I first outline, albeit briefly, the history of the Kildare family and the events which were to lead ultimately to this courtroom.'

Kelleher paused for a moment to ensure he had the jurors' undivided attention. Amy noticed the matronly figure move forward in her seat so as not to miss a single word.

'Patrick Kildare was born over seventy years ago at Drumgarrick, a large house and estate which had been in his family for over two hundred years. Like his forebears, he farmed the surrounding lands which at the time of his inheritance amounted to almost three hundred acres and, as is common in Limerick, bred thoroughbred racehorses from his own brood mares. When he was twenty-five he married a local girl who sadly died giving birth to what would have been their first child. Eighteen years later, at the age of forty-three, Patrick Kildare married the accused. The second Mrs Kildare was barely nineteen and not long afterwards she bore him his one and only child, a boy, Fergus.

'It appears that the accused did not share her husband's love of the country or of horses and, as her son will tell you, the marriage was not a happy one. Indeed, it became what I believe is sometimes called a marriage of convenience, in which both parties agree to share the same home and remain together but are free to indulge in their own pleasures and interests. Fidelity was no longer regarded as an obligation.

'Patrick Kildare was not a successful farmer or breeder and over the years the fortune which he had inherited was gradually eaten away. That is not to say he was an unhappy man. He was at all times much liked and a very popular figure among his peers. This perhaps explains why, some six years ago, one of his friends, Eamon Fitzwilliams, a very able and successful bloodstock agent, made him a proposition which was to change his life and, sadly, provide the springboard for his untimely demise. Mr Fitzwilliams' son, Hugo, was a racehorse trainer who in his first two seasons of training had enjoyed enormous success with a colt named Moondancer. As no doubt some of you will remember' – at least two of the male members of the jury nodded – 'Moondancer carried all before him on the racecourse, being unbeaten in his six starts and winning both the English Guineas and Irish Derby. He was owned by a Texan oil millionaire who decided to cash in on his success and sell him to be a stallion.

'Eamon Fitzwilliams regarded this as an opportunity which could not be missed and put together a syndicate to buy this great horse. Before doing this he took an unusual decision, motivated, as he will tell you, to help a friend going through a difficult time. He asked Patrick Kildare if he wanted to stand Moondancer at Drumgarrick. For Mr Kildare this represented the opportunity of a lifetime, a chance to restore his home and stud to former glory. He readily agreed and as a sign of his enthusiasm asked to buy five of the forty shares in the horse himself, then valued at five million punts. He was obliged to spend a considerable sum refurbishing forty stables for those brood mares who would come to be serviced by Moondancer, and constructing at some distance from the house a large and modern stable with an adjoining covering area for the horse himself. To raise this money Patrick sold a number of pieces of valuable furniture, the last of his remaining stocks and shares, and borrowed heavily from the bank. Like Eamon Fitzwilliams, he had no doubts about the lucrative future of their stallion. If his progeny were nearly as good as he had been, his already lofty nomination fee would rise and rise and Patrick Kildare would be able to repay all his debts. Others shared their optimism. Hugo Fitzwilliams acquired five shares, and two wealthy racing men, Guy Pritchard and Kieran Steele, ten shares each. That of course left ten shares which Eamon Fitzwilliams retained for himself.'

Amy looked round in vain to see if any of the other owners were present in court. Either they were waiting outside to give evidence, or were keeping well clear.

Kelleher, who had paused to take a drink of

water, continued and recounted Patrick Kildare's
increasing debts as Moondancer's progeny failed to
make their mark on the racecourse, his decision to
take out a life policy in favour of his wife, and the
threatening phone calls that he began to receive in
January.

'One of these calls,' said Kelleher, 'was taken
by the stud groom, Joe Slattery. You will hear in
the course of this trial a tape-recording of a conversation between Mr Slattery and Fergus Kildare
in which—' He stopped as Finbar Curley rose to his
feet.

'I must apologise to Your Honour for interrupting my learned friend's concise presentation of the
case for the state but my client does not accept
that these tapes should be allowed in evidence and
I wish to argue the question of admissibility in due
course.'

'Mr Kelleher?' said the judge.

'I'm quite happy to adopt that course if Your
Honour pleases. If only my learned friend had
mentioned this earlier, I—'

'No offence intended,' interjected Curley. 'I'm
very grateful to my learned friend for his usual
fairness.'

Very clever, thought Amy, breaking up the flow
like that, and giving the jury a chance to hear his
voice.

Slightly ruffled, Kelleher continued: 'On the

weekend of the fifteenth of January a meeting took place at Drumgarrick House to discuss Moondancer's future. You will hear from Eamon Fitzwilliams that a decision was taken to cut their losses and try and sell the horse abroad. Colette Kildare was present on more than one occasion on the Saturday when that decision and its consequences for the stud were discussed. That night the Kildares and their son entertained the members of the syndicate, all four of whom stayed the night. A large quantity of alcohol was consumed as they drowned their sorrows.

'The following morning, shortly after six, Fergus Kildare was woken from his slumber by Joe Slattery. Joe had gone in to feed Moondancer and found him lying dead in his box, shot through the head with a shotgun.'

Amy's attention began to wander as Kelleher proceeded to tell the jury about Patrick's mysterious disappearance, the discovery of his body by Fergus and the subsequent murder of Joe. He addressed the jury for over an hour and a half before building up to his final peroration.

'Finally, members of the jury, it will be for you and you alone to decide on the evidence, and that alone, whether Colette Kildare committed these terrible crimes. In order to convict, you must be sure of her guilt beyond any reasonable doubt. It is the prosecution case that all you are about to hear will lead inexorably to that conclusion. The state calls Thomas Kirkpatrick.'

Who? thought Amy to herself and then remembered that Kirkpatrick was the lawyer who had drafted Patrick's will and had had to read it aloud at Drumgarrick.

The lawyer took the oath and, despite the fact that he had spent a lifetime in the law, appeared singularly ill at ease in the witness box. Kelleher soon made him relax by asking a few gentle questions about his experience and practice. He then took him through the history of his dealings with the Kildare family and in particular the drafting of the will and Patrick's decision to enter into an insurance policy against his life.

'Whose idea was it that you should read the will out loud?' asked Kelleher.

'Colette's, Mrs Kildare's.'

'Was that a normal request in your experience?'

'Most abnormal. In nearly fifty years as a solicitor I must have dealt with over five thousand wills and this was only the second occasion when I had been asked to do such a thing.'

'Was any particular reason advanced?'

Kirkpatrick paused to reflect, shutting his eyes as if to conjure up the image of the drawing room on that day.

'If I'm right, I had told Mrs Kildare that reading a will aloud only happened in thrillers and she replied something to the effect that Patrick had liked thrillers and he would have wanted it that way.'

'So you agreed?'

'I had no option.'

'You had known the deceased for how many years?'

'Oh, forty, probably more.'

'Did you believe, as his wife claimed, that he would have wanted it that way?'

'Certainly not. Patrick was a kind, unassuming man, never one to create a drama out of a situation. No, it was my view that Colette was enjoying making a spectacle of her son and to a lesser extent myself.'

'And why was that?'

'Because I believe she knew full well the contents of both the will and the life policy.'

'Thank you. Will you stay there please, Mr Kirkpatrick, as my learned friend may have some questions to ask you.'

Finbar Curley rose slowly to his feet and smiled almost compassionately at the lawyer opposite him in the witness box.

'Who was it who telephoned you and asked you to come over to Drumgarrick with the will and other relevant papers?'

'Fergus Kildare, but I believe—'

'I'm sorry, sir, but unless His Honour directs you

to the contrary, this court is concerned with fact and not belief.'

'Sorry.' The lawyer looked embarrassed.

'And had you ever discussed the will or the policy with my client before that day?'

'No, but—' He stopped himself in time.

'So your evidence that my client knew about their contents is pure assumption on your part?'

'I suppose you could say that.'

'But am I not right in thinking that you were once present at a conversation where the will was discussed by the deceased and his son?'

'Yes, that's correct. About six years ago, shortly after the purchase of Moondancer, I was visiting the stud to discuss Patrick's financial affairs and he told Fergus in my presence that he had left him the house and its contents in his will.'

'Was any mention made of the fact that the deceased had borrowed heavily against the house to pay for the improvements to the stud and for his shares in Moondancer?'

'Definitely not. In fact he had specifically asked me not to discuss such matters with Fergus. Patrick always believed those debts would be paid off and there was therefore no point in upsetting his son unnecessarily.'

'You remember quite clearly the time when the deceased took out the life insurance policy?'

'Very well.'

'By then it was obvious that the shares in Moondancer were worthless?'

'Yes, so I was given to understand.'

'And would it not be normal in your experience, fifty years of it, for a husband to take steps to ensure that his wife was adequately protected financially if something happened to him?'

'Yes. I actively encourage my clients to make suitable provisions.'

'You're not suggesting to His Honour and the jury that the deceased was mentally incompetent or under some form of duress when he took out this policy?'

'Certainly not. I would never have permitted such a thing.'

'How well did you know my client?'

'It's right to say that Patrick was my friend and that I invariably dealt with him. I suppose your client and I met socially about two or three times a year.'

'And on those occasions she was always with her husband?'

'Oh yes.'

'And they didn't row or make a scene or such like?'

'No, although . . .'

Once again Amy could see the lawyer hesitate. He knew in his heart that Patrick and Colette did not get on and their marriage was a sham but it was a matter of instinct and based solely on a few casual remarks made by Patrick.

Go on, urged Amy mentally, say what you feel, for God's sake.

'Mr Kirkpatrick?' said the judge somewhat impatiently, his pen poised to write down the response.

'I'm sorry, Your Honour. Could you repeat the question, Mr Curley?'

'Of course. Did you see the deceased and my client row or such like when they were together?'

'No, never.'

'And is it not right that some months after the deceased disappeared you wrote to my client suggesting she should apply to the court to have him declared dead?'

'Yes, I felt it was my duty to inform her of her legal rights.'

'And is this the letter?'

Curley handed a letter to the usher who handed it to the judge who perused it quickly and handed it back to the usher who handed it to the witness. The jury's heads were moving from side to side as if on the centre court at Wimbledon.

'Yes, this is the letter.'

'Did my client telephone you shortly afterwards in a distressed state and say she thought it was premature and that she still believed that her husband was alive and would return?'

'Yes.'

'One last matter. You came on the Friday to Drumgarrick at Fergus Kildare's request, just two days after the discovery of the body?'

The solicitor nodded.

'How would you describe my client's appearance?'

'Her dress?'

'No, I mean her face, her demeanour.'

'She was obviously very upset and probably still in a state of shock.'

'And when it came to the will, did she say to you words to the effect that she was so tense and upset she couldn't read it herself?'

Once again the witness closed his eyes to think back. 'Yes, I believe she did.'

'You had no reason whatsoever, then, for doubting the sincerity of her feelings?'

Kirkpatrick sighed, as if admitting defeat. 'None whatsoever.'

Curley sat down. He had won the first round.

After the midday adjournment, Kirkpatrick was followed into the box by Eamon Fitzwilliams, who in a strong and confident voice told the jury of how he had become involved in the syndication of Moondancer, the decision to stand him at Drumgarrick and the horse's subsequent failure as a stallion.

'What was your reaction on hearing of Moondancer's death?' asked Kelleher, anxious that this witness would make a better impression than his predecessor in the box.

'I was flabbergasted. Although I had lost a fortune by retaining so many shares in him, I never wished him dead. I love horses too much for that.'

'Were you aware of the so-called threats from the IRA?'

'Patrick had told me about the calls and, like the others, I didn't really take them seriously. Until, of course, Moondancer was killed.'

'When did you last see Patrick Kildare alive?'

'I think it was in late February, about two weeks before he disappeared.'

'And how would you describe his state of mind at that time?'

'Depressed, a little distracted. I think he was naturally very upset about the horse's death, but also anxious that the insurers should pay up.'

'Did you know Joe Slattery?'

'Of course. I was a frequent visitor to the stud and Joe was always there working his heart out. I was very fond of him.'

'When was the last time you saw Joe alive?'

'At Patrick's funeral. He was a pallbearer, and then afterwards very briefly he was in the house.'

'Could you put a time on that?'

'We got back to the house at about five. I reckon I saw him about ten minutes past – around then, anyway.'

'And not again?'

'Never again.'

'What did you do at the house after that?'

'I spent the next hour or so in the drawing room talking to friends who had attended the service.'

'Do you recall who you were talking to from five thirty till six?'

'I have a pretty good recollection of that. I was standing by the windows having a discussion with Kieran Steele, one of my partners in Moondancer.'

'And can you remember what you were talking about exactly?'

'Yes, we were rowing, to be precise. Kieran has been disappointed with the way his flat horses have been running and was threatening to take them away from my son Hugo.'

'You were trying to dissuade him?'

'Exactly.'

'How can you be so positive about the time?'

'Because Kieran had a business call to make at six and he kept on looking at his watch.'

'Thank you, Mr Fitzwilliams.' Kelleher sat down and Finbar Curley rose to his feet.

'Mr Fitzwilliams, you yourself invested a large sum of money in Moondancer?'

'Yes, sir, a considerable sum.'

Curley leant forward as if to be certain of catching the next response. 'So the chance to claim on the insurance was like manna from heaven?'

'I've already said that I would rather the horse had lived.'

'Really now? And at what price were you going to sell him abroad before tragedy struck?'

'I hoped to raise five hundred thousand punts.'

'Five hundred thousand punts for a horse who was syndicated for five million. And you still tell this court that you were not glad he was killed?'

'I do.'

'I assume you slept alone the night before Moondancer was found dead?'

'Of course I did.'

'Did you know where the Kildares kept their guns?'

Eamon Fitzwilliams' reaction plainly showed that he did. He hesitated only briefly before replying. 'I had seen Patrick put them away after a day's shooting.'

'And you yourself are an excellent shot?'

'If you're suggesting I killed Moondancer, I—'

'I'm suggesting nothing, yet. Please answer my question.'

'The answer is yes.'

'Were you at dinner the night before the funeral?'

'Yes, I was staying the night, along with the others.'

'And you all ate together in the dining room? You had leg of lamb, I believe. Do you remember my client carving the meat on the sideboard in full view of everyone?'

'Not specifically, but I won't disagree if you tell me she did.'

'What were you doing for the two hours before dinner?'

'I was tired after our flight from England and went up to my room where I had a bath and a lie-down.'

'On your own?'

'Of course on my own.'

'And you came downstairs for drinks in the drawing room at seven thirty?'

'Correct.'

'One last question, Mr Fitzwilliams. Do you have any reason to doubt my client's feelings for her husband?'

Amy scrutinised Fitzwilliams' face as the court waited for his answer. It was clear from his line of questioning that Curley's instructions from his client were that she and her husband were happily married.

'No.' Fitzwilliams shook his head. 'None at all.'

The prosecution next called a pathologist who gave evidence of the nature of the injuries suffered by both Patrick and Joe. Kelleher produced the carving knife which, it was alleged, had been used to murder Joe.

'Have you examined this knife?' he asked the pathologist.

'I have.'

'And in your view, is it the weapon used to kill the deceased, Joe Slattery?'

'It is. If you look . . .' he turned towards the judge who redirected him to face the jury '. . . at the blade, you will see it has a very pointed end and is unusually sharp. This is consistent with the wound.'

Kelleher thanked the pathologist and sat down. Curley rose to his feet for the fourth time.

'You said in evidence that Mr Kildare weighed something over one hundred and eighty pounds.'

'Yes.'

'Were there any signs on his body that he had been dragged as against carried to the spot where he was found?'

'No, but you must remember that we only found the skeleton. The body had been in the earth for many months and had completely decomposed.'

'In your experience, could a single person, say a woman, carry a man of that weight for any real distance?'

'No, unless she was unusually strong.'

'And if I understood your evidence correctly, Mr Kildare was killed by a blow on the top of the head with a heavy blunt instrument, fracturing his skull.'

'That's right. There was a depressed fracture of the vertex of the skull.' He bowed towards Curley, indicating the site of the fatal blow by pointing to the top of his own head.

'In other words, a strong person, either the same

276

height or taller, would be the most likely assailant?'

'That is one possible solution, yes.'

Curley quickly sat down.

Kelleher rose equally quickly to his feet to re-examine.

'There are other possibilities then?'

'Oh yes. If the deceased had been kneeling down, say near where he was found, a blow from above would require far less strength.'

'And in this case the height of the assailant would be irrelevant?'

'Absolutely.'

Round three to the prosecution.

Kieran Steele was next to be called and his evidence-in-chief, save one or two minor details, corroborated that of Eamon Fitzwilliams. The only difference was that he came over as a good deal more impressive and articulate. Amy suspected that he would be more than a match for Curley in cross-examination.

Counsel for the defendant began by establishing that, like all his partners, Steele had had just as much opportunity as his client to go down to Moondancer's stable and shoot him.

'But I didn't,' answered the businessman emphatically.

'You stood to lose well over a million and a quarter punts, did you not, if Moondancer was sold to go overseas?'

'Something like that, but in business one has to take risks and risks don't always come off.'

'You regarded this, then, purely as a business venture?'

'To be honest, yes. I like owning racehorses but I had no particular affection for Moondancer.'

'Would it be fair to say that at that time quite a number of your business risks weren't "coming off" as you put it?'

Steele showed the first sign of temper. 'Who told you that?'

Amy wouldn't have liked to be in the shoes of the person who had. 'The Berlin wall' was beginning to live up to his nickname.

'It's my privilege to ask the questions, Mr Steele,' replied Curley. 'Am I right about your businesses or would you like me to go through these sets of accounts we have obtained?' Curley held aloft a bundle of printed documents for the jury and the rest of the court to see.

Amy watched Steele closely. She could see that he was calculating whether any advantage could be gained by a public examination of his financial affairs. From his answer it was clear that he thought not.

'You're right. Since then my cash flow problem has greatly improved.'

Curley moved on to a fresh line of questioning: 'You were present at dinner the night before the funeral?'

'Yes, with all the others.'

'Did you see my client carve the lamb on the sideboard?'

'I think I remember seeing her, yes.'

'And you very kindly offered to clear up at the end of the meal, did you not?'

'I took out a couple of things as a gesture. I'm not very domestic, I'm afraid.'

'Do you remember who removed the lamb and, more importantly, the carving knife?'

Steele shook his head. 'I can't help. I pay people to do that kind of thing normally.'

'Oh, to be so fortunate,' said Curley with half an eye on the jury. 'You told His Honour and the jury that between five thirty and six on the day of the funeral you were talking in the drawing room with Eamon Fitzwilliams.'

'Correct.'

'Do you know if anyone else saw you there together?'

'Not that I'm aware of. You'd better direct that question to Superintendent Brogan.'

'Of course, in a very crowded room and with people drinking and eating it is very difficult to be precise about time and just who one sees, isn't it?'

'I agree, only in my case I was very particular about it because I had to make a phone call at six o'clock.'

'And where did you make that call from, can you remember?'

Amy craned forward. If he had made it from the kitchen, it would have been picked up on Seamus's bug and no doubt Curley had in his possession transcripts of all those tapes.

'I remember the study was too crowded, so I went into the kitchen and had to wait for somebody else to finish. By the time I got on, there was no reply at the other end.'

'And who was meant to be at the other end?'

Again, Kieran appeared uncomfortable. 'A friend.'

'Male or female?'

'Female.'

Curley did not press for a name. The jury would be left with the impression that either the person didn't exist or it was someone with whom he was having an affair. On either view, not a very attractive character. Amy hoped that Jack would be called to give evidence next, as that way if he was finished by the end of the day his ordeal would be over and they could have dinner together. She wanted to update him on everything that had taken place but could not do so until he was out of the witness box. Over in counsel's row she could see Kelleher having a hurried discussion with his junior and the state solicitor. Clearly they were unhappy about serving up witnesses who Curley was able to show had equal if not greater motive to kill Moondancer and murder Joe as his own client. Amy reckoned they would not now call either Hugo Fitzwilliams or Guy Pritchard, and instead concentrate on the circumstantial evidence linking Colette to the crimes. Her instinct was right.

Kelleher straightened his back and announced: 'The state calls Seamus Pink.'

Amy thought that Seamus would at least have taken off his duffel coat to give evidence. He stood in the witness box, hands behind his back, for all the world a young man who would never need to trouble the ear of his priest.

Curley knew what was coming and quickly rose to his feet.

'Would this be an appropriate moment, Your Honour, to rule on that matter I mentioned during my learned friend's lucid opening?'

Amy crossed her fingers and her knees that the tapes would not be ruled inadmissible. It worked. After a spirited argument, in the absence of the jury, Judge Quayle decided in favour of counsel for the prosecution. The jury filed back into the courtroom and resumed their seats.

With considerable dexterity and not a little help from Seamus, Kelleher managed to make the planting of the bugs in the house and stables sound like the work of good Samaritans and there was a perceptible increase in tension in the court as first the recording of the will reading was played, followed by the conversation between Fergus and Joe, when Joe claimed to have recognised the voice on the phone, and finally, Joe's last words as he was murdered.

Amy wondered what approach Curley would adopt

now. Unless he was going to suggest that the tapes had in some way been tampered with, there was little to gain from a brutal or rigorous cross-examination.

Once again he directed his assault towards under-mining the witness's integrity: 'Mr Pink, I assume that you were paid to break into Drumgarrick House?'

'Yes, sir. I would have received payment as part of my total remuneration.'

'And do you make a habit of planting bugs in people's homes without their permission?'

'When it's necessary for the performance of my duties.'

'These duties, of course, are not authorised or recognised by the state or the Gardai, are they?'

'No, but I like to think—'

'I'm afraid your opinions are not relevant to these proceedings, Mr Pink. The simple truth is that you were trying to establish evidence to support the insurers in their desire not to pay out on this claim?'

'Put like that, the answer has to be yes.'

'Having heard those tapes, do you agree with me that there is no indication as to the identity of Joe Slattery's assailant?'

'Yes, except at one stage he does say something which could be "bitch".'

'Ah! Were you present when a test was made amplifying that particular sound?'

'I was.'

'And isn't it right that with Mr Slattery's strong accent, although it sounds like ''bi'' it could also be ''ba'', as for bastard?'

'I'd rather not say. It's surely for the jury to decide.'

'Quite right, and they no doubt will.'

By now it was past four fifteen and a tired and unsmiling judge decided that that was enough for one day.

Chapter Sixteen

The next day Amy arrived a good hour before the court was due to sit. It was a wise move. The reports in that morning's paper had drawn a large crowd and she only just managed to obtain a seat in the public gallery.

The prosecution case had barely survived yesterday's cross-examination and the idea that someone at the dinner party on the Sunday before the funeral had picked up the carving knife with Colette's fingerprints on it and then used it to kill Joe was imaginative yet still possible, and since all Curley had to do was cast doubt in the jury's mind, there had to be a real chance of an acquittal. That was unless a witness was called who could give evidence that the knife had been removed and then washed. Today would tell.

By half past ten everybody was in their places and His Honour Judge Quayle strode importantly into court. With an imperious nod at counsel for the prosecution, the proceedings began. The first witness to be called was Jack. It was the only time Amy had ever seen him in a suit and she decided that he should wear one more often: it gave him a certain dignity and maturity.

His evidence was a bit of an anti-climax. Insofar as he had been present, he reiterated Seamus's evidence and was then tendered for cross-examination. Amy was curious to see whether Curley would prefer not to concentrate on the existence of the tapes. There was no virtue, after all, in making an issue of evidence that was potentially prejudicial to his client.

'Your job, as I understand it, Mr Hendred, is to investigate suspicious insurance claims?'

'Yes, that's principally how I earn my living.'

'And are you paid a flat fee, or is there some kind of bonus for success?'

'That depends on the job in question. My clients tend to be generous if I am successful.'

'And they don't have to pay out.'

'That's right.'

'And therefore both you and Mr Pink would like to see it established that my client killed Moondancer.'

Jack shook his head. 'Only if she is guilty. And anyway, to avoid liability on the policy my clients would have to establish that one of the policyholders or an agent acting on their behalf killed the horse, and your client was not one of the policyholders.'

'You're not suggesting to this court that she is

in league with one of the policyholders, are you?'

Go on, said Amy under her breath, say yes, you fool. The woman beside her gave her a very curious look.

'It's not for me to speculate,' answered Jack.

'Or the jury,' observed Curley, with a sideways glance in their direction. He continued. 'With that established, you accept that my client had absolutely nothing to gain from this policy if the horse died.'

'Not under the policy, no.'

'One or two final questions, Mr Hendred. Have you in the course of your investigations learnt anything about the financial position of Mr Kieran Steele?'

'I have.'

'And how would you describe his situation?'

'Precarious.'

'And Mr Eamon Fitzwilliams and his son Hugo?'

'I understand that neither could afford to lose the kind of sums of money we are talking about.'

'And Mr Guy Pritchard?'

Jack was reluctant to make public all he now knew about Pritchard. He was shortly to be arrested and charged with fraud, arson and grievous bodily harm for his assault on Jack. 'The same.'

'Has that gentleman ever visited you in your flat?'

'Mr Pritchard?' Jack realised to his horror that Curley had somehow discovered about the information he had passed on to Scotland Yard. Either that, or Amy had been blabbing.

'Has he, Mr Hendred?' Curley pressed.

'Yes, he once tried to strangle me with a length of rope.'

There was a gasp of astonishment in the court and the jury, who had been showing only a limited interest in Jack's testimony, pricked their ears.

'Was he trying to kill you?' asked Curley, who was ostentatiously reading from a file of documents.

'It felt like it at the time.'

'And do you know why?'

'Since then information has come into my possession to show that he may be linked to a number of false insurance claims on property in London.'

'Is it not right that you have also been investigating him in relation to this insurance claim?'

'Yes,' said Jack, with a slight air of resignation.

'I have no more questions of this witness, Your Honour.'

Jack made as if to leave the witness box, but Kelleher had risen promptly to his feet and indicated he should remain.

'Mr Hendred, do you know who inherited Mr Kildare's shares in Moondancer in the case of his death?'

'I understand it to be his wife, the accused.'

'And once Moondancer was dead, those shares became instead an equivalent interest in the insurance claim?'

'Yes.'

'What value was put on Moondancer as a racehorse at the time of his death?'

'Two hundred thousand punts, or so I'm told.'

'Of which Mr Kildare's share would be how much?'

'One-eighth. My maths isn't very good, I'm afraid.'

'Twenty-five thousand punts,' barked the judge from on high.

'And what was Mr Kildare's share worth under the insurance claim?'

'One-eighth of five million.' That calculation caused Jack even more difficulty.

'Six hundred and twenty-five thousand punts,' interjected the judge again.

'Thank you, Mr Hendred.' Kelleher sat down.

Bravo, muttered Amy. That shows what a motive the bitch had for wanting him dead.

Emma Ballantine was the next witness to be called and Amy hoped that she might be able to lay to rest the spectre of the carving knife. She had never seen Fergus's old girlfriend before and she was nothing like Amy had imagined her to be – much taller and better built, and almost aggressively attractive. Her eyes were the size of oysters and she radiated self-confidence. The oddest thing about her was her choice of outfit, thought Amy. Fergus had told her that Emma had a wonderful figure, yet she was wearing a rather shapeless loose-fitting dress.

She gave her evidence confidently and clearly,

telling the court how she first met Fergus and then came to live with him at Drumgarrick after his father's disappearance. Kelleher then asked her about the dinner on the Sunday night.

'I remember it very well. Colette had cooked us dinner, which I thought very brave of her in the circumstances. We had roast lamb.'

'Do you remember who carved the lamb?'

'Colette. I was sitting next to Fergus, who was in a very depressed mood and saying very little. When I suggested he might help his mother he just grunted.'

'And after the meal?'

'One or two of the others offered to clear up; I think Kieran Steele carried a plate or two.'

Amy was interested to hear that Emma's recollection tied in with Steele's.

'But I mainly did the rest.'

'And the accused?'

'I'm pretty certain, in fact I'm sure, she went with the other men into the drawing room to have coffee and liqueurs.'

'And what happened to the plates and so on when you took them into the kitchen?'

'I assumed Mrs Magee, the daily, would be coming in the morning, so I just put them either in or beside the sink.'

'And the carving knife?'

Emma paused to reflect. 'I've been asked about this before by Superintendent Brogan.'

'And can you recall what you told him?'

'That I put it in the sink, out of the way, as it were, and especially out of Drummond's reach.'

'Drummond?' asked the judge. 'Is that the butler?'

Someone laughed in the public gallery and Amy had to restrain herself from joining in.

'No, sir, that's Fergus's dog. He's a Doberman.'

Kelleher resumed his questioning. 'The next day you attended the funeral and afterwards went back to the house. Can you remember what you were doing between five thirty and six o'clock?'

'Yes, fairly well. I was talking to one or two of the other mourners whom I knew from living at Drumgarrick, and then at about five forty I began a long conversation with Hugo Fitzwilliams.'

'The trainer?'

'Yes, we're old friends.'

You can say that again, muttered Amy rather more loudly than she intended.

'We discussed the yearling sales at Newmarket which his father had kindly invited me to attend.'

'How can you be sure of the time?'

'Because I remember Hugo asking me. He was on a course of antibiotics and was due to take another tablet about then.'

'Did you see anyone else?'

'Yes. About that time I noticed Fergus on his own, so I went over and had a brief word with him. Shortly afterwards he left to go outside or upstairs and I returned to Hugo.'

That, Amy was glad to hear, tied in with Fergus's recollection of having a short chat with Emma. He'd never mentioned seeing Hugo but maybe he hadn't noticed him.

'Thank you,' said Kelleher and turned towards Finbar Curley. 'Your witness.'

'You have known Mr Fergus Kildare for over three years, I understand?'

'Possibly a bit longer. We met at Trinity Dublin where he was studying.'

'And do you share his interest in horses?'

'More in the breeding side of things than race riding.'

'And presumably you have shared his confidences?'

'I'd like to think so.' There was a trace of a smile on her lips.

'You were sleeping together the night Moondancer was killed?'

'Yes. We'd had a lot to drink and I went out like a light.'

'So you cannot tell the court whether Mr Kildare was in his bed throughout the night.'

Emma looked puzzled at the suggestion. She must be pretty thick, thought Amy, if she couldn't spot what Curley was driving at.

'I suppose I can't. I have no reason to believe he wasn't, though.'

'I presume you knew that under the terms of his father's will, Fergus was to inherit Drumgarrick and the surrounding lands.'

'I had always understood that to be the case.'

'And at that time were you aware who was to inherit Patrick Kildare's shares in Moondancer?'

Emma appeared to hesitate. 'I think I understood it was to be Fergus.'

'Is there any particular reason why you are wearing such a bulky dress, Miss Ballantine?'

The sudden shift in Curley's line of questioning came without any warning. Emma was clearly taken aback. 'No, I just wanted to be comfortable. I sat outside yesterday and I had no idea how long it would be before I was called today.'

'Are you sure you are not wearing that dress to hide your condition?'

Oh my God, thought Amy. Why didn't Fergus say anything about this? Maybe he doesn't even know he's going to be a father.

Emma had turned scarlet with embarrassment. 'Do I have to answer that question?' she asked the judge beseechingly.

Quayle lived up to his reputation. 'Yes,' he replied with a firmness which brooked no argument.

Before she could speak, Curley, not wanting to miss out on a moment of theatre, handed up a piece of paper to the usher. The usual ritual was followed until it reached the witness.

'Please look at that.'

Emma took it and read it. From where she was sitting Amy could only guess at its contents.

'Is that your name on the top?'

'Yes.'

'And is that the result of a pregnancy test taken in early October confirming that you were pregnant?'

'Yes, it is.'

'And would you tell His Honour and the jury who the father of this child is?'

Emma appeared to regain her composure. 'Fergus Kildare.'

It was the answer which everybody had expected and Amy had dreaded.

'When did you tell him this piece of good news?'

'I was sure about it only a few days before he discovered his father's body. It clearly seemed a bad time to bring it up. Since then, with the pressure of this trial, Fergus and I have been living apart.'

'When you say you saw Mr Kildare at five forty-five on the day of the funeral, are you telling the court the truth or are you as his future wife and the mother-to-be of his child trying to shield him?'

Emma's reply was barely audible. 'No, never.'

Amy felt a tap on her shoulder. She turned round to find Jack crouched just behind her. Now that he had finished giving his evidence he had been allowed to come into court and watch the proceedings.

'That was a bit of a shock,' he whispered to Amy.

'You can say that again. Poor Fergus. At least he doesn't know what's going on in here.'

Brogan was called and took the oath. One or two people began to fidget and make noises in their throats and Jack pointed with his index finger to the door.

'Will you come outside? I've a little idea to try on you.'

Amy was reluctant to leave but she asked the man beside her to keep her seat and followed Jack into the public lobby.

In her absence Brogan gave an efficient and clinical performance in the witness box. He told the court how the Gardai had first been informed by Patrick Kildare of the phone calls from the IRA, that he had said they were made by a woman, and that the Gardai had subsequently been called in to investigate both the horse's death and Patrick Kildare's disappearance two months afterwards. In the absence of any positive evidence, all their inquiries had been inconclusive. The one thing they had discovered was that no farmer or horsedealer in Sligo had arranged to meet Patrick Kildare that fateful weekend.

Brogan then detailed the case against the accused. Although it was very circumstantial in relation to the death of her husband, he was adept at conveying to the jury her obvious motive for killing the horse and then her husband. The discovery of the brooch and Joe's recognition of both the voice on the phone and his killer pointed strongly to the accused. Finally, there was the damning evidence of the carving knife and her clear fingerprints on it.

Amy returned in time for the cross-examination. Curley went straight to the point.

'You yourself did not handle the inquiry into Moondancer's death?'

'No, sir, that was left to the local Gardai.'

'Do you know whether Fergus Kildare told them about his discovery that his father's gun had been fired that night?'

'No mention of it was made by him at the time.'

'When did he first mention it?'

'On the day he discovered Joe Slattery's body. He asked if he could make a statement to me and I took him down to the barracks.'

'Would you remind the court who else had a key to the gun room?'

'As far as I'm aware the only keys were in the possession of Mr Patrick Kildare and his son.'

'So that door could have been opened and the gun taken out by the son as easily as the father?'

'Yes, although anyone else who knew where the keys were kept could have obtained access too of course.'

'In the course of your inquiries, have you discovered who else had that knowledge?'

'The accused knew where her husband kept his key.'

'Where was that?'

'In a secret compartment in the desk in his study.'

'Who told you that she knew that.'

'Fergus Kildare.'

'Has she not always denied any such knowledge?'

'Yes, on the one occasion that I asked her, she did just that.'

'What steps have you taken to check up on the alibis for Fergus Kildare, Guy Pritchard, Eamon Fitzwilliams, his son, and Kieran Steele for between five thirty and six o'clock of the fateful afternoon?'

'We have interviewed every single person who attended the wake. Unfortunately it was very crowded at that time and a great deal of alcohol had been consumed. Numerous people remember seeing each of these gentlemen but no one can be specific as to the time.'

'So you have to rely on their corroborating each other?'

'That is correct. I should add that in the case of Mr Pritchard there are several people who recall talking to him at about that time.'

'At about that time,' repeated Curley, the words hanging on his lips. 'It was one of your Gardai who discovered the pregnancy test result in Mr Kildare's girlfriend's bag during a search on the Tuesday?'

'Yes.'

'And you quite properly disclosed it to the defence solicitor in this case.'

'Correct.'

'Were you aware of the financial problems facing Kieran Steele?'

'We have made inquiries, sir, but they are not conclusive.'

'Did you know about the activities of Mr Pritchard concerning the other insurance claims he is pursuing in England and his savage assault on Mr Hendred?'

'I know nothing about those.'

Very clever, thought Amy. The prosecution have to disclose all they know while the defence don't. Brogan, of course, had been outside when Jack had given his evidence. By leaning forward she could see a yellow folder on the table in front of Curley. It looked remarkably like the one she had recovered from behind the loo at Drumgarrick. She wondered whether Steele had been responsible for providing the defence with these particular pieces of information. Was that because he wanted Colette acquitted?

Curley was in full cry: 'The arrest of my client meant a very quick and neat solution to your investigation, didn't it, Superintendent?'

'She was arrested and charged because I believed her to be guilty of the crimes.'

'Who suggested you should search the secret compartment when you returned to the house?'

'It was a logical step following my interview with Fergus Kildare.'

'Do you remember my client's reaction when you

pulled that knife out of the secret compartment?'

'Yes, she fainted.'

'Because she had no idea it was there, and because it had dawned on her that you were accusing her of killing Joe Slattery?'

The superintendent shook his head: 'No, sir. Because she knew we had discovered her hiding place and because, to put it bluntly, the game was up.'

Curley sat down and the court then adjourned for lunch. After it, Kelleher asked only a few questions in re-examination. The stage was now set for Fergus. Or so Amy thought. When Kelleher called Shelagh Magee to the witness box, Amy was surprised. She had only heard of Mrs Magee by name as the somewhat formidable lady who 'did' for the Kildares. In her late fifties and about two stone overweight, she had squeezed herself into a new blue coat and chosen an extremely gay hat to match. She took the oath loudly and stared round the court, waiting like a television quiz master for the first question from the audience. Kelleher approached her.

'Would you tell His Honour and the jury how long you have worked for the Kildare family, Mrs Magee?'

'It must be all of thirty years now. I arrived well before the mistress.' She had a marked Irish accent and pronounced the word 'mistress' with a good deal of distaste. She clearly wasn't enamoured of the accused.

'What does your job entail?'

'Now you're asking me. Before the master ran into difficulties with money there was me and two others helping about the house and doing the cooking. Before he disappeared we were down to two of us, and after that only me. And hard work it was too, sir,' she said, turning to the judge for sympathy. She was out of luck.

'Did your duties involve doing the washing up?'

'And preparing the food.'

'Do you remember doing the washing up the morning before Mr Kildare's funeral?'

' 'Course I do. Not right, it wasn't, the mistress having all those people to stay like that before the master was buried.' She glowered in the direction of the dock where Colette had been seated impassively throughout the trial.

'Can you remember whether you washed up the carving knife that morning?'

'I did, sir. I particularly remember seeing it in the sink when I started. It was hidden under a pile of plates, and I nearly cut myself on it.'

'And after washing it?'

'I put it in the drawer. What else would I do with it? You're not accusing me of murdering Joe, are you?' She turned round again to the judge for support. This time she was successful.

'Don't worry, Mrs Magee. Counsel is making no such suggestion.'

'Good,' she said as she turned to face Kelleher

again, who was indicating to the usher that he should take the knife from its position on the table in front of the court and hand it to Mrs Magee.

'Is that the knife you washed?'

She held it in her hand, the exhibit label flapping from the handle.

'I can't be certain. You see, there are several knives in the kitchen.'

'Have another look. Take your time.'

'Yes, now I think about it, I'm sure it is.'

Kelleher sat down.

'Do I detect from your evidence that you are not that fond of my client, Mrs Magee?' asked Curley.

'I wouldn't go as far as saying that, sir.'

'Was there a small matter in the summer about some money missing from her purse which she left in the kitchen?'

'I never stole it. I told her that at the time.' Mrs Magee scowled in fury towards Colette.

'Did I just hear you tell His Honour that this was the knife you washed up that morning, the knife which we now know to be the murder weapon?'

'Yes.'

'Are you sure?'

It was apparent that Mrs Magee was bristling under this line of questioning. 'Sure I'm sure.'

'Really sure?'

'Yes, 'course I'm really sure, though I wouldn't swear on it.'

'I thought that's what you'd just done,' remarked Curley as he sat down.

Amy glanced up at the court clock; it was after three thirty. It had to be Fergus who was called next. Kelleher had obviously decided to hold him back, to build a case first with his other witnesses and then produce Fergus for the kill. So far the plan had misfired. Curley had been content to show that all the owners of Moondancer had both motive and opportunity to kill the horse and Joe. He appreciated there was nothing to link any of them to Patrick's death but he no doubt reasoned, and in Amy's view correctly, that if there was reasonable doubt as to his client's involvement in the horse's and Joe's death, then a jury could hardly convict her for the murder of her husband.

The sound of Fergus's name being called sent a noticeable *frisson* of excitement around the court. He walked purposefully into the box and took the oath without faltering. Amy had not seen him since Dundalk and he looked thinner than ever. The dark suit he was wearing hung off him as if he was a bag of bones underneath. Amy realised it was not all to do with the responsibility and, no doubt, fear of giving evidence. Tongue in Cheek had been allotted ten stone two pounds in the Ladbroke, which was marvellous for his chances but meant Fergus had to lose nearly a stone before the race. He had obviously been fasting and taking a considerable amount of exercise; the result was there to see.

After a hesitant start he gave his evidence very well and, Amy felt, with dignity and authority. He painted a compelling and at times sad picture of his upbringing and no one in that court could have failed to be impressed by the evident closeness of his relationship with his father. Equally, they must have been struck by the image which emerged of his mother – a cold, calculating woman who had neither time nor affection for her son.

By four fifteen he had reached the point when he discovered his father's body. Judge Quayle decided to adjourn until the next morning and reminded Fergus that he was on no account to talk to anyone about the case.

Outside the courtroom Amy met Jack who was waiting for her with Seamus.

'How did it go in there?' asked Jack.

'Bad at the beginning of the afternoon, but better with Fergus. He's coming over very well.'

'Until that Curley chap has a go at him.'

'I wouldn't be so sure. I wouldn't want to bet on how many people have committed perjury so far in this case, but I'm certain Fergus isn't one of them. Does Seamus's presence here mean that you're all organised?'

Seamus bowed deferentially.

'Do we know where to go?' Amy asked Jack.

'Not yet, but we soon will. Come on, Seamus, there they go.' And before Amy could say goodbye they had bolted out of the exit door of the courthouse.

Over at the other side of the hall Amy spotted Fergus emerging with his coat from the cloakroom. She waved to him and he waved back. She wanted more than anything to go over and say well done and keep it up, to let him know that she was rooting for him, but it might be misconstrued as tampering with a witness. She had to content herself with a broad smile and a wink which he reciprocated. As he walked out of the courthouse she noticed he was being followed by a tall man in a gaberdine mac. The police were obviously keeping a close eye on Fergus.

The next day when Fergus resumed his place in the witness box his evidence was, if anything, even more convincing. For nearly an hour and a half Kelleher took him through the discovery of his father's body, the reading of the will, his decision to leave the wake early and meet Amy for drinks at her hotel. Finally, there was complete silence in the public gallery and in the jury box as he described in detail the discovery of Joe's body.

Kelleher then played the tape.

'Mr Kildare, you just heard Joe refer to you as "Master Fergus". To whom was he in the habit of describing you in these terms?'

'I was always called Master Fergus about the house by the staff and of course Joe. That's how he would refer to me if talking about me to a member of my family.'

'By your family do you mean your mother and father?'

'I have no brothers or sisters.'

Now it was Curley's turn.

'Mr Kildare, you were studying at Trinity Dublin when Moondancer was killed?'

'Yes, although I was staying at Drumgarrick that weekend.'

'You knew from your father that you would inherit the house one day?'

'He always told me that.'

'He had told you about his will?'

'Yes, once. It wasn't the kind of thing we needed to discuss.'

'When do you say you first discovered that your mother would inherit the shares in Moondancer?'

'At the reading of the will.'

'So you're telling this court that your father had not been frank with you, you the son he told everything?'

'I've no doubt he had a good reason for it.'

'And what was your good reason for not being frank at the time you discovered the gun which had been used to kill Moondancer?'

'Because I assumed that my father had done it.'

'Why would he have done such a thing, a man who loved horses so much?'

'Because he needed the money and wanted to save the house from ruin.'

'Of course you never told anyone about this until the discovery of Joe's body?'

'No, it was only then I became convinced that my father had been covering up for my mother and that it was her voice Joe had heard on the phone.'

'Are you sure that it's not more simple; that you waited until your father was dead before coming up with this story about the gun to implicate my client?'

'No, it's the truth.'

'So you're telling this court that when the Gardai investigated the death of Moondancer, you withheld vital information from them.'

'Yes, I'm afraid I did. Under the mistaken belief that I was protecting my father. I bitterly regret my conduct now.'

'You say that after you told your mother about your father's death she insisted on visiting the grave alone and that when she reappeared she had dirt on her clothes and hands?'

'That's correct.'

'When did you first tell the Gardai about that?'

'After the discovery of Joe's body.'

'And when did you first tell the Gardai about this brooch?' Curley told the usher to hand it up to Fergus.

'Again, after the discovery of Joe's body.'

'You say Joe found this brooch and gave it to you that same day?'

'In the evening, to be precise.'

'And didn't you say anything to your mother, give it to her, ask for an explanation as to how it got there?'

'As I've said already, I do not have much of a relationship with my mother. I decided to hold on to it.'

'And, again, produce it after Joe's death?'

'Yes.'

'By which time, of course, Joe was in no position to confirm when and where the brooch was really found.'

That was a comment, not a question, and Amy was worried to see the troubled expressions now appearing on one or two of the jurors' faces.

'After Joe had told you about the voice he recognised, did you not try and locate him to find out whose it was?'

'Yes. That evening I went to the bar in Drumgarrick, but no one had seen him there. Of course he was, in fact, already dead by then.'

'But are you seriously telling His Honour and this jury that from Sunday night until the following evening you made no attempt to find out the piece of evidence which might solve your father's murder?'

'I simply didn't have the opportunity. My mother insisted that I make the arrangements for the funeral and you have to remember that over two hundred people came.'

'How are we to know that it wasn't your voice Joe recognised?'

'You have only my word. Why would I have wanted to kill Moondancer?'

'Haven't you just told this court that you thought you were to inherit the house and the shares in the horse?'

'Yes, but—'

'And wasn't Moondancer dead worth a lot more than Moondancer alive?'

'Yes.'

'And did you not have your own key to the gun room?'

'You know I did.'

'And wouldn't your father have himself checked to see if one of those guns had been used, like you did?'

For some reason that thought had never occurred to Fergus. His hesitation could easily have been misconstrued by the jury as prevarication.

'Answer me, please,' said Curley, raising his voice for the very first time in the proceedings.

'He probably would have done.'

'I put it to you that your father suspected you of having killed that horse and you were afraid that he might expose you or, worse, disinherit you.'

'I did not kill my father.'

'Is it not right that when you discovered that your

father had mortgaged Drumgarrick to the hilt, you were shocked and depressed?'

'I won't deny it.'

'And that you were furious that your mother stood, through the insurance and the life policy, to be a rich woman?'

'I was upset, yes.'

'Are you aware that a murderer cannot benefit from the estate of his or her victim?'

'No, I've never thought of it.'

'Come come, Mr Kildare, everyone knows that. If your mother is convicted by this jury, who do you think benefits most?'

Fergus said nothing.

'Let me try again,' said Curley. 'Who is the residuary legatee under your father's will?'

'I am.'

Curley looked round at his client for approval and for the first time in the trial, Colette permitted herself a semblance of a smile.

Fergus's evidence completed the case for the prosecution. It now all hinged on Colette's performance in the witness box and Kelleher's ability to destroy her in cross-examination.

Curley devoted the first hour of his examination-in-chief to the early years of his client's marriage and her relationship with her husband. She admitted quite candidly that they had few interests in common but she flatly contradicted Fergus's suggestion that they were unhappy. He then came to the purchase by her husband of his interest in Moondancer and the large expenditure incurred in bringing Drumgarrick up to a suitable standard as a stud.

'Were you concerned, Mrs Kildare, that he was risking all the family money on this investment?'

'To a degree; after all, he was nearly seventy and there wouldn't be a second chance. However, Patrick always told me that I would be properly provided for, and I never had any cause to doubt his word.'

'Did he tell you about his will?'

'Only that he had made one. I always understood that Fergus would inherit Drumgarrick, so I wasn't particularly interested in the details.'

'And the life insurance policy?'

'That came as a complete surprise on the day our solicitor read out the will. The same, I should add, as the shares in Moondancer.'

'Did you kill Moondancer?'

'No, I did not.'

'Did you murder your husband?'

'No.'

'Where were you on the weekend your husband disappeared?'

'On the Saturday I went to Dublin to do some shopping and on the Sunday I was at home reading. When I left on the Saturday my husband was still at home, out in the yard with the brood mares as Joe had gone off to help Fergus at some point to point.'

'It has been suggested that you murdered your husband and while burying him in the walled garden you dropped your brooch. Is that true?'

'It is a ridiculous suggestion. I gave that brooch to my husband a few days before he disappeared to get it repaired. You will see the bottom half of the K has snapped off.'

'And the dirt on your hands and clothes?'

'I told Superintendent Brogan about that. I knelt down and prayed beside my husband's corpse. I see nothing wrong about that.'

Amy had to admire Colette's self-possession and resilience. She was not in the least intimidated by the judge or jury.

'Did you kill Joe Slattery?'

'Again, no.'

'Can you explain how a knife with your fingerprints came to be the murder weapon?'

'That is for the Gardai to discover. I can only assume that someone removed it after the dinner on Sunday and subsequently placed it in the secret compartment in my husband's study.'

'Did you know about the existence of that secret compartment?'

'I knew there was one, but I had no idea how it worked. I regarded that as his affair.'

'So you did not hide that knife there?'

'No.'

'Are you innocent of these charges against you, Mrs Kildare?

'Completely and utterly.'

It was a well calculated and careful display, Amy conceded; there was no point in offering explanations when you had done nothing which needed to be explained or excused.

For the next hour Kelleher probed Colette as to the true nature of her marriage.

'Are you saying that your son's evidence, that you and your husband were living effectively apart, is untrue?'

'Sadly, yes. My son has a grudge against me. It is a matter of great distress to me that he should see fit to make such monstrous allegations.'

'You deny that you knew where the key to the gun room was?'

'I do.'

'You ask this court to believe that you had no idea of the life policy in your favour or that you would inherit the shares in Moondancer under your husband's will?'

'I do.'

'And you say you were in a distressed state after the discovery of your husband's body?'

'I was in a state of shock.'

'In which case why did you invite Eamon Fitzwilliams and the other owners to come and stay at Drumgarrick the night before the funeral? Wasn't it

312

specifically to discuss the progress of the Moondancer case now that you had inherited your husband's shares?'

For the first time Colette appeared uncomfortable. 'You forget my husband had disappeared eighteen months previously. I was beginning to worry about my financial position.'

'But hadn't you just been told on Friday that you were the beneficiary of a life policy worth a quarter of a million punts?'

Colette chose not to answer and Kelleher pushed on.

'Is it not right that you, more than anybody, benefited from your husband's death, once of course Moondancer was out of the way?'

'With respect, I think my counsel showed very well that it is my son who has the most to gain.'

'Only if you are convicted. If the insurance in Moondancer is paid out in full, how much will you inherit, including the insurance policy?'

'I'm not sure.'

'Does eight hundred and eighty thousand sound a likely figure to you?'

There was a definite reaction among the jurors as they took in the sum.

Colette remained silent.

'You say that you know nothing about the carving knife with your fingerprints on it?'

'Nothing.'

'Who else could have put it in its hiding place?
'My son.'

'So you're telling the court, and let's not beat about the bush, that your son killed his father and Joe and planted that knife there to frame you?'

'Those are your words, not mine.'

'But your son has an alibi for the time Joe was murdered. He was seen by his girlfriend downstairs. Since you were first questioned you have not named any person who could give you such an alibi, isn't that right, Mrs Kildare?'

It was apparent to everybody in court that Colette's arrogance had backfired. She stared round the courtroom.

'All right then, if you insist. I was in bed with a man at the time.'

Judge Quayle nearly dropped his pen. The revelation clearly took counsel by surprise too.

'Will you tell us,' said Kelleher, 'the name of this man you went to bed with on the day of your husband's funeral?'

'Yes. Hugo Fitzwilliams,' replied Colette, pointing to him in the front of the court.

In the hubbub that followed Amy spotted Fergus's stunned expression. Then he anxiously tried to catch the attention of the solicitor for the prosecution, who was seated behind his counsel.

Kelleher plunged on. 'I put it to you that that is a complete and utter lie.'

Fergus had by now attracted the solicitor's attention, who looked somewhat surprised by what he was hearing; he tugged at Kelleher's gown and had a brief word with him. Counsel then asked and obtained a five-minute adjournment. The judge also ruled that Curley could take further instructions from Colette.

Amy watched the group huddled around Kelleher. Counsel for the prosecution was shaking his head in disbelief at whatever was being relayed to him and then the solicitor was sent over to talk to Hugo Fitzwilliams. He, in turn, vigorously shook his head, his face red either through rage or embarrassment.

When the court resumed, Kelleher asked for leave to recall one witness, and call one new one.

'Is this evidence by way of rebuttal, Mr Kelleher?' asked Quayle, no doubt hoping it was.

'Only in part, Your Honour. The first witness fits into a quite different category, but I feel it is incumbent upon the state to present all the evidence on this issue to the court.'

'That must be a matter for your judgment. Call your witnesses.'

'The state recalls Fergus Kildare.'

This, realised Amy, was about to be the final irony. Fergus giving evidence for his mother.

'I remind you, Mr Kildare, you are still under oath.'

'Yes, sir.'

'You were present in court when the accused gave evidence just now?'

'Yes.'

'Is there anything relating thereto you wish to tell His Honour and the jury?'

'There is. After talking to Emma I went upstairs to my room that day to collect something. As I returned to the stairs I passed my mother's room and heard noises. The door was not properly closed so I tiptoed over and,' he was sweating profusely and having difficulty in getting the words out, 'I opened the door a little and watched what was going on inside.'

'And what was that?'

'My mother had her skirt up above her waist, with nothing on underneath. She was sitting astride a man and making love to him.'

'Could you see the man's face, could you identify him?'

'No.'

'What did you do then?'

'I ran downstairs and left the house.'

'Why did you not tell the Gardai about this, Mr Kildare?'

'Because I regarded it as the ultimate act of dishonour and I hoped to protect the Kildare name at least from that.'

For once Finbar Curley had no cross-examination.

But it was not all over. Kelleher then asked Hugo Fitzwilliams to the stand. By now the tall, extremely handsome trainer had regained his composure. He told the court that he was a happily married man and that the idea he had made love to or been in bed with the accused was ridiculous.

'Where were you between five thirty and six that evening?'

'Downstairs in the drawing room talking to Emma.'

Curley rose to question for the final time.

'You've never made love to my client, then?'

'Never.'

'You weren't with her that afternoon as she says?'

'It's a complete lie.'

'My client says you have a mole at the top of your coccyx, Mr Fitzwilliams. Would you mind turning round for a moment with your back to the jury?'

'Not unless the judge orders me to. This is outrageous!'

'Do as counsel asks you,' said Quayle.

Slowly and reluctantly Hugo turned round.

'Take off your jacket please.'

He removed his tweed jacket.

'Now pull up your shirt.'

Slowly and clumsily he lifted his shirt.

Everyone in the court leaned forward in an attempt to see the mole. There was nothing there.

Hugo went as if to tuck in his shirt again.

'Hold on a moment please, Mr Fitzwilliams,' said Curley. 'Will you lower your trousers a little please?'

As the trousers came down, a gasp went up from one of the women jurors; the mole was there for all to see.

Chapter Seventeen

Curley called no further evidence for the defence, no doubt feeling that his client's chances of an acquittal were unlikely to be improved. In the course of her practice Amy had seen too many good cases thrown away by attempts to gild the lily which went disastrously wrong. Indeed, even if another witness had been called, it was highly doubtful whether the jury would have bothered to listen. There had been enough excitement for one day. Realising that it was scarcely a sensible time to begin the final speeches and his summing-up, Quayle adjourned the case until the morning. With any luck the jury would retire soon after lunch and come back with a verdict without having to be sent to a hotel for the night.

By the time Amy had managed to escape from the crowded gallery, there was no sign of Fergus. She assumed he had fled the hordes of journalists hanging around the precincts of the court, and she could only hope that he would call her during the evening at her hotel. In a way she was glad of the chance to be on her own for a few hours. Apart from having to telephone her office and find out if there were any messages, a lot had emerged in the course of the day's hearing which demanded further scrutiny and analysis. It was beginning to appear that Jack's 'little idea', as he had called it, was right and she just hoped that the plans they had put into effect would bear fruit that evening or the next.

There was standing room only in the public gallery when she arrived the following morning at nine fifteen and for a moment it seemed that she was not going to be allowed to stay even then. An officious Gard asked her to leave. She was determined to stay at all costs and resorted to pulling rank: 'I'm sorry, but you can't put me out. I'm a solicitor in the case.'

In one sense it was true, and fortunately the Gard chose not to inquire further. In fact he was impressed enough to insist that a young girl in the front row give up her seat for Amy.

Prompt at ten thirty Kelleher began the closing speech for the prosecution. At the end of the previous day's hearing he had looked worn out and beaten, but here he was with renewed vigour, breathing fresh life into the case against Colette. Motive and opportunity were the message he repeatedly strove to hammer home and he put the issue to them as a stark choice between the image of the scheming and avaricious woman which had emerged during the evidence called on behalf of the state, and that of an innocent victim of some kind of conspiracy which the defence would have them believe. As Kelleher said, it was all very well coming up with an alibi at the eleventh hour, and in the most dramatic of fashions, but the jury had to ask themselves why it had been withheld up until then; and could they be sure that the accused did not know of the existence of the mole on Hugo Fitzwilliams' back from some third party? It was, he said quite simply, a question of whose evidence was really credible: that of Emma Ballantine who had said on oath that she had been with Hugo Fitzwilliams at the relevant time, or Colette, a woman who, if she was to be believed, was prepared to behave like a harlot on the day of her husband's funeral? And finally he came to Fergus. It was true that he was able to provide his mother with an alibi but who knows what might have driven him to this final act of misconceived yet understandable filial loyalty?

When they came to review the evidence, Kelleher urged the jury to consider the facts surrounding each murder separately. It was for the prosecution to prove their case beyond reasonable doubt. If the jury were unsure about the murder of Patrick Kildare, if they thought that the explanation about the brooch might be true, then they were obliged to acquit. As to Joe's murder, once they had rejected the alibi evidence, they might well feel that there was no doubt as to who was responsible. The fingerprints on the knife, its concealment in the secret compartment, and the indisputable truth that Joe had recognised his victim all pointed to the accused. To whom else but the accused would Joe refer to Fergus Kildare as 'Master Fergus', a term born of both familiarity and respect? There was only one answer and Kelleher urged them when they retired to do their duty, however distasteful it might be.

Curley's closing speech was as succinct as it was brilliant. Analysing the evidence of each witness called on behalf of the state, he was able to show that save for Tommy Kirkpatrick the family solicitor, Mrs Magee and Superintendent Brogan, they all had a reason for wanting Moondancer dead and once that was accepted they must all then have had a motive for killing Patrick Kildare, and Joe Slattery. The prosecution case, Curley wryly observed, was held up before them on the hallowed prongs of motive and opportunity. Each of the witnesses had ample doses of both and, in addition, a great deal of cunning. Whoever killed Patrick Kildare and Joe Slattery was not content with taking two people's lives; he, or maybe it was they, wanted to sacrifice a third. His client's. To find Colette Kildare guilty would be to commit the rest of her active adult life to imprisonment and no just or considered jury could lightly take such a step on evidence which hung together like a cobweb. One blow and it would fall apart. No one who had seen Hugo Fitzwilliams' demeanour and attitude in the witness box could fail to be left with the impression that here was a young man, a married man with children, who had been caught out. In those brief moments the truth of his client's evidence shone like a beacon in the court-room. Colette Kildare was not on trial for her morals or her marriage or, if her son was to be believed, her failings as a mother, she was on trial for the greatest sin a man or woman could commit – taking the life of another. He urged each and every juror to cast aside emotion and prejudice and ask him- or herself the one simple question in relation to each charge: am I so convinced that she did it that I can go home tonight and sleep the sleep of the just? Because if not, the answer was clear and simple and right: the verdict on each count had to be not guilty.

After lunch the judge summed-up for the best part of an hour and a half. Amy, who had expected him to balance the arguments in such a way as to communicate almost imperceptibly his own views, was disappointed. He gave a short yet considered résumé of the evidence and was at pains to reiterate that the jury could only convict if they were sure. As they filed out of the jury box, no one could allege that Quayle had tried to make the decision for them.

Amy decided to go and find Fergus. He was seated

outside, his head in his hands, looking for all the world like a broken man.

'Hey you!' she said, putting her hand on his shoulder. 'That won't get you anywhere. I hoped you might have called last night.'

'I'm sorry, I decided that I wouldn't be much company for anybody. It's ironic, isn't it? I should do my best to get her convicted, then just as it looks like we've nailed her, I end up coming to her rescue. The one person I never considered was Hugo Fitzwilliams.'

'You're not the only one. Did you know that Emma was pregnant?'

'I had no idea. I only found out when I read the evening paper. That's the problem when they call you to give evidence last. I've heard about births being announced that way, but never paternity.'

Amy was pleased to see he still had a sense of humour. 'And you really had no idea about it, as she claimed?'

He shook his head. 'None at all. I think it was very decent of her to keep it from me. I couldn't have handled it along with everything else. I suppose that's my next problem; I'm glad I'm going to be a father, but I don't love Emma.'

'I know that. Are you really sure that the baby's yours?' asked Amy gently.

'She said so there in court.'

'Fergus, I admire your loyalty, but some might say

you were a trifle naive. Come for a walk; there's a man over there watching us.'

'Him?' said Fergus, pointing his head in the direction of a poker-faced individual standing a couple of yards away.

Amy nodded.

'He's a journalist from one of the tabloids. He's offered me fifty thousand pounds if I "tell all" this Sunday.'

'What did you say to him?'

'To try Mother. But I warned him they'd have to treble the asking price.'

They paced up and down the street outside talking about Tongue in Cheek and the progress he had been making at home. The time went slowly and they were just going to have a cup of tea in the cafeteria at the courthouse when the cry went up that the jury were coming back. Amy, along with Fergus and half of Dublin, squeezed into the back of the court as the jury filed into their box and the judge was brought into court.

'Would the foreman please rise?' said the associate at the front of the court. 'Foreman of the jury: have you reached a verdict on which you are all agreed?'

'We have,' came the unwavering reply.

'On the first count of murdering Patrick Kildare, do you find the accused guilty or not guilty?'

'Not guilty.'

Amy could not see Colette's face, but from behind she did not appear to move a muscle.

The associate waited for the noise in the gallery to quieten.

'On the second count of murdering Joe Slattery, do you find the accused guilty or not guilty?'

For some reason, nerves or malice, the foreman hesitated.

'Do you wish me to repeat that?' the associate asked.

'I'm sorry,' he replied, finding his tongue again. 'Not guilty.'

Amy grabbed Fergus by the hand and before the judge had barely left the court himself she had him outside and in a waiting taxi which immediately set off for her hotel.

After two large whiskies Fergus's gloom had only increased. His mother's acquittal meant that the family name had been exposed to the world at large in vain and, as he saw it, that the jury had taken her word against his. As he was at pains to point out to Amy, all he had done was say that he had seen her in her bedroom when he went upstairs after talking to Emma, and if Emma was right about the time, that still meant his mother could have killed Joe and then met Hugo upstairs.

'Don't you think it would all have been a bit tight?' reasoned Amy. 'I'm afraid to have to say it, but I think the jury were right. What if your mother is innocent? You won't bring your father or Joe back by convicting her.'

'You're right, I know you are, but it's very difficult for me to accept. At least one thing is certain: the insurers will have to pay up on Moondancer and my mother is going to walk away with a small fortune.'

'I wouldn't bank on it. What's more, from now on she's going to be treated with contempt and I can't see too many people inviting her into their homes. But that's her problem, not yours. You've got to pull yourself together, return to Drumgarrick and carry on with Tongue in Cheek.'

'I suppose you're right. And you? Presumably it's back to London and the rest of your life?' There was a little-boy-lost look on his face and Amy felt an urge to put her arms round him and hold him tightly to her. She did just that. 'Come on,' she said, 'it's past seven thirty and I've booked a table downstairs in the restaurant. If you wait here I'll go and have a quick wash and change in the bathroom.'

Twenty-five minutes later they went downstairs and were taken straight to their table in the far corner, isolated by a pillar from the rest of the room.

'Embarrassed about me?' asked Fergus.

'No, I think a little privacy is called for tonight, that's all.'

Amy managed to keep his spirits up throughout

the meal and by the time they reached the coffee, he was beginning to talk as if the Ladbroke was already in the bag.

'Careful now,' she said, 'remember what pride precedes.'

'Don't worry. It's fun to fantasise now and again. Hey, what the hell is he doing here?'

Amy turned round to see a rather weary and ill-tempered Superintendent Brogan walking towards them.

'Did you know about this?' asked Fergus.

Before Amy could reply, the superintendent had reached their table. 'I got your message, Mr Kildare. It'd better be interesting. Do you have another late disclosure to make to me?'

Amy stood up. 'Actually it was me, Super-intendent, who left that message. We haven't met. I'm Amy Frost. I'm a solicitor, practising in London. I'm acting for the insurers of Moondancer and, for this evening, for Mr Kildare as well.'

'Well then? I've a lot of work to do as a result of this afternoon's verdict.'

'I realise that. This won't take long.'

Brogan reluctantly accepted a chair from the head waiter and eyed both Fergus and Amy suspiciously. Fergus looked confused and worried.

Amy glanced at her watch anxiously, then relaxed. 'Ah, here they are.'

The arrival of Seamus and Jack didn't please

Brogan any more than it did Fergus. Amy had to plead with the superintendent to stay. She only hoped Jack had not come empty-handed.

'All right,' conceded Brogan, 'I'll give you ten minutes, and if this isn't good, I'll book the lot of you for wasting Gardai time.'

Amy tried to disarm him with her friendliest smile. 'Jack, do you have something you wish to play to the superintendent?'

Jack produced a tape from his pocket, and Seamus pulled a small cassette player out of his.

'Have you been bugging again?' asked Brogan, raising his voice slightly. 'Because if you have, this time you'll both go inside.'

'Play it, Jack,' said Amy.

He pressed the play button and after a few seconds of incomprehensible noises – possibly a knock followed by a door opening – there were voices, clearly audible.

'That bloody Fergus. Get me a drink.'

The clink of glasses could just be made out in the background.

'Were you followed?'

'I don't think so. I came down from my room in the lift, pretended I'd forgotten something in my room, and then came back down the stairs. I walked round the block twice before coming up here.'

'Good, we've got to think pretty fast before Brogan starts thinking about the evidence I gave.'

'What about me? I'm ruined.'

329

'Stop panicking. If we keep our heads, we can get out of this. They're bound to ask us about our movements the weekend Patrick died.'

'I'm all right. If you recall, I was at Limerick races all day and with plenty of witnesses to say they saw me there. No one knows that I dropped you off at the house before going there and that I met you afterwards at Cahir. You drove his car there. No one said they saw you at the time, and I suppose there's no reason why they should remember now, but still you're more vulnerable.'

'Not really. I'll just say I went shopping in Dublin; it worked pretty well for Colette.'

'But she was telling the truth.'

'How are they to know I'm not? They still can't work out exactly how Patrick was killed. He was meant to be in Sligo. I can see him now in the garden kneeling over the asparagus bed as I hit him from behind. They won't risk a second botched-up trial. I'm only sorry they believed Colette's story about the brooch.'

'You mean she hadn't given it to him to get repaired?'

'Of course not. He'd have told her where to go. I stole it a month before and left it there on purpose in case they ever discovered the body.'

'God, you've got to be the most calculating person alive.'

'No, just pragmatic. I was sorry about Patrick and

there wouldn't have been any problem if he hadn't seen me coming out of the gun room and got such a conscience about the insurance. I believed him when he said he was going to have to tell the Gardai. If they had discovered about you, then bang went the insurance money.'

'And boy do I need it. They can't trace us to Joe and, anyway, one of us has the perfect alibi now.'

'And let's keep it that way. After all, there's so much for the three of us to live for.'

Jack pressed the stop button.

'When did you make this recording, Mr Hendred?' asked Brogan in a somewhat more friendly tone than before.

'This conversation took place this evening about an hour after the jury's verdict. We tailed these two individuals to find out where they were staying during the trial and yesterday morning we planted the bugs in their rooms.'

'May I take that?' said the superintendent, who was going to take the tape whether they liked it or not. 'Are you all right, sir?' he asked Fergus, who was staring disbelievingly at the cassette recorder.

'But how could she?'

'Easily, by the sound of it,' replied Amy.

They went their different ways over Christmas and the news of the charging of Hugo Fitzwilliams and Emma Ballantine hit the national newspapers the day after Boxing Day. According to Seamus's contact in the Gardai, who had resurfaced, Hugo was the first to crack. He had apparently been carrying on the affair with Emma for six months before Moondancer was killed and planned to leave his wife and live with her. He couldn't afford a divorce and the risk of losing his yard unless he could recoup his investment in Moondancer. It had been Emma who had dreamt up the idea of the IRA, and she who had made the calls to Patrick, one of which Joe had answered. Unfortunately Patrick had seen Emma leaving the gun room. She had taken the key from Fergus's hiding place under the floorboards in his room. Two months later, Patrick had told her that he was going to report her involvement to the Gardai. She realised that was only one step away from Hugo's involvement being discovered and the insurance claim being aborted. So Patrick had to die. Hugo had made the call pretending to be the bloodstock dealer in Sligo, inviting him down to see a horse. In fact, what no one knew was that Hugo had telephoned on the Saturday morning, cancelling the trip. He had driven Emma to the house after they had seen Colette leave, and then gone on to Limerick races. Emma had killed Patrick and then driven his car to Cahir where she had met Hugo, and gone on with him to the Curragh. The following day Hugo had driven the car to Sligo and left it there, catching a train back home.

Of course, they had never thought the body would be discovered. Even then, they hadn't been worried until Emma had gone down to the stables on the Sunday evening to find Fergus for his mother, and overheard Joe telling him about the voice on the phone. She then realised Joe had to die too.

It worked out much easier than they could have hoped. That evening she was careful to clear the table after dinner and suggest that Colette retire into the drawing room with the men. Wrapping the knife in her napkin, she washed the traces of lamb from the blade before hiding it. She took another carving knife from the drawer, cut some meat with it, and left it in the sink for Mrs Magee to find in the morning.

She and Hugo knew that the best chance to kill Joe was during the wake when people would not notice who was coming and going from the house. The essential thing was to ensure that Colette did not have an alibi, while they did. It was Emma's idea that Hugo should seduce Colette. Few women could resist Hugo, certainly not one with Colette's predilections, and Emma knew all about her past infidelities.

While Hugo was upstairs with Colette, Emma slipped down to the stable and murdered Joe with the knife. 'Master Fergus' had been what he always called his master to her too. She put the knife into her shoulder bag and returned to the study where she immediately engaged Fergus in conversation. After everyone had left, she slipped the knife into the secret compartment in the desk, which Fergus had told her about in the early days of their relationship. When questioned by Brogan, Emma said she was with Hugo from five thirty to six, and he corroborated her. If Colette had claimed that she was in bed with Hugo, who would have believed such an outrageous suggestion? It was only Fergus who had inadvertently ruined their plan. And that damned mole on Hugo's back.

Chapter Eighteen

The panic over the Ladbroke began on the Thursday before the race. Amy had agreed to go over to Ireland to act as travelling lad again, and was due to fly to Shannon in the morning. She had already drawn six thousand pounds out of her savings to have on Tongue in Cheek, five of which she was lending to Fergus, and the other one for herself. Fergus had managed to raise another five thousand, two thousand of which he was having on in memory of Joe; any winnings from it he would give to Joe's widow. Much as she wanted to let Jack into the secret, Amy realised that the fewer in the know the better, and the longer the price. Even with his low weight, Tongue in Cheek was freely quoted at fifty to one in the betting, all the money being on an English-trained horse, Wizard of Byton, and an Irish hotpot called Ash Hill Lad, the horse that had finished only two lengths in front of Tongue in Cheek the previous season.

The phone was ringing as Amy let herself into her flat. It was Fergus and he sounded in a real panic. He spoke so quickly Amy could not understand a word he said.

'Slow down and start again,' she urged him.

'I'm sorry but there's one thing we've completely overlooked. How are we going to get the ten thousand pounds on without destroying the odds? Joe always said that I could leave it to him, but he's not here. We might get a thousand on with the bookies on course at fifties, but after that there's no way we'll start at anything over twenties. All we'll end up doing is lowering the starting price.'

Amy, who knew a fair amount about betting, had not given any thought to the problem either.

'And that's not all,' went on Fergus. 'Who's going to have the bet on course anyway? I can't because I'm meant to be riding the damned thing and you won't know what to do.'

Amy was amused by his chauvinist attitude. 'In which case we'll have to involve someone else. From the little I know, the only people who can have big bets are big losers. Jack once told me he had a friend who is a big gambler. He could almost certainly get it on.'

'And if he does it on credit, how do we know we'll ever be paid? They'll just set it off against his losses.'

'We'll have to do it ourselves then.'

'Not on your own, you can't.'

'How about if Jack helps me? He's utterly reliable and likes his racing.' She could sense him groaning inwardly at the other end of the phone.

'I somehow thought I'd never see him again.'

'Fergus, I think you owe Jack a big favour. After all, he was the one who suggested we bug Emma's and Hugo's rooms.'

'That wasn't altruism. Now that Hugo's confessed, the insurers don't have to pay out on the policy and Jack's a hero again.'

'Don't forget your mother's shares are also worthless. That must give you some pleasure.'

'It did until I found out how much she was paid for those articles in the newspaper.'

'Forget it, and concentrate on Saturday. For once you're going to do as you're told. I'll take care of the punting and you do the riding. I'll see you tomorrow. Here's to the crack!'

Before leaving for Shannon, Amy made a selective tour of betting shops and managed to put a couple of thousand on at fifties without attracting too much attention. The Ladbroke was a popular race for ante post wagers and when she saw the next day's racing papers the odds had remained the same. She only hoped that Jack had managed to do as well in shops in the West Country.

Despite the cold weather, the crowd at Leopardstown was the biggest they had ever had. There were twenty-four runners in the field. The favourite,

Wizard of Byton, had been a useful flat performer who had taken well to hurdling and had finished fourth in last year's Champion Hurdle at Cheltenham. He was carrying top weight but the ease with which he had won his last race at Sandown made him an obvious choice for the punters. With the ground riding on the fast side of good, the big weight would not be quite such a burden. The rest of the field except for Ash Hill Lad were all decent handicappers that lacked any real class and then there was a ten-pound drop to the next horses in the card, including Tongue in Cheek. It was Ash Hill Lad, though, that Fergus most feared. Last year he had won both his hurdle races in fast times and his single victory this season at Limerick showed he had lost none of his previous form.

Fergus had spent hours watching old videos of the race to see how past winners had been ridden. He had come to the conclusion that the only common denominator was that no matter where they had been in the early part of the race, the winning horses were always within striking distance of the leaders before they raced down the hill on the far side of the course. Leopardstown was in the main a big left-handed galloping track about two miles round, with an uphill finish. But three furlongs from the finishing post there was a sharp left-hand bend at the bottom of quite a steep incline. If the challenge was left too late, the leaders had first run and those behind could find themselves having to race round a wall of horses that were tiring in front of them.

It was still cold but at least the sun was shining as Fergus stepped into the paddock with the other jockeys. The handicappers had treated him lightly and he had only had to give Tongue in Cheek ten pounds. The commentator announced that Wizard of Byton had won the prize for best turned-out horse – hardly surprising as he was the only entire colt in the field and possessed a coat that shone like a conker.

As the bell rang and the jockeys mounted, the stewards got them into order for the parade. Bruce Lee, Wizard of Byton's jockey, led them out under the horse chestnut trees, round the side of the grandstand and onto the track.

'Well, there's no going back now,' Fergus commented to Amy.

'If you don't win, you might not have anything to go back to,' she replied, trying to ensure he did not lose his bottle.

The runners walked in front of the stands for a short while and then one by one, as their lads let them go, they galloped down the course to the two-mile post at the bottom of the straight. Fergus's plan was to go middle to outer; he reasoned that was the way to steer clear of trouble and to ride the race as it came. He knew that Tongue in Cheek had stamina as well as speed and as long as he was galloping within

himself, he would be happy. What Fergus had to
ensure was that they were handy by the top of the hill
on the far side. The Ladbroke was always a fast-run
affair with the lightweights trying to make their
advantage tell and he was quite prepared to find
himself nearer the front than the back for the first
half-mile.

As the starter sent them off on their way and they
raced towards the first hurdle, that's exactly where
Fergus found himself. He let Tongue in Cheek settle
into the pace. The horse had never jumped at this
sort of speed before and the first couple of flights
were hit or miss affairs with neither horse nor jockey
having much idea what was happening. After that,
Tongue in Cheek found his feet and began measur-
ing the hurdles more accurately. As the field
streamed away past the stands, Fergus looked up and
could see the colours of Wizard of Byton taking
them along. Fifteen lengths ahead of Fergus was Ash
Hill Lad, tight against the rails. The runners now
turned away round the long bend into the back
straight. Fergus squeezed Tongue in Cheek with his
legs to make him lengthen his stride and they began
to move slowly closer to the leaders. They raced over
the matting halfway down the far side and by the
time they reached the top of the hill, Tongue in
Cheek was breathing right down the necks of the
leading group.

The field then swung left-handed and raced down

the hill to the third last flight from home. Fergus could feel Tongue in Cheek cruising beneath him and decided it was time to go for home. At that moment Ash Hill Lad, who seemed to be going just as easily, met the hurdle all wrong and crashed to the ground in front of them. Fergus yanked Tongue in Cheek to the right and would have missed the fallen horse if he had not rolled right over. As he thrashed his legs to gain his balance, he caught Tongue in Cheek full on the chest and knocked him out of his stride. For a split second Fergus thought he was going to fall out the side, and by the time he had himself and Tongue in Cheek balanced again, they had lost at least six lengths. It was then that he noticed the blood spraying onto his breeches and his heart sank. It was the classic sign of a broken blood vessel. All the plans and the last of his money gone to waste because of a rotten blood vessel.

He took a tug on the reins to pull Tongue in Cheek up so that he would not do himself any more damage, but Tongue in Cheek had other ideas and suddenly took off again. Taking his lead from the horse, Fergus shortened up his reins and pushed him for all his worth in pursuit of the others. Soon he was catching them hand over fist and by the time they had reached the last flight, he had only a tiring Wizard of Byton beside him. At the sight of a wide open space and no other horses ahead of him, Tongue in Cheek pricked his ears and popped neatly over the hurdle; all Fergus had to do was keep him going to win by a very comfortable four lengths.

There was stony silence as they passed the post but Fergus made no attempt to hide his joy as he slapped Tongue in Cheek repeatedly on the shoulder. Amy had reached them almost before he had finished pulling the horse up and began giving Tongue in Cheek the kind of embrace his jockey longed for. Fergus was short of breath from the excitement more than any physical exertion and was leaning over like he had just ridden two Grand Nationals.

'I can't make it out,' he panted to Amy. 'He broke a blood vessel but he kept on going.'

Amy looked closely at Tongue in Cheek's nostrils. 'He's bleeding all right, but it's from a cut, not a blood vessel. That horse that nearly brought you down must have caught him with his foot. The only blood vessels which are going to break on this course belong to the bookies!'

Jack joined them later in the racecourse restaurant to celebrate. He and Amy had managed to get five thousand punts on the course at fifties and that had to be added to the four thousand they already had in ante post vouchers. He had taken forties on the other two thousand. They had done it!

Jack, full of champagne, gently slid his right hand under the table in search of Amy's hand. He looked over at Fergus; maybe he wasn't such a bad bloke, but Amy was going to be his girl. As Fergus clenched the hand tight he too felt that maybe he had judged Jack unfairly.

Amy stood up and grinned broadly at them. 'While you two hold hands I'm off to buy another bottle!'

More Crime Fiction from Headline

JOHN FRANCOME

BREAK NECK

'Francome writes an odds-on racing cert'
Daily Express

When apprentice jockey Rory Gillespie
abandons his fiancée Laura Brickhill, in favour
of trainer's daughter Pam Fanshaw, it's a
decision made from ambition not love. And
Rory has to wait ten years before Laura will
forgive him.

Now one of England's leading trainers, and
married to property tycoon Luke Mundy,
Laura asks Rory to ride her best horse,
Midnight Express, in Cheltenham's Two Mile
Champion Chase. Shortly afterwards, Luke is
killed on one of Laura's horses and she is
arrested for manslaughter. Rory won't desert
her this time and, setting out to prove Laura's
innocence, he discovers that there is more than
one person who will benefit from Luke's death.

Packed with intrigue and excitement, the plot
unravels at breakneck speed, revealing bribery,
blackmail and corruption as ingredients in this
highly accomplished racing thriller.

FICTION / CRIME 0 7472 4704 8

More Thrilling Fiction from Headline

JOHN FRANCOME

'Francome writes an odds-on racing cert' *Daily Express*

'Spirited stuff' *OK magazine*

'Pacy racing and racy pacing – John Francome has found his stride as a solo novelist' *Horse and Hound*

Already a leading jockey in his home country, Jake Felton comes to England to further his career and avoid confrontation with New York's racing mafia. But his plans to combine the life of an English squire with that of a top-flight jockey look like coming to a sticky end when he falls victim to a series of accidents that begin to seem all too deliberate.

Aided and abetted by typical English rose Camilla Fielding, Jake discovers that he's been targeted by a ruthless and professional killer. And now he urgently needs to find out why . . .

With an intricate and thrilling plot and all the drama and excitement of Derby Day, *Outsider* shows John Francome at the top of his form in this new novel of danger and skulduggery on the race track.

'A thoroughly convincing and entertaining tale' *Daily Mail*

'The racing feel is authentic and it's a pacy, entertaining read' *The Times*

FICTION / CRIME 0 7472 4375 1

A selection of compelling novels by John Francome

SAFE BET	£6.99 ☐
HIGH FLYER	£6.99 ☐
FALSE START	£6.99 ☐
DEAD RINGER	£6.99 ☐
BREAK NECK	£6.99 ☐
OUTSIDER	£6.99 ☐
ROUGH RIDE	£6.99 ☐
STONE COLD	£6.99 ☐
STUD POKER	£6.99 ☐

Headline books are available at your local bookshop or newsagent. Alternatively, books can be ordered direct from the publisher. Just tick the titles you want and fill in the form below. Prices and availability subject to change without notice.

Buy four books from the selection above and get free postage and packaging and delivery within 48 hours. Just send a cheque or postal order made payable to Bookpoint Ltd to the value of the total cover price of the four books. Alternatively, if you wish to buy fewer than four books the following postage and packaging applies:

UK and BFPO £4.30 for one book; £6.30 for two books; £8.30 for three books.

Overseas and Eire: £4.80 for one book; £7.10 for 2 or 3 books (surface mail)

Please enclose a cheque or postal order made payable to *Bookpoint Limited*, and send to: Headline Publishing Ltd, 39 Milton Park, Abingdon, OXON OX14 4TD, UK.
E-mail Address: orders@bookpoint.co.uk

If you would prefer to pay by credit card, our call team would be delighted to take your order by telephone. Our direct line 01235 400 414 (lines open 9.00 am–6.00 pm Monday to Saturday, 24 hour message answering service). Alternatively you can send a fax on 01235 400 454.

Name ....

Address ....

....

....

If you would prefer to pay by credit card, please complete:
Please debit my Visa/Access/Diner's Card/American Express (delete as applicable) card number:

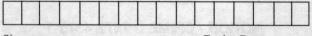

Signature .... Expiry Date ....